Pieces Of Grace

KAREN GIBSON

PIECES OF GRACE

KAREN GIBSON

Penbrook Press

For Mallory, Morgan & Mitchell

Chapter 1

Grace pushed an errant piece of jalapeno pepper away from her water glass, pinched it between her thumb and finger, then dropped it onto the empty nacho platter. She concentrated on the movement of her hand as it completed this simple task, trying to determine if she was having some kind of out-of-body experience. Through the floor to ceiling window before her, the moon dripped a shimmer of light over the pool. It was too magical to be real.

She blinked. The scene remained the same. She closed her eyes for a few seconds, and when she opened them, still no change. She was indeed sitting here, at this moment, experiencing…whatever *this* was. *This,* she determined, was unusually romantic, and perhaps even a little fairytale like, and she fought an urge to laugh out loud. Grace Warrens was too practical to believe in magic or fairytales.

All of it was real, because the physical evidence was striding toward her now, the shadow of stubble on his chin giving him the cliché rugged good looks of the outdoorsman he was. She hadn't imagined Josh after all.

"Sorry about that, Grace. I had to wrap up a few loose ends with a vendor."

A server appeared behind him, setting the check on the edge of their table and clearing away the empty beer glasses and plates.

"No problem at all. I didn't want to leave without saying goodbye and thanking you again for the…for this." She

1

gestured, hoping he understood she meant the drinks, and snacks, and the flutter of her heart, and the most romantic evening she'd ever spent, but her arm bumped the water glass, toppling it and scattering water and ice cubes over the edge of the table. He deftly hopped back, able to avoid another dousing.

"Careful there. We don't need a repeat, do we?" His laugh warmed her, despite her momentary embarrassment. She did indeed have a problem with spilled water today, and it was becoming evident she might have another problem. His touch on her arm left a warm tingle long after he removed his hand.

They walked to her car and stood facing each other, not quite knowing the proper ending for a "we-just-met-but-this-feels-really-special" kind of night. He finally leaned down and kissed her gently on the forehead.

"I'm glad I met you Gracie-Belle."

She barely remembered telling him her middle name, Isabelle. When she looked into his eyes, however, she had no regrets about anything said or done all day—not one thing.

"You know what I especially liked about you right from the start?" His voice was so low she had to lean in closer to hear, breathing him in, wanting to remember the smell of aftershave, the outdoors, and his sheer masculinity, if such things could be captured in an aroma. "You fell down, but you got right back up again, Grace."

Her heart skipped the tiniest of beats. Did her heart know something she didn't? It couldn't. It was too soon. He opened her car door, smiling as she settled in and fastened her seatbelt. She had never met a guy quite like him. She watched him in her rearview mirror as she drove away, knowing her life was somehow changed.

***

The late morning sun made dust specks dance and shimmer in mid-air. Grace watched them, in no hurry to start her day. She imagined them to be bits of fairy dust left over from her magical night. She savored the feelings until practicality settled in, pushing aside remnants of romantic nonsense for real world matters. She would not allow herself to fall for this guy.

By the time she climbed out of bed, she'd almost convinced herself.

She checked her face in the mirror, relieved to see she looked exactly the same. It was silly to think she wouldn't, but she lived with Lexie, so she had to be sure. Lexie would know something was up. Her best friend was extremely perceptive. Grace guessed it had something to do viewing the world through an artist's lens. Nothing escaped her.

It took only a couple of minutes.

"You look weird. Why do you look weird this morning?" The irony of these words coming from her quirky roommate might have been laughable to some, but Grace was used to Lexie's "unique" forms of expression. Today, she sported some type of metal headdress. Grace no longer questioned the appearance of such random peculiar accessories. Lexie was earning a degree in fine arts. Nothing else needed to be said.

"I do not look weird. I'm just tired. I had to drive all the way back from Phoenix a lot later than I expected."

"No, that's not it." Lexie positioned herself directly in front of Grace, staring into her eyes as if trying to read something written deep down in their recesses. She gasped. "You met someone. Oh my God. You met someone."

Rolling her eyes, Grace pushed Lexie away. "I met a lot of people, dummy. I was at a conference." She feigned intense interest in pouring herself coffee in an attempt to avoid further eye contact. "It was good. Highly informative. I got some great ideas for beefing up my resume.

Lexie wasn't buying Grace's attempt at an explanation. "That's not what I'm talking about. Come on. 'Fess up." She grabbed Grace's arm, forcing her to look at her again. "What about our agreement? No relationships. No distractions. Career first. You can't screw it up now. I'm here to help you. I mean, if there's still time."

It hadn't seemed silly when they made the promise four years ago as college freshmen, and now, a matter of weeks before graduation, Grace's resolve was about to be tested. Lexie was waiting for reassurance from her friend that it was nothing but a close call and remaining true to the promise was a non-issue.

There was no such reassurance forthcoming.

Something burst inside Grace, rendering her helpless to hold back. "You're right. I know we promised, but he's so cute. And sexy." She flopped onto the loveseat that took up most of the apartment's living room. "Yesterday was crazy. I had *the* single most embarrassing day and the most wonderful day all rolled up in one. How does that happen?" The dreamy look that first alerted Lexie was getting dreamier by the moment.

Lexie sat next to her. "Am I supposed to remind you why we made the promise? You know this isn't part of your plan."

Lexie was right. Meeting someone was not part of Grace's master plan. Of course, she went on occasional dates, but a relationship was never in the cards. Her plans were too carefully cemented in her brain, crafted with the greatest of care, to let anything get in the way. Grace was nothing if not a planner. Straying from the well-scripted path would not do at all. She didn't believe in fate. Fate was the antithesis to planning. Planning was her religion.

Lexie was still staring at her.

Grace had played back every moment of yesterday's events multiple times already—on the drive home last night, after climbing into bed, and as soon as she awoke this. Maybe it would start to lose some of the magic if she said the words out loud.

"OK. I'll give you every gory detail."

***

Her morning was on the cusp of getting completely out of control. An ugly brownish-orange colored spot on her blouse was throwing her into a tizzy, made worse by the fact she couldn't even remember eating something that color. She tried to sponge it off, but that made it worse. If she wasn't on the road in the next ten minutes, she'd never make it on time. Taking a deep breath, she returned to her bedroom to change into her pink silk blouse with the white flower petal button appliques.

The panic started to consume her when she realized that blouse was at the cleaners, a stray drop of ketchup hopefully being obliterated into nothingness, but more likely permanently there as a reminder of her clumsiness. She didn't have a lot of options, settling quickly on Gray slacks, a white blouse and black cardigan.

Grace looked young. The smattering of freckles across her nose were of no help at all. Her mom insisted she would appreciate that someday, but with college graduation around the corner and the need to start a job search looming, she wished for a bit more sophistication to her look. Outfit number three would have to do the trick. She had nothing else. She couldn't raid Lexie's closet. Her eclectic wardrobe was as far from business causal as clothing could get.

She slipped on black pumps and pulled her shoulder length brown hair, straight and shiny, into a sleek ponytail as a last-ditch effort to appear a tad older.

Telling herself she was overthinking this didn't make a bit of difference. There was an unmistakable undercurrent of excitement about the day. If this seminar could come through with just half of what it was promising, she was confident she could use the information to help in what she called her search for a "big girl job." The job market was terrible, so the campus career resource officer told her to do whatever she could to jumpstart her job search. This one-day seminar on marketing herself was a good idea, the resource officer had proclaimed, handing over the sleek flyer. A career fair, scheduled as part of the day's events, would be an opportunity to start interacting with potential employers. It was going to be a great day.

Grace grabbed a legal pad from her canvas book bag and made it out the door only a few minutes behind schedule. Gone were her plans for a leisurely drive to the Valley View Golf Resort and Conference Center in Phoenix.

She blamed it on being rushed. She blamed it on her meager wardrobe. She blamed it on resorts hosting more than one conference in a day. No matter where she tried to place the blame, the result was the same. Her planning failed miserably.

A smiling doorman in a green and gray uniform greeted her at the entrance to the Valley View. To save time, she turned to ask him for directions, but he was already gone, opening a car door for a hotel guest.

She looked around for an announcement board of some kind, and almost bumped into a young woman who had turned to acknowledge a male voice coming from behind a carved pillar. "We're in C27, Julie."

Grace made a quick appraisal of the two, noting they appeared to be college-aged, and quite likely at the hotel for the same conference. "Julie" was sporting the exact look she'd hoped to pull off, had the wardrobe malfunction not thwarted her efforts. They were carrying matching black portfolios she couldn't help but lust over.

Her excitement for the day faded. They looked every bit the professional with their polished looks and sleek black cases. She glanced at her legal pad and then at the zipper-closure leather portfolios they carried, feeling inadequate and out of place.

A little in awe of them already, Grace tagged along to C27, convinced it was the same seminar she was attending and painfully aware they were far more ahead of the game than she was. They would obviously get their resumes to the top of any job search pile and didn't even need this seminar.

She had little time to notice much about C27 other than a middle aisle with rows of tables lining each side of the room. Four chairs stood at each table, all facing the projection screen at the front. Each chair was occupied, which was probably the first thing Julie and her male companion noticed as they walked confidently down the aisle, looking from left to right for an empty seat. The second thing they likely noticed was the name of the seminar prominently displayed on the screen: *Extreme Survival Techniques: Learning to Live in Hostile Environments*.

Laughing at their error, the couple turned in unison to make a quick exit, not realizing they had picked up a straggler, now too close on their heels. With an involuntary "oof," the man bumped into Grace, who was too stunned to do anything to avoid the contact. Grace felt herself falling, even as he reached out to grab her arm. To her horror, she ended up sprawled across the lap of a young man who had just pushed his chair back to place a backpack under the table and out of his way. His look of surprise quickly turned to one of amusement. The couple she'd followed continued out the door, the man mouthing "Sorry" before disappearing.

The seconds dragged on endlessly as Grace stood up, apologizing to the young man and gathering her purse and notepad. As she turned to make a quick exit from the room, the heel of her shoe caught in the strap of his backpack, sending her headlong into the chest of a man making his way up the aisle directly behind her. As if in slow motion, she watched the pitcher he carried tip, spilling ice water all over the front of his shirt and down his pants.

Grace had no idea how she actually disentangled herself from the strap and made it to the door, but she did, positive she could hear the roar of laughter following her every step. Her cheeks flamed with the humiliation of what must have looked like a circus act gone awry. All of her efforts to appear professional were obviously in vain. She may as well have worn a clown suit today with the spectacle she'd created.

Mortified, she ducked into the nearest bathroom, staring at the disheveled reflection in the mirror. Once her heartbeat returned to normal and the burning in her cheeks subsided, Grace decided to call it a day. Maybe her wardrobe malfunction should have been an adequate sign. This seminar was never meant to be. There would have to be another one on another day…maybe. If she ever decided to give another one a shot, she would be far better prepared.

She pulled her ponytail holder out, letting her hair fall to her shoulders. She hurried through the lobby and out the front door to the parking lot, hoping nobody who had just witnessed her stunning act of imbalance would be anywhere in the vicinity.

The doorman was absent from his post. She could duck into the sanctuary of her car and be on her way. Two spaces before her parked car, a man with his back to her was unlocking a saddlebag attached to a motorcycle. Of course, the embarrassment gods were certainly not on her side today. Or, perhaps better said, they were having such fun at her expense they decided to prolong her agony. She stopped short, realizing she was looking at the backside of a man with wet pants and her face burned all over again.

She planned her escape, hoping the guy who'd been on the receiving end of her mishap wouldn't look up. If she crossed through a row of cars on her right and circled back around to her car, he might not notice her. Although his back was to her, he turned just in time to see the look of horror on her face for the second time. He smiled, approaching slowly as if she were a wild animal who might run away if he moved too quickly.

"We probably should know each other's names if we're going to keep running into each other like this—literally and figuratively, of course. I'll start. I'm Josh. Josh Jarvis." He stuck his hand out, rapidly closing the distance between them.

Caught completely off guard, Grace stared dumbly at him.

Undeterred, he smiled even more broadly and stopped directly in front of her. "This is where you reach out your hand and shake mine," he teased.

She shook his extended hand. "I'm Grace." She wasn't prepared for his reaction. He bent at the waist, laughing a deep, rich laugh.

His grin was infectious. It stayed on his face as he caught his breath. "Grace, huh? Well, I guess you tripped and stumbled through that room with grace, Grace." She thought she should maybe, possibly, be upset with what sounded like an insult but his grin made anger impossible, though it didn't ease her embarrassment.

"Well, stay tuned for my next act. I'm sure it'll top anything I did just now." She gave a slight bow and fleeting smile, then continued toward her car.

"Aren't you going back in for the session?" He used his thumb to point in the general direction of the hotel. "I just grabbed some dry clothes and I've gotta get back in there." He winked then. "Maybe you could walk me back in since I'm out here because of you." He swept his hand in front of him, emphasizing the spot that was most soaked.

"Oh no, no, no. I'm not going back in there," she shook her head emphatically. "I wasn't even in the right room. I just didn't realize it soon enough. I was supposed to be at a seminar to help me with my resume writing and job search because I'm graduating and need..." She let her voice trail off. It was sounding like babble even to her own ears, so she simply added, "I think I've had enough of seminars for one day."

She was flustered—perhaps because of what she'd done to him or perhaps because of what he was now doing to her. Again, she reached for her door handle, knowing it was time to get away from the scene of destruction that had become her morning.

"I hope you're not upset. This is no big deal. See? I'll just change my clothes and pretend nothing happened." He wasn't making any move to leave and she was not getting any closer to being in her car.

They were at a momentary impasse, and then her curiosity got the best of her. "Do you always carry a change of clothes?"

Josh shrugged. "It's the first rule of survival. Be prepared. I'm like a grown-up Boy Scout. I always try to be ready for the unexpected. Even something as unexpected as running into you, Grace." This time when he grinned, she felt the blood rush to her cheeks. He was definitely charming.

Grace turned back to her car, not quite sure what to make of him. This was an opportunity to make her escape, but she was no longer sure she wanted to. Such indecision was very unlike her.

"Come on." He was continuing his efforts to get her to return to the building.

She turned from her car, still torn, but definitely intrigued.

He was a good-looking guy. She guessed him to be about six and a half feet tall. His dark hair was on the long side, and he had a slight cowlick. A shadow of stubble darkened his chin. He obviously worked out, she decided, noting the muscle tone. And his piercing eyes that looked at her with intensity... When her face reddened this time, it was because she had been caught checking him out. "I...I can't. I'd be walking in so late as it is." She was losing the argument with herself. "No, I'm done. I've embarrassed myself enough for one day."

"Let's go." He wasn't taking no for an answer. He stuck his arm out, glancing from his crooked elbow to her and back again to his arm.

She laughed at his antics, not sure how much longer she could resist. "I don't know. How can I possibly go in there when it started at least 10 minutes ago?" She glanced at her watch. "Make that 15 minutes ago." She shook her head and made one more attempt to open her car door. "I'm supposed to be preparing to be a professional and that most certainly screams anything but."

Josh laughed again. She liked the sound and the way his face lit up. She wanted to hear more of it.

"You have to go back in there."

"I *have* to?"

"It's the only excuse I have to keep you around for the day so I can buy you a drink when it's over. Do you really want to be responsible for my current predicament *and* my depression if you leave? Come on," he repeated. His puppy dog look broke her resistance.

"I can't believe I let you talk me into this." She took his arm and together they walked back into the building.

"I'm going to change my clothes and try this again. Maybe they even dried the floor by now." She saw the twinkle in his eye. "You should probably look over there to see where you are *supposed* to be." He nodded toward the message board she'd been looking for earlier.

"Gee, thanks for the tip." She rolled her eyes as he smirked.

"Hey, Grace." He caught her attention before she'd taken two steps. "I don't know what time you get done, but you can find me back at the scene of your crime or in the lounge as soon as you finish." There was the slightest hint of a question there but she'd already learned from experience he wouldn't take no for an answer. Why was she giving in to this guy? She smiled to herself, determining it had to be his rugged good looks.

With a shrug, she acquiesced. "I guess I owe you a drink after what I did to you." He glanced at his wet front, nodded, and walked toward the men's room, leaving her to watch him from the back this time. She nodded in approval. He was definitely a nice-looking guy. "Hey, Josh." He turned, a sassy grin on her face this time. "I'm sorry I made you late. I hope your presenter doesn't get too upset with you."

Again, he laughed. "Impossible. *I'm* the presenter." As surprise registered on her face, he added, "Next time I'll have someone else fetch my water." He left her standing there shaking her head. Interesting guy, she thought, as his laughter drifted away with him.

***

Lexie scrunched her nose, a habit when she was deep in thought. "You stayed and had a drink with him? A total stranger, Grace? What were you thinking?"

Grace shrugged. "I wasn't thinking, OK?" The dreamy look re-appeared. "We talked about *everything*. It's not like I don't know anything about him. He's an only child. An army brat." She smiled, remembering how amused he was by her stories about her two older sisters. She could tell Lexie so much about him, like that he moved a lot because of his dad. Germany, South Korea, Louisiana and Texas. Or that his mother deserted them when Josh was 12. No longer able to tolerate the life of a military wife, she simply packed her bags and moved out. Neither he nor his dad ever fully understood what switch had flipped to make her suddenly hate a life she seemed to love for so long. His mother never bothered to show up or even send a card when his dad died three years ago. But the look on Lexie's face stopped her.

"What do you want me to do, Grace?" Lexie threw her hands in the air. "Am I supposed to talk you down from this?"

Born and raised in Flagstaff, Lexie had no intention of leaving her home state after graduation, but Grace had no intention of staying here. If Grace fell for this guy, and things worked out, she might stay, which was a definite win for Lexie. She had to walk a fine line now, wanting nothing more than to have Grace stay, but wanting to be supportive of her best friend's goals at the same time.

Lexie suspected she was already too late. Grace was smitten.

A smile played across Grace's face as she thought about how easy it had been between them. It both intrigued and frightened her. She could fall for him—despite their strange introduction. She remembered the way the candle flickered, creating soft shadows across their faces as they leaned closer and closer to one another.

"Grace?" Lexie snapped her out of her daydream.

"I don't know, Lexie. It was probably nothing." She pushed herself up from the loveseat and stretched. "Time for a shower."

As the hot water washed over her, she took stock. She was in Tucson. Josh was in Phoenix. She was about to graduate. Josh had an established career. She was leaving Arizona after commencement next month… There was no point in continuing the list. The truth was evident. It would be stupid if she gave in to this temptation now. Her plan was to begin her career in a big city, her sights set on New York, Los Angeles, or Miami. She shouldn't have to keep reminding herself. Arizona was temporary.

"Why do you need to go out of state, Grace?" Her mother's words rang in her ears. *"What's so bad about staying in Illinois?"*

"We have plenty of great schools around here," her dad chimed in.

She gave them a carefully crafted list of reasons. Her two sisters stayed close to home for college. Now they were married, one with a family and the other hoping to start one, and they were all still in Chicago. Their lives seemed so…boring. She wanted more.

The "surprise caboose" of the family, Grace watched her older sisters carefully, sure they had to regret their decisions to stay in Chicago. Had they given up on adventure? Was this really all they wanted?

Grace was unsure if she convinced her parents or wore them down. They compromised, allowing her to apply to schools in Arizona because Aunt Irene, her dad's older sister, lived just outside of Chandler. If she got homesick, or needed a place to spend holidays if she couldn't make it home, at least she'd be near family. She applied and was accepted to the University of Arizona and was about to earn a degree in marketing. Her plan was working.

Except, there was the chance meeting with Josh…

Getting a break from Chicago winters for four years was ideal. She worked a variety of on and off campus jobs so she could stay in Arizona for winter breaks and then visit her parents and sisters during the summers. The Sonoran Desert was the perfect choice for avoiding frigid Chicago winters.

Every step of her planning was sheer genius.

And then yesterday happened.

But she'd made mistakes before, and they somehow worked out for her. She could picture herself so clearly, arriving on campus, unpacking, and saying goodbye to her parents. And then she discovered her error in thinking. It turned out Tucson was not for the faint of heart in late August when she was sitting through her new student orientation. Grace was completely unprepared for the intense heat in early September when the semester was in full swing. To say she was a hot, sweaty mess by the time she walked from her dorm to her classes each day was an understatement.

Grace struggled those first weeks. She wondered if there was any way she could enroll in a few classes at any one of the many colleges and universities in and around Chicago. Pride kept her from taking that step. She was not going to admit she might have made a mistake. She avoided contact with Aunt Irene, afraid she would convince her to go back home, too.

It wasn't until she met Lexie that she was able to start settling into her home-away-from-home and begin enjoying her new experience. Once she got used to the routine of college life, she rapidly forgot about the doubts. She loved college. But college was just college. As soon as she had her degree, she was going to make a name for herself in marketing. Then one day, she'd marry and start a family. Everything in its appropriate time. That was the plan and she was sticking to it. Josh would not be a part of her plan.

Plans, she was about to learn, had a funny way of changing.

Chapter 2

12 years later...

"What am I trying to say? What in heaven's name am I trying to say?" Her voice was startlingly loud in the quiet house. Grace pushed her hands through her hair, shoving the laptop away with her elbows. Closing her eyes, she massaged her temples, hoping to stave off the headache she could feel nudging its way forward, just below her fingertips.

Her frustration was taking control, rendering her incapable of finding the right words to complete the task at hand, and making her realize she needed a moment to assess the situation. What was at the root of her frustration? She was struggling with this project. Words usually didn't prove problematic for her, and she generally didn't have difficulty finding them. Today, however, was another story. Perhaps it was the pressure. Katherine made it very clear she needed a completed marketing report on her desk Monday morning. That certainly counted as pressure.

Grace blew out a long breath of air, pushed herself up from the sofa and walked away from the coffee table she was using as her work desk. A whole weekend committed to work. That was another frustration right there.

Her coffee cup, sitting half empty for over an hour now on the kitchen counter, offered nothing but a bitter taste as she swallowed. She laughed to herself, realizing how appropriate the bitterness was in that moment. She was bitter. It oozed from every ounce of her being. She never met this client and never had any opportunity to get a feel for his taste, his ideas, his goals. Katherine simply handed her the file and said she was counting on Grace. Katherine O'Reilly, owner and president of O'Reilly Marketing, ran a tight ship. She made the rules and she expected everyone to follow them. Grace proved herself smart, creative and capable for Katherine and slowly the armor started to crack. Katherine eventually started to treat her differently than she treated the other three consultants. Their working relationship was formal but a high level of mutual respect existed. That's why Grace was especially frustrated over Katherine's actions on Thursday afternoon.

They never operated this way. Normally Katherine asked her to sit in on initial meetings with potential clients. Even if Katherine decided to fly solo on the project, she still liked knowing that Grace had background with the client so they could toss ideas around.

Grace gathered her hair in her hands, smoothing it with her fingers to shape a ponytail. She pulled the elastic band from her wrist where it generally stayed until she needed it, stretching and tightening it around the gathered strands. It was time for a mental and physical break.

Jasper slowly uncurled his legs from underneath him and stretched, sniffing the chew toy next to his over-sized dog bed. Almost eleven years old and quite arthritic, very little really interested him beyond a good ear scratch and a lot of nap time. He was hoping for that now as he slowly made his way to Grace. She obliged, reaching down with both hands to give his ears a good rub. He groaned, leaning first to the left and then to the right, making sure she didn't miss a single spot.

As much as Grace wanted to take him for a long walk like she used to, she knew that would just prove too painful for both of them. Jasper couldn't walk far and it broke her heart to see how much he had changed. "Sorry guy. I need to clear my head. You nap and I'll be back soon." Jasper didn't look overly disappointed as he re-curled himself into a ball and closed his eyes, letting out a satisfied sigh. She grabbed a water bottle and Gatorade, tossing them into the lightweight backpack Josh insisted she carry on her walks. She fit her cell phone into the outside pocket, where it would be in easy reach in an emergency.

Josh taught her everything he knew about survival, but he also knew much of it was wasted on her. She had no intention of going on a grand adventure that might require putting those skills to use. She touched her forehead, the tiny raised bump of skin strategically hidden by a side part a reminder of her first attempt to rock climb with Josh. Within the first few minutes of climbing, her foot slipped and she hit her head on the rock wall. The cut bled for a long time, making her panic, and the scar reminded her she wasn't as adventurous as her husband.

The Arizona morning was cool and comfortable, and perfect for a power walk. Grace set out, staying close to the edge of the road, at times with one foot on the pavement and the other in the gravel to avoid getting hit by a car coming too quickly along the curving hillside road, but not so close to the edge as to accidentally fall into a cactus. The drop off here was steep so she figured she would actually be lucky to fall into a cactus or two as long as it broke her fall.

It was a working weekend for Josh, too. She tried to remember what he'd said about the client. A man from New York who was training for a hiking adventure in Europe? That sounded vaguely familiar to her. It was amusing to think about yet another typical Josh client with too much money and time on his hands, creating adventures, escaping the reality of aging, a bad divorce or a sluggish economy. Josh joked about developing and marketing a "Mid-Life Crisis Package," an apropos title for what many of his recent clients seemed to be experiencing.

Grace paused to take a drink. A roadrunner darted through the saguaro, stopped, then scurried off in the opposite direction. Jasper would have loved that. She'd be sure to tell him about it. He was a great listener, never interrupting and never judging. He would simply cock his eyebrows, wag his tail and sometimes, if it didn't mean getting up and walking to her these days, lick her hand. It was good enough for her.

They loved Jasper dearly, but he didn't fill the void reserved for a baby. A sadness hovered, ready to dive-bomb her heart, but she denied it entry, pushing the word baby from her head and focusing instead on her breathing, on placing one foot in front of the other, on anything but her failure to make them a family. She told herself to think about anything besides babies. But it was to no avail.

One miscarriage is bad. Three miscarriages are devastating. When the first pregnancy test showed a positive result, they were beside themselves. Josh went out the next day and bought her a gift, watching excitedly as she held up the necklace, the small diamond twinkling as it caught the light. "We'll have a beautiful little girl who looks just like her mommy," he whispered to her. "Or a tough little boy who lives on the edge just like his daddy," she whispered back. They made love carefully and tenderly in the weeks following, both in absolute awe over what was about to happen to them.

When she started bleeding just one month later, she wanted Josh to return the necklace, but he refused, saying he would put it in a safe place until they could celebrate their first baby. Time has a way of healing, so they allowed themselves to get just as excited for the second pregnancy. Josh kissed her neck as he fastened the clasp of the necklace. They were breezing into week 13 when the bleeding started. They silently made their way to the doctor's office, went through the procedure again, and put the necklace back in the box.

Grace could never tell for sure if it was disappointment or relief on Josh's face when the third miscarriage occurred. Her doctor suggested going back on birth control for a while to give her body and mind some time to heal. She had not seen the necklace in years.

She shook the thoughts from her head, attempting to focus on the here and now.

She hoped Josh's weekend was going better than hers. They had a lot to talk about when he returned tomorrow. The thought surprised Grace, as she realized they hadn't really talked about much lately, of significance anyway. How had they gotten so absorbed in their own worlds of work that they no longer took time to share the way they used to? She couldn't remember the last time they made love. "That's going to change," Grace said aloud. This kind of complacency could destroy a marriage. She loved Josh with all her heart. In fact, the first day they met she had fallen hard for him—literally. The memory made her smile, easing some of the stress of her morning.

She wondered if Josh ever thought about their early days together.

Chapter 3

————— ◆—◆—◆ —————

J osh rolled over in bed. It took a moment to remember exactly where he was, that moment between sleeping and waking sometimes a confusing time that plays interesting tricks on the mind. On weekends he was accustomed to waking up in unusual places—a tent on a hillside or a makeshift shelter the most common. This morning he definitely wasn't in a tent. The sheets rustled beneath him, the soft cotton caressing his skin. He definitely wasn't on a bed of pine needles.

Fully awake now, he smiled, remembering exactly where he was. He slid closer to the warm body under the sheets with him, his arm wrapping around her as he listened to the sound of her breathing. She stirred, making a sound someplace between a sigh and a purr, and he wondered if she was having a good dream. He didn't have to dream. Everything he wanted—awake or asleep—was snuggled next to him in this bed. This was his happiness.

He rubbed her arm and then slowly slid his hand down, finding the warm place between her legs. He probed gently, his own desire becoming more evident by the moment. This time when she stirred there was definitely a purr. She reached down to wrap her hand around the firmness she found there, eager to continue the lovemaking which had already kept them up much of the night. A moan escaped Josh as he rolled her toward him and moved on top of her in one graceful motion, sliding into her warmth. Yes, this was his happiness.

Chapter 4

---◆—◆—◆---

Grace set the grocery bags on the countertop, pushing aside the laptop that safely housed the now completed marketing plan. Glancing at the wall clock, she worked out her timing. She expected Josh home at about 5:00. That would give her about three hours to put the groceries away, shower and have dinner started by the time he walked in the door, assuming he made it home at his usual time. After aimlessly wandering the grocery store aisles for a while trying to figure out what to make for dinner, she decided on a Cajun shrimp dish they both liked. She hadn't made it in a long time. In fact, she hadn't planned a nice dinner for them in ages. Picking out a bottle of red wine was the next step, deciding it would be a perfect way to get them both relaxed and in the moment.

She calculated the time she'd need to get the food in the oven, make a salad and open the wine. Grace smiled, pleased with all she'd accomplished since yesterday's walk. It had done wonders to clear her mind and ease her frustration. Having a plan in place always made her feel better. She set about putting the groceries away, telling Jasper the details of her plans for the evening. He seemed to approve, thumping his tail now and then and cocking his head at certain comments that seemed especially pleasing to him. He was so easy to talk to.

Once showered, she prepped the vegetables for the salad, peeling and slicing and letting her mind wander to the fateful day she'd met Josh. Falling in love with Josh was never in the cards, but over the weeks following their chance meeting, they found every excuse possible to connect. They called one another. They emailed one another. When they had any free time at all, they spent it together. It was difficult for Grace to concentrate on final exams and term papers. Josh wasn't trying to break her focus, but somehow, that became inevitable. There were coffee dates, lunch dates, dinner and movie dates. There were long talks. By now, they knew just about everything there was to know about each other, both of them anxious to share their pasts, their dreams and their hopes for the future.

She told him about her parents' homes, the family home in Chicago to enjoy city life, and another in Venice, Florida, where they could "snowbird" each winter. He learned about her sisters, Ellen pregnant with her second child and worried about how Tyler, just three years old, would feel about a new baby in his house. Jeremy, her husband, spent a lot of his time reassuring her that kids adjust quickly. He knew, too, that John and Geneva, "Gen," were disappointed that they had not yet had a baby. She told him what a foreign world that seemed to her. It wasn't that she didn't want a family, she just didn't want one any time soon. She had other things to accomplish first.

Josh went to college because it was his dad's dream for him. He studied Environmental Sciences, but what he really wanted to do was start an outfitting company, leading campers to remote areas, teaching them survival skills and respect and appreciation for the outdoors. The seminar she crashed was his first attempt at teaching those skills in a classroom setting. He still wasn't sure that was the right approach for him. He wasn't worried though, he assured her. He was going to figure it out. She believed him. He was certainly a guy who could figure things out.

Most of all, there was lovemaking. Exploring each other's most intimate desires was an adventure they both anticipated and enjoyed. Josh was an amazing lover, able to make her feel weak and helpless yet strong and powerful at the same time.

They learned to bring out the best in each other, touching, stroking, and making sure each experienced nothing but pleasure. He was fit and muscular. She loved running her fingers along the veins in his arms, laughing when he jumped because it "tickled" and moving down to do the same to his legs. She loved his body.

Grace's carefully developed plans seemed a distant memory. When her family flew out for commencement, Grace proudly introduced them to Josh. George and Sylvia Warrens knew immediately this was not a passing fancy in the world of dating and their Grace was not going to be moving back by them any time soon. They hid any disappointment they were feeling when Grace told them, "I might apply for some positions around Tucson. You know, just to see what might be interesting here." Deep down, they always hoped she'd land back in Chicago after graduating.

It was a tight job market and she had to carefully balance the need to start her career with the unending desire to be as close to Josh as possible. Although a couple of job offers came in from firms with offers of rapid advancement from sales to marketing, each was in a different state. In the end, Grace opted to work as a personal assistant to the CEO of a relatively large marketing firm in Tucson. She told Josh it would be a great starting point for her to really learn the business. It wasn't her dream job, but they knew the truth. If she took a job out of state, the relationship they were building would fizzle. Long-distance relationships had a strange way of doing that. So, she stayed in Tucson and he stayed in Phoenix, still spending as much time as possible together, and hating the moment when they had to say goodbye.

***

The wine was opened and the glasses, polished twice for good measure, were set out on the counter when Josh walked in the door just moments after 5:00. He looked tired, but Grace wrapped her arms around him, kissing him on the cheek. He looked around the kitchen. "Did I forget some special occasion?" She smiled, handing him the glass of wine she'd just poured.

"We're both here together. That's the occasion." She sipped her wine, watching Josh over the rim as he again looked at the results of her labors. Cut flowers were in the vase, the table was set, salads were on the table and a tantalizing aroma was coming from the oven. "Can you guess?" She nodded toward the oven, acknowledging that he was taking in the smells and sights.

"It definitely isn't trail mix. I'll go with a wild guess here…Cajun shrimp?" He opened the oven door just enough to see the bubbling sauce and release more of the smell. The aroma filled the air, rich with Cajun seasoning. "Smells great. I'll jump in the shower."

He took a sip of his wine and set the glass down, before heading off to shower. Grace smiled, pleased with herself for the extra effort. This was just what they needed to re-connect. And she hoped that re-connecting would include making love. She didn't realize how much she missed that until this weekend. It had been ages since either of them had initiated sex. Yes, it would be a great evening.

***

It had the *potential* to be a great evening. Grace finished putting away the last of the dishes, poured herself what was left of the wine, and turned off the kitchen lights. She knew Josh was in the family room because she could hear the television. He was in the recliner, his nearly-empty wine glass on the coffee table where she'd spent the weekend working on the marketing report. His eyes were closed, mouth slightly open, sleeping the sleep of the exhausted. With a sigh, Grace picked up his glass, poured its contents into her own and sat down on the sofa directly across from her husband, watching him sleep.

This was not how she pictured their evening. She continued sipping the wine, reliving the evening and knowing it had not met her expectations from the moment Josh finished his shower. She imagined conversations they'd had in the past, laughing as they recounted each other's days, creating a shared experience despite their lives being so completely different. Tonight's conversation was nothing like those. Josh talked nonstop. It was actually quite unlike him. He told story after story about the client he worked with all weekend, sharing conversations they had, describing the details of the training plan they developed and would put into action. There was no opportunity to tell him about her work, or her frustration with Katherine.

"We'll try this again soon, Josh." She whispered the words aloud to him, hoping that maybe they'd register someplace in the deep recesses of his unconscious. She sat a while longer, finishing her wine.

As Grace watched him, she thought back to the night he proposed, surprising her with a weekend get-away to Sedona. When she thought they were on their way to a quiet dinner, he surprised her with a sunset hot air balloon ride. It was breathtaking, almost magical, but what really took her breath away was Josh taking her hand just as the sun slipped below the mountain and getting down on one knee. "I know you were planning a big-city kind of life, but I'm hoping you'll be able to call this home now. Marry me Gracie-Belle?"

In his re-telling of the story, he claimed she said yes before he even asked the all-important question. She denied it, but wondered if maybe he was right. Like most girls, Grace dreamed about finding the perfect man who would propose in the most perfect way. When it was actually happening to her, the moment seemed too surreal to be happening. That night was a lifetime ago. There hadn't been any magic tonight. They were just another "old married couple" slipping into complacency. Her attempt to change that tonight had failed.

She stood and walked over to her sleeping husband, reluctantly admitting the evening was officially over. She gave his arm a gentle shake. "Let's go to bed, sweetie. You're exhausted."

Josh smiled in his sleep and mumbled, "You were great honey." Grace shook her head. He was charming even when he was spoiling her evening. She gave him another gentle shake and when he finally opened his eyes, he seemed surprised to see her there. He looked around, trying to get his bearings. "Oh, I guess I fell asleep. Sorry." He followed her to the bedroom and by the time she finished brushing her teeth and washing her face, he was again sound asleep, and this time Grace let him sleep. She never even had a chance to tell him what she most wanted to tell him. She wanted to try again to have a baby.

Chapter 5

C offee sloshed dangerously close to the surface of her travel mug as Grace unlocked her office door, juggling her mail, purse and coffee. *Just what I need, another mess to clean up*, she thought.

Removing the bag from her shoulder, she unzipped the computer case and slid the laptop onto her desk, moving her coffee a safe distance away. She hadn't had the best of mornings thus far and now she was being extra cautious. After a restless night she arose early, feeling suddenly less than confident about the marketing plan she developed. She decided to get to the office early to spend an extra hour reviewing the report before her meeting with Katherine. She feared she perhaps spent a little too much time thinking about a romantic evening with Josh, and had rushed through some elements of the plan. She would have time and opportunity to tweak it as long as she had no interruptions.

Josh was still asleep when she got out of bed. Jasper was content to stay curled up on the floor as close to her side of the bed as he could get. He raised his head enough for her to give him a quick pat as she walked by, and then he snuggled deeper into his bed. She quietly set about showering and getting ready for the day ahead. It wasn't until she was almost ready to walk out the door that Josh, hair tousled and eyes heavy with sleep, finally made his way into the kitchen. Normally up well before she was, it was a little unusual to see him sleep in. He took the mug of coffee she handed him and leaned in to kiss her on the cheek. "Morning. Guess I crashed last night." He gave her a grin and she smiled in return.

"You could say that." It was impossible to be upset with him. He worked hard all weekend, too, so of course he would be exhausted. It was silly of her to try to plan a big romantic thing on a Sunday night when she knew he would come home exhausted. This was all about her poor timing.

"Early meeting?" He had already downed half of his coffee, oblivious to the fact that it was hot, and was foraging through the refrigerator to figure out what he would throw in his morning smoothie. She reached for the coffee pot to top off his cup. Josh chose that moment to swing around from the refrigerator and bump her arm as she poured. Both jumped out of the way as hot coffee spilled on the countertop and floor but the splatters on her skirt meant a quick change before she could leave.

Trying to tamper her irritation, she answered over her shoulder as she returned to the bedroom for a wardrobe adjustment. "Not exactly. I was hoping to review some materials before my meeting with Katherine. She has been kind of salty lately so I'm hoping to impress her with my proposal. Make sure you take Jasper for a walk before you leave."

He was already completely absorbed in the morning paper when she whisked by him on her way out the door.

Now, here in her office, she was ready to focus. After a quick review of the report, she was again confident she had captured the essence of the project, creating a marketing proposal aligned with what she had to assume to be in the best interests of the client. She returned to the same argument that caused her frustration all weekend. The report may be done, but this wasn't her client, so she couldn't be absolutely certain what the client was expecting.

Resentment unexpectedly boiled up inside her all over again. Expecting her to create a marketing plan without having met or talked to the potential client didn't make any sense. She debated asking Katherine why there had been this unexpected change in her usual protocol. Of course, there was always the slim chance that Katherine was finally giving her an opportunity to start flying solo on big accounts. Maybe this was going to be her test of sorts. Not sure why she hadn't thought of that sooner, Grace's spirits lifted. She was so quick to negatively judge Katherine's request when it was probably going to be highly beneficial to her. She had to learn to stay positive.

At exactly 8:50 she made her way to the break room, pouring a cup of coffee for herself and getting a green tea ready for Katherine. She hoped Katherine would appreciate the effort, and maybe even recognize it as a thank you for having trusted her employee on this account. Balancing the two cups and her laptop, she stood outside of Katherine's office, surprised that the scene was not what she was expecting. Her boss wasn't playing out her usual routine of sitting on the edge of her desk, long legs crossed, talking on the phone, beckoning Grace into the room. The office door was closed, and it was clear Katherine was not around. Grace set the cups down on a nearby table and walked the few steps to Maddie's desk, situated between the main entrance and Katherine's office.

"Maddie, did Katherine leave a message for me?" She asked without even waiting for Maddie to look up from her computer screen. Although Maddie was officially the administrative assistant for the firm, it was common knowledge that she was really more Katherine's personal assistant than their go-to for needed assistance.

Maddie's look of surprise meant she had no idea why Grace would be asking for Katherine this morning. "Hey Grace. Happy Monday." Maddie felt a need to make every day a happy one. Tomorrow she would greet everyone with a Happy Tuesday. She was looking at the electronic calendar she pulled up on her screen, studying it carefully for anything to suggest Grace had a scheduled meeting. "Katherine's not planning to be in this morning. She has two hours blocked off here. It just says 'late arrival.'" Maddie was using her finger to point to the place on the screen, as if that would make it more official for Grace. "I assume she has an off-site meeting. Can I help you with something?"

Frustration turned to anger. "Late arrival? She was adamant that I was to present a proposal first thing this morning. She was very clear about this. Are you absolutely sure she's not expecting me? She made this sound pretty important."

Maddie only shook her head, screwing up her eyes as if concentrating really hard on the electronic calendar in front of her. "Sorry Grace. There's nothing here about changing a meeting with you or being late or anything. Maybe you wrote down the wrong time."

"Maybe," Grace replied as she turned on her heel, grabbing her laptop but leaving the two beverages on the table as she stormed back to her office. Someone else could clean that up, she decided. She had cleaned up enough messes for one morning. She unceremoniously dropped the laptop onto the desk, beyond frustrated with her boss. She did the only thing that seemed logical to her in the moment. She picked up her phone and called Josh, needing to vent to someone who would understand her anger with the pressure that had been unnecessarily forced on her for the whole weekend. But even that turned out to be unsatisfying as Josh's phone went directly to voicemail, asking her to please leave a message that he would return at his earliest convenience.

Grace slammed the phone into its base, feeling some sense of satisfaction from the loud crack it produced. "Son of a bitch." The words were spoken to no one in particular but felt somehow appropriate in the moment. "Son of a freaking bitch."

Grace paced the few steps each way that her office space allowed and then threw herself into her desk chair, not sure where to direct her anger. Sitting didn't last long. Soon she was up again, unable to contain her frustration. "All weekend. I worried about this all weekend. Never again. I will not work this way." Her rant made her feel a bit better.

Two hours later, buried in a project completely unrelated to the work she'd spent the weekend developing, Grace was startled by the rapid footsteps that always heralded Katherine's approach. "Grace, Maddie said you needed to see me." She was either completely oblivious to the directive she'd given Grace a couple days earlier or playing some kind of game. Any thoughts she'd had earlier about this project somehow being a favor to her were long forgotten.

"Are you ready to review the project you told me was vitally important to have ready for you first thing this morning?" Grace hoped she was hiding her real anger, making her unprepared for the response.

Katherine smoothed her hair behind her ear, her movements slow and deliberate. "We seem to have an issue here, Grace. If you have a problem with how I run my company, you can certainly find a different one that might be more accommodating to your needs." Katherine's expression remained unflinching, almost cold. Her face seemed more pale than usual, making her red hair look like a blaze around her face.

Completely taken aback, Grace froze, unsure how to respond. Had she expected Katherine to apologize? Of course. Katherine was the one in the wrong. Grace had followed her every directive. She took a deep breath, knowing she had to find it in herself to let a cooler self prevail now or she would certainly regret this moment, so she chose her words carefully. "You're the one who insisted I prepare a marketing plan to share with you first thing this morning. You told me it was *imperative* I have this ready to share first thing this morning. I was a little surprised that you changed your mind about its relevancy. Perhaps you could explain that to me." Grace wished her heart would stop pounding, certain Katherine could see it beating through her blouse if she happened to glance there. Grace willed herself not to check, forcing herself to maintain eye contact with her boss.

"First and foremost, Grace, I don't have to explain anything to you. Secondly, your attitude this morning leaves me concerned that you aren't entirely happy here. I'll provide a reference should you decide there's something better out there for you. Take some time to think about it." With that, Katherine turned and left, leaving Grace shaking and unsure as to what just transpired. Feeling sick to her stomach, she closed her office door, resting her head on the cool top of her desk. She didn't even want to try Josh's number again because she had no desire to feel rejection again—that lack of satisfaction that comes from hearing the mechanical tone of a voice recording. She needed a sympathetic ear, not a machine telling her what to do.

She remembered the last time she felt this same type of betrayal and confusion. Sitting here, wallowing in those emotions again, it brought the memories back vividly. It wasn't work related then. It had been Josh. Her stomach churned even more and she wondered if she should just call it quits for the day, go home and take a hot bath to forget the day...and the whole weekend that preceded it. But she remained where she was, her eyes closed, unable to stop the flood of memories.

It was about six years ago, at an especially busy time for them. They bought their first house. She was one year into her first real marketing job and Josh was busier than ever, having just started his newest service to clients, triathlon readiness training. After competing in his first Iron Man competition shortly after their wedding, Josh was hooked. He realized that athletes and athlete wannabees would pay him good money to train in the perfect weather conditions of Arizona winters.

He researched, planned, organized, prepared and when he launched the new division of his company, supported by a former Olympic qualifying swimmer to provide the aquatic expertise, he was immediately drawing a customer base from around the world. The two of them offered a unique and challenging training opportunity, including swimming training focused on endurance and speed, guided desert bike riding, and tandem runs with Josh.

Jillian, the swimming expert, was pretty much everything Grace was not. She had the perfect swimmer's body, with solid legs and muscular arms. She also had shockingly blue eyes that made her look as though she had been born from the very water she swam in every day. She was always as excited as Josh when talking about training, muscle use, controlled breathing—all a foreign concept to Grace—and Grace felt an irritating niggle—a tiny bit of jealously creeping in over the special bond Josh and Jillian shared. Grace wasn't sure if it was the athleticism, the great looks or the fact that Josh spent countless hours with her that sparked the jealously.

Josh established a connection with two popular Tucson resorts, advertising his services on their websites and using the resort health clubs as a home base for clients. It saved him the expense of leasing a pool, and guests were more willing to commit to the training when they had a luxurious hotel and spa to return to after their grueling workouts. The resort was able to fill its casitas and Josh was able to rapidly expand his offerings. It also meant Josh and Jillian spent time together at the resorts, time that hardly seemed like work the way they carried on about it. When Grace couldn't stand it any longer, she did what many women in her shoes have done. She started watching for signs of an affair.

She watched for changes in his attitude and behavior—subtle nuances she was sure she would recognize as signs of an affair. She secretly went through his pockets—not sure what she would be looking for but positive she'd recognize signs of an affair. She subtly sniffed his neck when they hugged—sure she would recognize another woman's perfume and a sure sign of an affair.

When all of that proved fruitless, she resorted to even worse measures. Grace still felt the humiliation from the night she made up her mind to catch Josh in the act. When she made up her mind to call his bluff, another claim of late-night work to be done, she drove to his office late that Tuesday night. She quietly let herself in the locked front door, certain she would find something she didn't want to see, but knowing the truth was better than wondering. Passing through a series of open work spaces as she made her way down the hall, the sound of Jillian's laugh became clearer through the closed office door. Grace made her way to the door marked Private, poised to fling open the door, knowing her glance would be immediately pulled to the comfortable sofa Josh called his "Thinking Lounger." She did indeed find an almost completely undressed Jillian wrapped in the arms and legs of...an equally long-legged, lithe-bodied woman. Both looked up in complete shock, and Grace backed out of the room, mumbling something that was supposed to sound like an apology. Josh arrived home just 30 minutes after Grace, proudly waving the contract signed that very night by his newest client. She decided then and there that sleuthing was not for her. She had to trust that Josh would not betray their marriage vows. She never told him about her suspicions and she assumed Jillian never mentioned their strange nighttime encounter either.

With a sigh and a great deal of effort, Grace picked her head up from the desk and forced herself to return to the project she'd started earlier. She would wait until the afternoon to ask Katherine for a follow-up meeting. They would clear the air and move on. Katherine was right. As the boss, she could certainly decide what Grace was to work on and when she was to work on it. Perhaps the dream of being Katherine's partner in the business was suddenly a more distant possibility, but she wasn't ready to leave her job either. She also decided to try calling Josh again, just in case he might be available to hear about her day from hell.

Chapter 6

————◆–◆–◆————

J osh couldn't stop smiling. He tried. He honestly tried, but the silly grin just kept re-appearing. He was seated next to Kat in her comfortable living room, one of his favorite rooms in the house. That wasn't entirely true. Her bedroom took the prize as his favorite room. They could spend hours on end in there, completely forgetting anyone else existed in the world.

"This is real now, babe. I'm due September 22nd." Her voice held something between excitement and disbelief. Neither had planned this, but neither would trade it for anything in the world. "I guess I'll be spending a lot of time in air-conditioning all summer long." Kat was giddy as she pretended to be heavy-bellied, waddling a few steps and then stopping to wipe away imaginary sweat.

Up until just 10 minutes ago, Josh had been pacing the floor, waiting for her to get home. Of course, the thoughts while pacing included Grace to some extent, but he had come to terms with that over the past couple of weeks. He saw the calls from Grace on his cell phone but he had no intention of answering. When Kat told him two weeks ago she was pregnant, they both knew one thing to be true beyond any shadow of a doubt. They were going to have this baby. They spent an incredibly special weekend on a getaway that had been purposely planned as their last quiet time together for a while. They were well aware of the unavoidable turmoil that would ensue once Grace learned of their relationship and Josh's decision. He and Kat needed this calm before the impending storm. And it would certainly be a storm. He had no doubt about that.

This morning had been nothing short of torturous, as he was trying to get out of the house so he could begin separating himself physically and emotionally from his wife. His heart and mind were already elsewhere. Kat had scheduled the appointment with her obstetrician for this morning so she could make sure everything was going as it should, find out the due date and start planning their lives from there. Their lives together. That still felt strange and exhilarating to him. So much so, in fact, it was impossible for him to concentrate on work. That's why he was sitting at Kat's house now, waiting for her to return.

The evening before had been difficult. If he could, he would have simply called Grace and told her over the phone, but he knew that was the weak way out. If there was one thing Josh was not, it was weak. He had to face his wife, tell her the truth and then let the wounds start to heal. When he walked in the door and saw that she had planned so carefully for a special evening, he momentarily lost his courage. So instead of telling her the truth, he made up a whole story about some imaginary client with whom he'd spent the weekend. He hated himself for prolonging the inevitable, but Grace was being so sweet and put so much effort into the dinner, he just couldn't do it last night. He couldn't let it happen again, though. He pictured a bandage being ripped off his skin. A sickening feeling accompanied it. He could do this. He had to do this. The quicker he could rip it off, the better it would be for all of them.

"You are *definitely* telling her today, right?"

"Yes, babe, I'll tell her." He took her hand and pulled her closer to him on the sofa. He would deal with Grace as soon as she got home from work. Right now, he had a special gift for Kat. She opened the box, pulling out a necklace. She held it up, watching the diamond sparkle in the rays of sunshine pouring through the living room window. He took it from her hands and carefully fastened the clasp as she held up her long red hair for him. "I love you, Katherine. I can't wait until I can put a diamond on your finger. For now, you'll have to settle for one around your neck."

They sat together on the sofa for a long time, Josh gently rubbing the place on her belly where one day in the very near future they would be able to see evidence of the love they had for one another. He was anxious to get through the ugly part with Grace so he could move forward to the life he was going to give to this beautiful woman who was going to have his baby.

Chapter 7

The wine bar was crowded, but it took just a second for Grace to spot Lexie. Perhaps it was the almost frantic waving of her arms to make sure Grace saw her, but more likely it was the new hair color—purple, black and silver to be exact. An artist by trade, Lexie used every palette available to her, and that included her own body. She had multiple tattoos, a couple of piercings, and an ever-changing head of hair. Sometimes the changes were in length and style and other times changes in color. This tri-colored combination was new, making Grace smile and shake her head.

She loved Lexie to death and learned long ago not to judge anything she saw on the outside. On the inside, Lexie would always be the wonderful person who became her best friend their first year of college when they were paired for a class project. Inseparable since then, they started rooming together their sophomore year, first in the dorms and then moving to an apartment together for their final two years of school. They were like sisters. Of course, Lexie looked nothing like Grace's actual sisters with their all-American girl-next-door wholesome looks so when the three of them stood up as bridesmaids in Josh and Grace's wedding, it was immediately evident to everyone that Lexie was not part of the family. Her sisters were a little concerned at first that people would find Lexie's outrageous appearance offensive but they quickly learned what Grace already knew. Lexie, despite all the self-expression, was one of the kindest, sweetest people any of them knew. Now, Lexie gestured toward the stool next to her. "Sit. You sounded terrible on the phone. Do you want a glass or should we go directly to a bottle?"

Grace gave her friend an appreciative smile as she settled onto the stool, tossing her purse on the empty seat next to her. "I better start with just a glass."

Once the wine arrived and they knew they would be uninterrupted for a while, Grace finally let the floodgates open. "Everything that could possibly go wrong has been going wrong, Lex." Always the perfect sounding board, Lexie listened, adding the right nods, headshakes and surprised expressions as Grace told her all about her strange day and the ruined weekend that led up to it. "Katherine has never treated me like that. I'm sure I deserved it today, but she could have been a little more understanding, too."

"Sounds like Kat-Woman needs to get laid." Lexie emptied her glass and Grace knew the comments would become even more unrefined with her second glass of wine. She didn't care. "I knew we should have gone directly for the bottle. I'm getting one." Lexie waved at the server to get his attention, ready to help her friend forget about all of her troubles for a while. "Go ahead and bring us a bottle of this," she held her empty glass high up in the air to show the young man before he even reached the table. He nodded, turned on his heel and was soon back to show off his bottle opening skills for them.

"You're probably right, but that's not exactly a recommendation I can give her." Grace was feeling the effects of the wine, a slight burn moving down her chest and slowly warming her insides like a hug. She probably should have eaten something before hitting the wine, but it had just been that kind of day. "Dragon lady would probably eat the man after he does her." Grace covered her mouth, shocked that the comment slipped so easily out of her mouth. "You're such a bad influence on me!" She gave her a playful punch on the arm, grateful she could always be herself around Lexie. "And what about Josh? It isn't right to have my job and my marriage screwed up at the same time." She leaned in close to Lexie, trying to shut out the noises of the patrons around them. "Do you think he's losing interest in me? He hardly talks to me anymore." Grace was embarrassed by the tears burning her eyelids. She reached over to find a tissue in her purse, hoping Lexie hadn't noticed.

"Don't be crazy. He's nuts about you. Maybe you just have to do a better job of reminding him that you're still the sexy little thing he fell for. We could go to Victoria's Secret right now if you want." Lexie wiggled her eyebrows at Grace, hoping to make her laugh. It worked. "And if that doesn't do it, we can buy you some sex toys."

"Lexie! That's disgusting." She thought about it a moment. "I guess I could put a *little* more effort into it. I'm sure the old All-American Iron Man t-shirt isn't exactly screaming 'take me.' Yep, I can probably do just a wee bit better."

"Maybe you should get your nipples pierced. That might really turn him on. Come on Grace. Let's find that crazy Wildcat spirit." That earned Lexie another light punch. "Even better, promise him a threesome for his birthday. You know I love you and will take one for the team if it'll help you out."

"Right. I'm sure that's the perfect cure for our sexual woes. Let me get back to you on that one."

After her final glass of wine and a phone call to Josh, she gingerly climbed off her barstool, feeling just a little unsteady on her feet. "I'm not sure what I'd do without you Lex. Thanks for listening. Do you want Josh to give you a ride home?" Her words came out slurred, making her giggle. "I guess it's smart of me not to drive home, huh? I'm a little tipsy." She bumped her now empty wine glass, somehow actually catching it before it fell off the table. "Oopsy daisy. I'm officially cut off." It came out more like awfishly, sending them into another bout of giggles.

Lexie poured herself the last drops of the wine from the bottle and held her glass up in an exaggerated toast, tapping her glass against nothing but air. "Here's to solving all the world's problems. I'm calling a cab after I polish off this cab." She laughed at her own joke and took the final sip. "You have to go home and tantalize your man. You can tell me every juicy detail tomorrow. And don't forget to slip in the possibility of a threesome. I'll be waiting for your phone call." She moved her cell phone next to her glass, intently staring at it as if waiting for it to ring. Again, they both laughed, oblivious to the stares from those around them.

Josh arrived shortly after, first helping Lexie into the cab she'd called and then making sure Grace was settled in the front seat of his Jeep. "You're not going to throw up, are you?"

Grace ran her hand up and down his arm, impressed as always at the muscles that rippled under his shirt. "I only had three glasses. Maybe four. I just didn't eat anything all day so it hit me right away. Thanks for picking me up." She leaned over to give him a kiss and he gave her his cheek, intent on steering out of the parking lot and onto the street. "I had the worst day *ever*. Lexie always makes me laugh." She leaned her head against his arm, her eyes getting heavier. She must have fallen asleep on the short ride home, because the next thing she knew, Josh was gently shaking her. Grace didn't want to move. She was perfectly comfortable right here.

"It's time to get to bed, Grace." He unfastened her seatbelt and then got out, walking around to help her out of the Jeep. "I'll have to get up early to drive you to your car before I can get to work tomorrow. I'm glad you didn't drive but now I'll have this to deal with this. Maybe you should have thought of that before you had all that wine." He didn't even attempt to hide his irritation with her. "Let's get you inside so we can get some sleep."

Grace tried to protest, insisting she had to tell him all about her terrible day. She started to say more and lost her train of thought. Josh assured her he would be happy to hear all about it in the morning. If Grace had any thoughts of seducing her husband, they had long disappeared by the time she brushed her teeth, washed her face and slipped into her faded t-shirt. She giggled as she remembered the conversation about her not-so-sexy sleepwear. She fell asleep as soon as her head hit the pillow.

Josh knew he wouldn't be telling her anything tonight. He wasn't sure if he was grateful or disappointed. As ready as he was to do this, it was still a conversation that he didn't relish having.

***

Despite waking with a headache, Grace was up and ready before Josh even finished shaving. She walked Jasper, made coffee and was all set to get a ride back to the parking lot where she'd left her car so she could start her day with a fresh attitude. She was hoping to touch base with Katherine before much more time put an awkward space between them. Well, a more awkward space than had already been created. She was also anxious to share the prior day's events with her husband. She could hear Josh on his phone as she made her way to the bedroom with a cup of coffee for him. He wrapped up his conversation and set his phone on the bed as she handed him a coffee mug. "You're awfully perky this morning, little Miss Wino."

Grace grinned sheepishly, slightly embarrassed, yet knowing she had a great excuse for her actions. She was also certain Josh would fully agree once he heard about the day she'd had. "My day would have driven anyone to drink. I don't even know where to start!"

"Why don't you start by letting me get ready and you can talk on the way." She gave him a playful swat on the butt as she left him to finish getting ready while she wandered back to the kitchen for another cup of coffee.

***

Her disappointment was morphing into fury at warp speed. Josh was not reacting with quite the spirit she expected. It was a guy thing—wanting to get right to solving the problem instead of being a much-needed sounding board—but where was his righteous indignation? Where was her protective husband? She wrapped it all up with, "She was totally out of line, Josh. She made me give up my entire weekend because she said she *had* to have it. Then she acted all incensed because I asked for an explanation. That just doesn't make sense. I'm sure *she* didn't waste her whole weekend on work!" She had set Josh up to provide plenty of sympathy, but was left feeling sadly deprived.

He kept his eyes on the road, seemingly absorbed in traffic and maneuvering carefully through each intersection. "I'm sure she has a good reason for all of it Grace. She *is* your boss. Just apologize and let it go."

This was almost too much for Grace, and she noticed her headache returning with a vengeance. Where was her support system? Where was the man who was supposed to be on her side—for better or worse, for mean boss days, for all that stuff? Incensed, she nearly spat, "Let it go? Would you 'let it go'?" She had turned in her seat to face him as he drove, but now

Grace felt somewhat like an impertinent child as she crossed her arms across her chest and threw herself back in her seat with a "harrumph." *Men!* "You'd be ready to put a fist into a man's mouth if he treated you that way, but because it's two women, we're supposed to 'let it go.' Jesus, Josh. That's like, I don't know, it's such a double standard."

"Come on, Grace. That's not fair. Why would two men just start throwing punches? You need to take some of the emotion out of this. She asked you to do a job and you did the job. Maybe she just wasn't ready for your presentation. Maybe the client changed directions on her and she just didn't have a chance to say anything to you. It's probably not a big deal at all. Don't blow it out of proportion. And don't act like a couple of school girls fighting on the playground. It's your job and you need to stay professional."

Grace didn't say anything the rest of the ride. As she got out of the Jeep she turned and smiled sweetly at her husband. "Don't worry. I'll be a perfect little angel at school today. I'm sure the principal won't have to call you in for a conference or anything." She slammed the door and strode off, not bothering to look back to see his reaction. At that moment she actually wanted to punch *him* in the mouth! Instead, she unlocked her car, adjusted the mirror and drove a little faster out of the parking lot than she probably should have, refusing to glance his way.

He hadn't noticed. He was back on his phone, having to explain to Katherine that once again he was not able to tell Grace the truth. He knew Kat had no intention of being at the office today so at least the two women would be spared another face-off.

***

Maddie was on the phone as Grace approached her desk, signaling her to wait a moment while she finished her conversation. When she turned her attention to Grace, her smile was less warm than usual. "If you're looking for Katherine, you're out of luck. She won't be in the office the next couple of days." With that, Maddie stood, pushed her chair back and walked to the breakroom, leaving Grace wondering what had just transpired. Why was she no longer worthy of a "Happy Tuesday" greeting?

Her intention to apologize had been a good one. Perhaps an opportunity would arise in the coming days. She thought about calling Katherine, but that didn't feel right. She wanted to take care of this in person. In fact, maybe by waiting a couple of days, Katherine would realize how much she overreacted. This delay would be in everyone's favor, Grace decided. There was plenty of work for her to tackle without needing additional instruction or updates from Katherine so she got to it immediately. A few hours later, her stomach growling loudly, she realized she never prepared a lunch for herself at home— mainly because her stomach had been a little queasy from the over-indulgence in wine—so she left her office to grab a veggie wrap from the health food shop down the street. As she walked, she called Lexie.

"He was being an ass, Lex. I have no idea what his problem is, but there was no sex last night. And there probably won't be tonight either."

"Maybe you two need a vacation," Lexie offered. As much as that sounded appealing to Grace, she knew they wouldn't be doing that any time soon.

Concentrating on work the rest of the afternoon was difficult, the headache and the anger dulled enough so she

48

could look at both sides with clarity. Maybe, just maybe, she thought, Josh was so non-reactionary on purpose. Perhaps it was his way of saying he wanted her to come to a conclusion on her own. The more she thought about it, the more she realized how logical that actually sounded. Josh made his living guiding and instructing others to be decision makers in regard to their diet, their workout programs, listening to the messages their bodies were sending, taking clues from nature. Why wouldn't he use that same approach with her? It made sense.

She had options after her emotional eruption with her boss. She could...quit? The thought took her by surprise. What would she do if she were to quit? Work for another marketing firm? Do something entirely different? She occasionally thought about working for a non-profit organization. Perhaps it was time to start exploring an option like that. Josh was brilliant, helping her reach this conclusion on her own. He should have studied psychology.

Changing jobs. The more she let the thought roll around in her head, the more intriguing it became. Maybe there were two big decisions she and Josh could discuss if they were both awake, sober and in the same room at the same time anytime soon.

Chapter 8

T he house was quiet when she walked in later that afternoon. Jasper didn't greet her but she didn't find that to be all too unusual. What she did find unusual was Josh's overstuffed duffel sitting by the kitchen door. She was taken aback for a moment, trying to remember any reference to an upcoming trip. She couldn't come up with anything. "Josh. Where are you going?" She was talking loudly enough for him to hear her regardless of where in the house he might be. She set her purse on the counter, listening for a response, but there was none. "Hey. Where are you going?" she repeated, walking into the living room. He was sitting on the edge of the couch, awkward and uncomfortable. Again, surprised by this out of the ordinary behavior, she wasn't sure what she should do. "Are you okay? Did something happen, Josh? Are you sick? You look terrible."

He raised his head, holding something between his thumb and finger. She stared at the object, trying to make sense of what was happening. "I think you should sit down, Grace." Suddenly lightheaded, she sank into the nearby recliner. Nothing was connecting, like watching a movie that was skipping scenes, and a sense of anxiety was rapidly growing within her. "I think you should sit down."

"I *am* sitting down, Josh. Tell me what's going on. You're scaring me. What happened?" She gasped. "Did someone die?" Her mind raced to all the possibilities. Maybe he went to a doctor and was told he was dying. She pushed the thought aside, unable to let herself think about something so horrible. Maybe a client died. That would be horrible. Maybe Josh was somehow responsible. She needed him to tell her before her mind came up with more horrifying possibilities. Hardly able to breathe, she waited for him to talk to her, willing his words to spill out. "Please just talk to me," she begged.

He drew in a ragged breath and looked at her, but he looked away just as quickly, seemingly interested in something outside the bay window. He cleared his throat. She wanted to shake him.

"Josh, you need to talk to me. What the hell is going on?" She couldn't sit still, fear and urgency swallowing her whole. "You're scaring me. Talk to me."

"I, uh, I need to tell you some things you aren't going to want to hear but I need to tell you." Again, he looked at her momentarily before focusing his attention on the object in his hand. "I wasn't working this weekend, Grace. I was…I was with someone."

Grace heard the words, refusing to give them their intended meaning. "With someone? I know you were with someone. You were with your client. You told me all about him over dinner. I made us dinner and you told me all about him. You were with a client, Josh." She couldn't stop talking, her stomach dropping, as if she was on some terrible rollercoaster. It was becoming clear. Josh was about to forever change their lives. If she could keep him from talking, maybe she could stop this ride from crashing, shattering them beyond repair. "You were working with that client who was really excited to do the workout, but you knew he was really just happy to get away from his wife. You told me all about him, Josh. You were working all weekend. You said he…"

"Stop, Grace. Just stop talking." He was directly in front of her now, a prize fighter ready to throw the knockout punch. "I need to say this. I was with someone. I've been with someone for quite a while now. There's someone else, Grace, and I need to leave. I didn't want to tell you this way but I don't know how else to do it. I'm going to be with her."

"Please don't do this Josh. Please don't." She could forgive him for having an affair. She could forgive him. But he had to stay. "We can work this out, Josh. This is just something we need to work through."

"Stop it, Grace. You need to stop talking."

Grace's fear turned into something else. She couldn't identify it immediately, but as words exploded from her, she recognized it. She was livid. She had never been so angry in her life.

"What do you mean you're leaving? You're walking out on our marriage? What gives you the right to make that decision? What the hell are you thinking? You're my husband. This is where you belong." She stood, staring him down, her voice octaves higher than normal. "What the hell are you thinking?" She raised her hand to slap him, but he caught her wrist, holding it tightly in his hand.

"Don't make this worse, Grace. I'm leaving. I know you don't want to hear my side but I need to tell you. Do you hear me? I need to tell you. I've been seeing Katherine. We've been together for quite a while now. I really am sorry, but I had to tell you the truth."

Grace stumbled backward, shaking her head. "Katherine? That's not true. You *wouldn't*. You're lying."

He reached for her hand, and in some strange surreal place in her mind she thought he was reaching out to hold it. She knew it! He couldn't just walk out. She could hold on to this lifeline. But he wasn't holding her hand. He placed the object in her palm and turned away. "She's going to have a baby, Grace. She's going to have my baby. I need to do this. It's only right. I can't desert her. I can't desert them. They need me."

She stared at the wedding band in her palm and then hurled it at him. "You fucking son of a bitch." He took no notice of her screams as he picked up the bag and walked out. Grace sank to the floor, her legs suddenly not strong enough to hold her weight. "Go to hell!" she shouted at the closed door, but there was nobody to hear her.

Jasper padded from the bedroom, confused by the commotion. He sniffed her face, licking her, and she wrapped her arms around his neck as she cried, sobs shaking her entire body. Part of her wanted Josh to return and beg for forgiveness. That part wanted his arms around her, promising to never make such a stupid mistake again. Part of her wanted him to come back so she could tell him to get out again.

He wasn't coming back. The door remained closed. He was off to start a new life, with the exciting promise of parenthood.

The full impact of his words hit home, making breathing difficult. He was leaving her. He was leaving her for Katherine. He was having a baby with Katherine. Her *boss*. Grace's dreams had somehow been gift wrapped and handed to someone else.

"Go to hell," she shouted again at the closed door. "Go to hell." Her heart palpitated. It wouldn't matter if she died right now. She was nothing. She had nothing. Anything she thought was hers had casually walked out the door, leaving her empty.

***

Darkness filled every corner of the room. Grace lifted her head from the floor, unsure how to process what happened and what to do next. All she'd wanted in the past days was for Josh to talk to her. A shuddering breath escaped her. Josh finally talked to her. Oh yes, he had certainly talked.

Jasper was still snuggled up against her and he whined as she finally stirred, perhaps to let her know he hadn't had his dinner yet, or perhaps as a show of sympathy.

She wondered if Jasper realized they just lost everything.

Chapter 9

Jasper took up most of the room in the small casita-turned-art-studio, but that didn't bother Grace. She felt small and insignificant, content to stay huddled in a small corner of the planet. She had no energy, motivation or desire to get out of bed. Technically, it was a day bed, which made being in it day and night perfectly logical to her. But she wasn't sleeping. She tried. She closed her eyes, but when her thoughts took her places she didn't want to be, she couldn't find respite in sleep. She cried until she was sure she couldn't muster another tear and then cried some more.

Her clothes and essentials were haphazardly thrown into two suitcases until she could figure out the chaos that had become her life. The contents were irrelevant. She wore the same thing day after day.

She heard Josh's words on her voicemail days after he left. *"You should stay in the house until we figure out what to do with it."* The first nights after his announcement and departure, she wandered from room to room, remembering every moment of their years spent together, trying to figure out how everything could change so drastically in such a short amount of time. His betrayal became too much for her and she had to get out, away from the ghosts of the people they once were.

Lexie came to her rescue, offering the small "art cottage" behind her house. Small was an apt description but Grace didn't care. It was someplace other than her home. Lexie no longer used the space now that she had her own downtown studio. Her metal consignment work wouldn't fit in this space, anyway.

Lexie was once again her lifesaver. "I have some snacks in the cupboard. The mini fridge is full of water bottles. I put a bowl out for Jasper's water, too."

Grace nodded, but most of the words weren't registering.

"I know you need your space to heal, but I also want you nearby, Grace. I won't smother you. In fact, I'll give you plenty of well-deserved time to wallow in self-pity." She'd taken Grace's icy cold hand in her own. "But I'm not going to let that wallowing go on for very long. I'd invite you to stay in the house, but Sean has the kids this weekend." Lexie's live-in boyfriend had his two kids every other weekend. "I know you love them, but you don't need that kind of energy right now."

Grace smiled weakly.

"You'll be comfortable here." She squeezed the limp hand she still held and gently lifted her friend's chin. "You'll be okay, Grace. He didn't break you."

Grace wanted to believe her, but all she could see were the broken pieces of her life scattered on the floor around her feet.

***

Grace raised her head, the pounding in her temple intensifying with the movement. Ibuprofen was nearby. It would be easy to rid herself of the pain if she stretched out her hand. Instead, she dropped her head back to the pillow, letting the ache wash over her. The pain was somehow better than three weeks of numbness. A few minutes later she reached for the bottle, deciding she was wrong and ready to be numb again. She dozed.

Jasper's whining and nuzzling became insistent. "I know. I'm getting up." Her voice was hoarse from lack of use. There was no reason to talk to anyone. Shuffling to the door, she let Jasper out to relieve himself. She couldn't remember when she last ate anything. Nothing tasted good. Her red puffy eyes stared back from an almost unrecognizable face when she dared to look in the mirror. She told herself she should shower, but that sounded too exhausting so she told herself every few days would be good enough. She wasn't sure, though, if a few days had yet passed since her last shower. Jasper didn't complain about her smell.

She wandered back to the door, watching Jasper sniff at something in the grass. Try as she might, she could not stop Josh's words from rolling around in her head. Did all of this happen to her? Was this her life now? Like a stupid song stuck in her head, his voice echoed and reverberated. The gamut of emotions since that evening left her exhausted, confused and unsure of herself and who she thought she—no, they—had been.

Josh called her about a week after leaving, shortly after she settled into the casita. Desperate to hear from him, she actually answered the phone, letting herself believe he was calling to apologize, to beg her forgiveness, to ask if he could come back home. She analyzed to death everything he told her, but she still could make no sense of it. He apparently needed to purge himself of every wrongdoing since they met, but each word was no less impactful than a slap to her face.

She listened to the recounting of infidelity, the chance meeting with Katherine, the knowledge that she wasn't just another affair, the baby on the way. Of all his transgressions, the one that bothered her most was the lie that set up the weekend she spent working on Katherine's project. Finding out there had never been a client, a project to work on, or even the intention of a Monday morning meeting was the final nail in the coffin for Grace. She replayed again and again Josh's description of his client and their seemingly hard work together throughout that weekend, all while eating a dinner she so carefully put together in an attempt to show him her love, to prepare him for the conversation she wanted to have about trying to get pregnant. It was only now she understood why he talked so much, why he recounted conversations he supposedly had with the non-existent client. He obviously created a make-believe world to talk about with her so she couldn't see into the real world of his weekend away with her boss.

She was disgusted with herself for letting him get it off his chest. Why she hadn't simply disconnected and refused to talk to him was beyond her comprehension. Grace finally managed a weak "get out of my life." Ironically, he'd already done that without waiting to be told. Her reaction after Josh's "great reveal" was to run to the bathroom and throw up.

Jasper was at the door, ready to come back in. She had to pull herself together, but she just wasn't sure how. She slipped back under the blanket. Jasper stood near her head, his way of asking permission to climb up on the bed. He couldn't do it by himself so she got up and helped him, happy to have him next to her.

She buried her face in his fur, remembering the day he came into her life. Josh disappeared the morning after they'd moved into their first place together, a small rental. He reappeared with a sheepish grin and said he needed to show her something in his truck. She followed him outside, assuming he was about to show her some "interesting" furniture piece he was lucky enough to find at the secondhand store. She was already prepared to offer him a "that's nice but it probably won't really fit our design style" when he reached into a box in the back seat and pulled from it a puppy.

The adorable bundle of fluff squirmed, trying with all its might to cover every inch of her face with sweet baby kisses. She cried tears of sheer joy into the puppy's fur as Josh said, "I guess we're a real family now." Jasper became their constant companion, going everywhere they went, sharing everything they did. He might as well have been their baby. Now, her face burrowed into his warmth, she cried more. Everything she once loved was gone except Jasper. She couldn't imagine being without him right now. They were still in this together. Maybe tomorrow she would have the strength to be a normal human being again. Maybe.

She dreamed that night she was at the bottom of a very deep pit with slippery walls and nothing to give her a foothold. She could hear voices overhead encouraging her to climb out, to come back to the top and join them, but she couldn't find the strength to do anything. In her dream, she crumpled into a ball, knowing she had fallen too far down, and this time, no matter what she did, she was never getting back up again.

***

Lexie sat across from Grace at the table in the main house. Forcing Grace to get up and join her in the empty house this morning was no easy task, but Grace followed her friend, zombie-like, up the path to the house, Jasper padding along behind. They sat staring at one another for a few moments before Lexie broke the silence. "You need to shower, Grace."

Grace let the hot water run over her body, not ready to step out of this warm cocoon and face the world. She washed her hair, noticing that several strands were left behind in her hands. Water running over her, she stared at the hair clinging to her fingers. Her entire world had just fallen apart. Would going bald really matter?

When the water felt cold and even moving the lever further to the left didn't result in hot water, she knew she had no choice. It was time to get out. Her movements were slow and clumsy, as if she'd forgotten how to do the simplest of things—drying herself off, putting lotion on her skin, combing through her tangled hair. She stared at even more strands left behind, wondering just how much hair she could afford to lose. Lexie had set out yoga pants and a t-shirt for Grace and she held the material up to her nose, remembering the smell of freshly laundered clothes, her senses waking up just the tiniest bit. She glanced longingly at the king-sized bed, desperate to sink into it, but she forced herself to finish getting dressed.

Grace appeared in the kitchen, running her fingers gently through her wet hair and holding out yet more strands for Lexie to see. "I think I'm going bald now on top of everything else."

"I'm not surprised." Lexie handed her a mug and gave her a gentle pat on the shoulder. "It's only because of stress and not eating right. And if you do lose your hair, I'll help you find a wig. Purple would be a great color for you. I'm making you an omelet. Sit down." It wasn't a question so she didn't wait for an answer. Grace looked fragile. Food would help.

Grace sipped the tea slowly, watching her friend at the stove. She poured the egg mixture into the hot skillet, the sizzle instantly awakening something in Grace. Perhaps she was a little hungry. Lexie continued to talk while she artfully placed mushrooms, spinach and goat cheese on top of the nearly ready egg whites, perfectly flipping one side over the other to form an omelet. Everything she touched seemed to be a masterpiece in the making. Grace wasn't thinking about the artistic element, however, as she took the first forkful into her mouth, partially hearing what Lexie was saying, but mostly focused on the taste of food on her tongue, and its warmth moving down to her empty stomach. She was savoring more than an omelet. For the first time in weeks, she was feeling almost human again.

"I didn't even realize how hungry I was. Oh, my dear sweet Jesus, Lexie. This is delicious." For a moment, Grace was lost in the actions of raising and lowering her fork, chewing slowly and savoring the flavors. It was so strange to feel something, even something as simple and normal as this.

Reality returned, and with it, waves of sadness. She carefully set the fork down next to her plate, taking deep breaths, but it didn't help. The food turned to sawdust in her mouth, the act of swallowing impossible. She raced to the bathroom, retching and vomiting until she was unable to stand. Lexie knelt next to the slumped form, drawing Grace into her arms as violent sobs shook her, holding her tightly, whispering soft words of encouragement into her hair.

Once the shaking subsided, Lexie helped her friend to her feet and led her to the living room. She gave Grace a cool washcloth for her face and a fresh cup of hot tea, and then sat across from her. It was time for a heart-to-heart.

Grace managed a couple of small sips of the tea, feeling it move down her throat and make its way to her once again empty stomach.

"Maybe I should have started you out with a piece of dry toast," Lexie stated sheepishly, realizing how little Grace must have been eating in the past weeks.

Grace gave her a weak smile. "I'm so sorry Lex. It was good. Really. I thought I could eat it. I don't know what happened. It was like one second I was feeling so normal and then…it just hit me all over again." Tears rolled down her cheeks and she gulped. "I'm just so…I don't even know…" She struggled to find words, a headache forming behind her eyes. How could she explain how disappointed she was in herself? She hadn't trusted her own instincts enough to follow through all those years ago when she suspected Josh was cheating on her. She convinced herself she was mistaken; she convinced herself that she was the one with an issue because she wasn't more trusting. How would she ever trust herself again? She never before confided in anyone her suspicions but now it all came tumbling out. "Lexie, I was so stupid. Am I one of those wives who knew deep down but let it go on anyway? I'm such an idiot."

Shaken by her friend's story, Lexie chose her words carefully. Grace was in need of some tough love, but she would be gentle giving it. "Grace, when we love, we give everything in us. I remember how you were when you first met Josh. You were head-over-heels for him."

Tears continued down Grace's cheeks, but she didn't say anything.

"I know you never planned to stay here, but you did it to make a life with him here." She grinned. "I'd like to think you stayed to be closer to your best friend, but I'm not kidding myself. He loved you. He gave up everything in Phoenix to move here so you could start out together. Both of you gave something up to be together. You had every reason to believe you would be together forever. Sometimes relationships don't work out. He cheated on you—more than once. Some people just can't love one person or be happy with one person. You can. He couldn't. I can't make what you are feeling go away, but I hope you eventually see that what you did wasn't abnormal—and you're not an idiot. You gave your husband the benefit of the doubt out of love."

Grace dropped her head, still unconvinced. "I should have known. How can I ever trust myself to know the difference? I'm probably better off being alone for the rest of my life."

"You don't mean that. This doesn't define you. You are still a best friend, a daughter, a sister, an aunt, and so much more. The only thing you're not is Josh's wife. Don't let this change who you are. If you put up walls, you'll never meet the person who is your forever guy. He's out there and he'll never betray you like Josh did. You have to give yourself a chance to find that man."

Grace shook her head, a sob making her shudder. She wasn't sure at this moment if her friend was right or wrong. Trusting was never going to come easily for her again. Jasper nuzzled her hand, trying to comfort her. She smiled through her tears, giving him a tight squeeze. He loved her unconditionally. Who said she needed a man in her life when Jasper was here to love her so much?

And just like that, she knew what she would do.

"I'm going back to Chicago, Lexie. I want to go home."

***

It was another week before Grace pulled herself together enough to get dressed in something other than her "comfy clothes" and do her hair and makeup. It wasn't because she actually wanted to, but because Josh wasted no time filing for divorce. When the Petition for Dissolution of Marriage paperwork was delivered to her, she hired an attorney, unable to stomach any additional direct contact with Josh. She was afraid mostly that he would feel a need to disclose even more of his shortcomings, affairs, and other betrayals. She couldn't handle more.

"We just aren't the same people we used to be, Grace." Those words were probably the most honest ones he had spoken. The more distance she could put between them now, the better it would be. She wasn't someone he loved. He threw away their life together as soon as something new came along. He was a child with a shiny new toy. Maybe the novelty of parenting with Katherine would also wear off and he'd be in search of a newer, shinier toy before long. Grace hoped, for the baby's sake only, that wouldn't be the case. One thing was certain, though. Even

if he begged, there would never be a day in the future that she would allow him back into her life.

"Three or four months, and you'll be divorced," her attorney told her on the phone. "I have all the papers filed and I'll make sure you get what you deserve. I'll need you to sign some documents for me at your earliest convenience."

Done wasting her time, she decided today would be her earliest convenience.

She took one last look at herself in the mirror. Why didn't she look as different on the outside as she felt on the inside? How could it possibly be the same familiar face looking back at her when she wasn't the same familiar person inside? She sighed once more and turned out the light. Looking around the small space she still called home, she made a mental note to do something special for Lexie and Sean. They were gracious hosts. They didn't need a deadbeat hanging around.

Her second stop of the day would be the house. It was time to pack up the rest of her clothes and the few items she decided she wanted to keep. Josh asked if they could meet at the house together to determine what to do with the contents neither of them wanted. What was the point? He was moving in with Katherine. She would take anything she really wanted, which at this point was a very short list, and he could do whatever he wanted with his belongings. She just didn't care anymore. The house would go on the market in the coming weeks, the furniture would be sold or given away and the life Grace once knew would be cut in half.

Everything split down the middle. Divorce was ugly that way. Was she getting just half of herself back in the divorce? She hoped it would be the happy, productive, driven half she once knew.

She promised Jasper she would be home soon and she'd bring along the last of his chew toys from the house. He looked at her curiously, probably wondering why she would suddenly think he was interested in a toy, but he wagged his tail, thumping it in a steady rhythm as she rubbed his head and then he curled back onto the rug in front of the daybed, waiting for her to climb back in to be near him. She couldn't, though.

Once finished at the attorney's office she continued to the house, where Lexie and Sean were waiting for her.

"Take your time. I'll help you load anything you want to keep," Sean assured her.

She wandered from room to room selecting the tokens she wanted. There weren't many. She didn't want the knickknacks she and Josh picked out together on some long-past shopping spree. She didn't want the items he bought her when he still loved her.

Lexie was her voice of reason. "You'll want some of these things for your new place, wherever that might be. Why don't we pack it and ship it to your parents' house, like they suggested?"

Grace allowed Lexie to take over much of the packing, her own head not able to see clearly enough that future Lexie talked about. She stood by, watching Sean and Lexie fill boxes and label them. Some would be stored at the art studio for now, and Grace was shipping some back to Chicago. Her parents were looking forward to having her back "home." Of course, her sisters, too, were thrilled with her decision to return. They all wanted to help her through her dark times and Grace was ready to let them. It would take all of them to put her back together again.

The house she'd loved so much was no longer her home. It was part of a past she watched slip away. Josh would handle getting a realtor. She said a silent goodbye to her old life as the door clicked shut. She didn't look back.

Chapter 10

———◆–◆–◆———

"This one has decent security. The rent is a little higher so I'm not sure I can swing it." She paused to sip her coffee. "It's actually a good thing I need a ground-level place because of Jasper. Rent will be cheaper, but dad won't be happy." She could hear her dad's warnings to his daughters about a ground-level apartment's lack of security. "He'll understand. I have to make this easy on Jasper and most of the old buildings don't have an elevator."

Grace continued scrolling through Chicago apartment listings. The Perk-Up Café crowd was the usual—a couple college kids, two moms with toddlers, an employee on break. She let the moment wash over her, realizing she hadn't been thinking about Josh, the divorce, or anything else unpleasant. It had been a while since she enjoyed the simple pleasure of people-watching at her favorite coffee shop. Progress. Healing. She smiled.

"You could always leave Jasper here with us." Lexie laughed at her own joke.

"Very funny." The little girl nearby let out a high-pitched squeal, knocked her mom's drink off the table, and all sorts of commotion ensued. Grace watched with amusement. "I have even more exciting news. I have a lead on a job. It's a former client from when I worked for…well, it's a former client whose friend is starting a company in the Midwest. I'm meeting with him next week, once I'm back in Chicago. They aren't set on a Chicago branch, but maybe I can help convince them."

"That's great! Everything is falling into place." Lexie's voice faded away momentarily.

Grace shifted the phone to her other ear, the crying child making it difficult to hear. "I promised I'd be out of your hair soon and it's already been three months. Three months! I don't know what I would have done without you." She refused to cry, wanting one day without all the emotions bubbling to the top. "Sean's been so sweet keeping an eye on Jasper while I wrap up all these loose ends. I'm going to miss you guys when I move back home."

She was surprised how easily 'home' slipped into her vocabulary, especially since it was a reference to a place she hadn't known since she was 18. She was returning to Chicago. It was time to re-discover the Grace she was before she met Josh, before she became a wife, and before she learned that so much pain could exist. She was slowly putting herself back together again, piece by piece, and feeling stronger by the day.

Staying with her parents would be awkward, but temporary. They downsized a few years back, enjoying the conveniences of a small condo. Having another human being and a dog would make the place crowded. It would be a brief landing zone during her apartment search. She was ready for a fresh start with Jasper in the Windy City.

Lexie obviously had her on speaker phone, her voice fading in and out as she moved around the downtown gallery she was prepping for an upcoming opening. "And just so you know, I do still expect your help with marketing ideas for my show next month. You always have great ideas. How am I going to find a replacement for you when it comes to that? I'm sure I'll find a best friend replacement a lot easier." She was making light of the situation, despite her disappointment over Grace moving away. A loud crash and an expletive meant Lexie was struggling with something on her end. "Hey Gracie, I need to call you back. Let me know if you want me to meet you later for dinner. Or better yet, we can get a bottle of wine tonight. Love you. Bye."

Grace smiled and put her phone in her purse. She was sitting inside, enjoying the air-conditioned coolness of late spring turning rapidly to summer. She remembered early May days like this when she was a student, trying to concentrate on finishing the spring semester so she could return to the beautiful summer days on Lake Michigan, boating with her sisters, taking walks with her mom, going to concerts, festivals and art shows with her friends. There was always too much to squeeze in during the short Midwest summertime.

She felt a pang as she remembered she wasn't a college student anymore. She was a jobless soon-to-be-divorcee who wasn't even sure what path to take anymore. With a sigh, she turned her attention back to the Chicago-area apartment offerings on her laptop. The timing was perfect, leaving Arizona before the real summer heat set in. She couldn't wait to leave, now that her plan was in place. There were too many places reminding her of the life she'd lost. The charm of Arizona was gone. She was ready for a healthy change, especially since avoiding Josh and Katherine had become almost an obsession.

Going home would be a relief, even if it did mean facing a whole new set of challenges. Calling her parents had been difficult. They certainly didn't say it and never would, but she still felt like a disappointment to them. Her sisters managed to stay happily married and raise families, but she just couldn't seem to hold it together and accomplish even that.

"Maybe you should take a couple weeks and stay at the condo. We'd watch Jasper for you." Her dad's offer of their winter home in Florida was sweet, but finding a job and getting into a routine would be better.

She was startled out of her reverie by the sound of her phone. She assumed it was Lexie calling back to tell her about the latest mishap at the studio and solidify plans for the evening, but was surprised to see it wasn't Lexie. "Grace? It's Sean. Hey, something is wrong with Jasper. I'm not sure what I should do. You might want to come take a look and maybe get him to the vet. He doesn't look good."

Grace's heart almost stopped. "I'll be right there."

Thirty minutes later, she was running through the backyard to the casita, not sure what she would find. Sean was sitting on the front step of the studio, Jasper's head in his lap. "I came over to let him out and he was kind of shaky when he got up. He came out here and just collapsed. I didn't know what to do besides call you. Sorry. I tried to get him to drink some water, but he wouldn't touch it. Tell me what I can do to help, Grace."

He shifted out of the way and let Grace slide into his spot. Jasper's breathing was shallow and rapid and he was barely able to open his eyes to look at her. His tongue touched her hand as she wrapped her arms around his neck. "I'll take care of you Jasper. I'm here. I'll take care of you. Don't you dare leave me. Don't you dare."

Together, they carried him to her car.

"I can come along and help if you need me to," Sean said as she closed the back door. "I'll just give Lexie a call and let her know I'll be late getting to the studio."

Grace shook her head. She had been enough of a burden on them already and Lexie needed Sean's help. "We'll be OK. Someone will help me get him out of the car at the animal hospital. We'll be OK," she repeated, trying to convince herself. She hugged him, breathing in the scents of Pine Sol and Old Spice. His beard scratched lightly against her cheek, and his arms around her felt firm and strong. Grace wanted to sink in and get lost in the embrace for a moment longer, too tired to deal with yet another crisis in her life. Pulling away, she thanked Sean again. Jasper needed her. It would be so nice to let someone else take on the burden, but she knew what she had to do, so she climbed behind the wheel and sped off.

She'd been to the emergency department at Mountain Ridge Animal Hospital one other time. Jasper ate his way through almost a full bag of charcoal briquettes when he was not quite two. She was sure he would die from it, and made Josh race him to the emergency vet. The doctor on call calmly reassured them that the foreign objects would make their way out of his system over the next days. They took him home and followed him outside every time he had to go to the bathroom, anxious to see the extra "gifts" he left behind. She wished it was only charcoal briquettes this time, but she knew better. Jasper didn't look good and she was terrified, unable to stay calm at traffic light after traffic light, willing them to turn green and wanting to push the gas pedals of the slow drivers in front of her.

All the while, she talked to Jasper, reminding him of silly things he did over the years, reminding him how much she loved and needed him, and reminding him to keep breathing. She spent the last weeks trying to forget everything about her old life, and now she was reliving it again as she talked to Jasper, willing him to hold on, be strong, be brave.

The emergency entrance allowed her to pull into the circular drive and ring a bell for assistance. Within seconds, a pimply-faced teenage volunteer appeared at the door. He wheeled a cart next to the car and together they lifted Jasper onto it. With shaking hands, she filled out the paperwork handed to her on a clipboard as tears coursed down her cheeks.

"He's in good hands," the receptionist reassured her as she watched Jasper disappear down the hallway with the teenager and a veterinary assistant. "You can join Jasper as soon as we have the paperwork in order."

An internal debate started. Josh would want to know something was wrong with Jasper. She picked up her phone, and realized she didn't know what was wrong with Jasper so she didn't know what to tell him. And would he even care? She would wait until she knew something about Jasper's condition. A spark of anger ignited. Why was she worried about calling Josh? Hadn't he been the one to desert them? The minute he betrayed their marriage vows he lost the right to be a part of this.

She pushed thoughts of Josh aside as the assistant returned to escort her back to the examination room.

Jasper was stretched out on the metal exam table, an IV in his leg. She took it all in, feeling weak in the knees. A large swathe of fur was shaved from his right foreleg, and the smell of soap and disinfectant hit her. The assistant suggested Grace have a seat until the doctor arrived and then excused herself for a moment. Grace tiptoed to Jasper's head. She stroked his ears and ran her hands down his head, whispering soft words of reassurance to him. His eyes fluttered open and shut and her heart was gripped with fear about another loss in her life. She found it hard to catch her breath and a sob escaped her.

She had to pull herself together but her world began tilting and spinning. Dark shadows crept into her peripheral vision as she gripped the side of the bed, and her legs turned to jelly.

The door opened and the doctor strode in, followed closely by the assistant. "Oh dear," he said, gently pushing Grace into the nearby chair and instructing her to bend forward. "Just put your head down and try to breathe normally. You'll be just fine, Mrs. Jarvis. We don't need you fainting on us now, do we?"

For a second time, Grace was ready to let someone else take over and allow her to be along for the ride. Instead, she sat up, ready to do what needed to be done for Jasper. "It's Miss. Miss Warrens. Well, Grace, actually. I'm fine." The spots that danced before her eyes moments ago were starting to disappear and the ground no longer seemed to be swaying underneath her feet. After a couple of deep breaths, she continued. "What's wrong with him? I've never seen him like this before."

Dr. Bovary took a seat in the chair directly across from her. "Miss Warrens," he stopped, gripping the chart he carried with him. "Grace, we need to run some tests. Right now, we have Jasper on an IV catheter. He's quite dehydrated so this should give him some immediate relief. If you are feeling up to walking now, I'm going to ask you to wait in the lounge. As soon as we have the results, we will come and get you. Please help yourself to some juice and snacks. It might make you feel a little better. You were pretty close to hitting the floor when I walked in." He looked at her over the glasses perched precariously low on his nose, and then stood up and walked over to Jasper, giving him a quick pat on the head.

Jasper was in good hands. Reluctantly, she stood to leave, giving Jasper one last hug and telling him that she loved him.

For the next hour and a half Grace continued the debate from earlier. She went so far as to punch in the first four digits of Josh's cell and then stopped. What if he thought she was looking for some excuse to bring him back to her? But she had to tell him, because he must still love Jasper as much as she did. But if he really loved Jasper, why simply walk out without even giving him a second thought? She didn't have answers.

The assistant's voice startled her. "Miss Warrens, Dr. Bovary is ready to see you in his office."

She led Grace down a hallway, taking a left and then a right before tapping lightly on the open door. "Dr. Bovary, Miss Warrens is here now."

The veterinarian lifted his head from the chart and motioned Grace to one of the chairs in front of his desk. He smiled at her, but she sensed the news wouldn't be good. "Miss Warrens, I hope you're feeling better. You have some color back. You were awfully pale when I walked in." He leaned forward, locking eyes with her. "It's awful when our pets are ailing. They're part of our families and we never want to see them suffer, no more than we want to see our own children suffering." He spoke slowly and quietly.

"Is he going to be OK? Can I take him home tonight?" Left unspoken was how much she needed Jasper with her. He was her lifeline.

"We ran a series of tests and I'm afraid the news is not good."

Her heart caught in her throat.

He continued. "Jasper has a canine osteosarcoma. He has bone cancer. It started in his humerous and our tests show that it is invasive and metastatic." He paused to lift the paper on the chart to see the next page. "Unfortunately, it has already invaded the lungs. I know it doesn't do any good to tell you that over 50% of large dogs over the age of ten end up with a cancer diagnosis."

He paused as Grace processed his words. Shock, pain and despair fought for position. She started to say something but gulped instead, tears rolling down her face. He waited, allowing her to catch her breath. Finally, she whispered, "Is he going to die?"

She didn't want him to answer. She already assumed, but the confirmation would still be a terrible blow.

"While there are some things we can try, they're extreme and not likely to make a lot of difference at this point. We can think about chemotherapy or amputation. Miss Warrens, my recommendation would be no drastic measures. Even with those measures you are adding days or maybe a week to his life, not months or years. I believe Jasper has no more than three months ahead of him." Her sob again made him pause and she took more tissues from the box in front of her.

There's an expiration stamp on Jasper, she thought. She cried harder, and it took a while to compose herself enough to speak. The doctor waited, empathetic, not new to a reaction like this.

"I see." She closed her eyes and shook her head, struggling to find the words she wanted. "Should I have caught this sooner? Did I miss this? Is this my fault?" She barely got the last words out before they were swallowed in another sob.

Dr. Bovary was no stranger to this question. "Miss Warrens, many times there are no signs whatsoever. There could be pain and stiffness, but as Jasper has aged, I'm sure you've seen an increase in those symptoms that would have seemed perfectly normal and natural to you. Your vet likely told you Jasper was experiencing the early stages of arthritis. Arthritis could have very well masked any new symptoms."

The explanation was meant to reassure her, but didn't. Now she would analyze everything she had seen in Jasper in the previous months and question herself, convinced she must have missed something. Wallowing in her own self-pity all these months may have cost her the only thing she had left. She should have been more attentive. But isn't that same lack of attention what cost her a marriage, a career, a life…? Her thoughts were spinning wildly out of control.

"If you're ready, I'll take you in by Jasper now." Grace followed him out of his office and further into the back of the animal hospital. The assistant was standing next to Jasper, adjusting the tape over the IV in his leg. He was perfectly still, eyes closed, and Grace wondered for a moment if she had already lost him.

She whispered near his ear as she put her hand on his head. "Jasper?" He made a noise in his throat and his eyes fluttered but didn't open.

"We started him on an analgesic—a morphine drip to be exact. It should relieve some of the discomfort." Her eyes followed the IV fluid line from the catheter in his leg to the drip just above the table. She watched for a moment as one drop at a time the medication transferred to Jasper. "We're going to keep him overnight to make sure he is handling the medication and adjust it as necessary and then you can take him home and make him comfortable. We'll prepare a prescription for you and review all the instructions before you go today. Just be aware that his appetite will decline, his energy will decline. What we're seeing now is the last stage of the cancer. If you decide it's time for him to go, Miss Warrens, then you'll have to make that decision, but if you're considering more measures be taken, we should discuss them soon." He removed his glasses to wipe them on a handkerchief he pulled from his lab coat pocket. "You can stay here with him for a while if you'd like, and then we'll move him to an overnight suite. Jeannette will be in and out to check on both of you." He gently touched her shoulder. "I'm very sorry to have to share this news with you. I know it's not easy. If you have any questions whatsoever or decide to take additional measures, please don't hesitate to call us. We're happy to review all of your options again at any time."

With that, he and his assistant left the room and Grace was alone with her grief and the last connection she had to her life with Josh.

She wrapped her arms around the dog's neck and buried her face into his fur. The spigot was wide open and she didn't even try to hold back any of her pain, anger, fear and frustration. As time passed, she started to talk, telling Jasper how much she loved every minute they spent together. She recounted the mischievous puppy days and the trips he accompanied them on as a family of three. She told him how much better he made her life. At times, she found herself speaking words she wanted to say to Josh when he dropped his bombshell on her. Everything in her poured out.

What she thought was rock bottom before was simply a ledge before the final fall. "I'm supposed to take you home, Jasper. I don't even know where home is anymore. You won't get to be in Chicago with me." Her hand stopped moving through his fur as she determined her next step. "This is where you need to be right now. I'll take you back to Lexie's. We'll be there together so that makes it our home. I can't imagine my life without you. I'm so sorry I didn't see what was happening. I'm so sorry Jasper." She had been unable to see a lot of what was happening right in front of her.

She took a deep breath. Drawing her phone from her purse, she tapped in Josh's number. Before it had a chance to ring, she disconnected, reminding herself to breathe. The second time she forced herself to let the ringing begin. He picked up on the third ring.

"Hey Grace. Uhm…what's up?" She felt some satisfaction that he sounded uncomfortable talking to her. Maybe he *did* feel at least a little guilty. She pushed the thought aside, focusing on Jasper now.

"I'm at Mountain Ridge Animal Hospital. Jasper isn't doing well. It's cancer and he has just a matter of days or possibly weeks to live. I think you should come and see him and let the doctor explain it to you. He has to stay overnight

76

tonight and I would prefer you visit him here to tell him goodbye," She didn't wait for his response. She disconnected and sat back in her chair.

When Jeannette returned, Grace was gently stroking Jasper's fur. The drip was empty and the assistant disconnected the bag. "We're going to move him to another room, Miss Warrens. I'll wait until you're ready to go for the day, so take your time. We'll make him comfortable for the night. I have the prescriptions and I've typed up all the instructions for you also. I put my phone number on it so if you have questions once you're home with Jasper I can certainly answer them for you."

"Thank you." She pushed her emotions down. "I'm going to leave shortly, but I was hoping you could do me a favor. Could you leave Jasper in here for a little longer today so my husband, my ex-hus…I'm sorry. My soon-to-be ex-husband will be here shortly. He'll want to see Jasper and hear what the doctor told me. I don't want to be here when he's here, but I think he should have a chance to see Jasper one last time."

Jeanette nodded, understanding what Grace meant either because of her own personal experience with an ex or because she dealt with this kind of thing on a regular basis. "Of course. That won't be a problem at all."

Grace listened carefully to the last of the care instructions, thanked Jeanette for all of her help, gave Jasper a long goodbye hug and allowed herself to be escorted back to the main entrance. The world outside the animal hospital was unchanged. It was a strange feeling when her life had just been turned inside out and upside down once again. This was not the time to think about herself. She needed to get ready for Jasper's final trip home.

***

Grace stopped at the pet store to pick up the most comfortable dog bed she could find. She bought Jasper's favorite foods, bacon and string cheese, at the grocery store. She placed the new bed next to her bed, close enough so she could reach down and touch him all night long. She pushed thoughts of losing him out of her head. She had to focus on making him comfortable in the short time he had left.

Her life was on hold again. She called her parents to tell them she would be delaying her return.

Lexie knocked on the door shortly after 7:00. "I've been worried sick. Is Jasper here? What happened? Sean told me something was wrong with him." One look at Grace's face told her everything she needed to know. Losing her marriage and home and job had apparently been just the first wave of rotten luck for Grace. Losing Jasper and putting plans for starting over on hold was the second wave. "Oh Gracie. What can I do?"

Lexie held her tightly and then listened as Grace recounted everything that happened since their conversation earlier.

"He's been my baby for almost 11 years, Lexie. How do I say goodbye?"

Lexie didn't have an answer. She also didn't know how far Grace could bend before breaking completely. They sat together late into the night.

After Lexie left, Grace paced the small space, prepared for a long sleepless night. For the first time in hours, she checked her phone, seeing three missed calls from Josh. He hadn't left a voicemail, which was fine with her. She didn't want to hear his voice, and didn't want to have to reassure or console him. She hoped he was in as much pain as she was right now.

In her restless state, she opened a box she'd previously pushed into the corner of the tiny living space. It held all the personal contents of her desk. Grace knew Maddie had packed it all up because her handwriting was on the inserted "Good luck" message. Grace doubted anyone cared about her luck—good or otherwise. The box was actually one of the few items Grace carried out of the house and placed in her car instead of shipping it off with most of her belongings. After Josh revealed the painful truth about his "wanderings" and falling in love with Katherine, Grace never bothered going back to the office. She knew there was no point in giving notice. Josh actually accomplished that for her by choosing her boss over his wife.

The box appeared at the house just two days later, along with an envelope containing a severance package offer. At first Grace wanted to rip the papers to shred, but she placed them inside the box for another day. When she first met with her divorce attorney, she shared the documents with him, asking for his advice on the matter. He agreed to craft a response and the original offer for a three-month severance turned into a six-month deal. Her lawyer proudly shared the paperwork with her but she felt no great sense of joy or satisfaction as she signed the forms. But it wasn't the documents drawing her to the box right now.

Grace reached in, moving aside the few things on top to get to the framed photographs that once lined the front of her desktop. She found what she was looking for. All were pictures of Jasper—one playing in the snow when they took him hiking on Mount Lemmon, one sitting in the front seat of the Jeep next to Grace, and one curled under the Christmas tree with his chin resting on the largest rawhide bone imaginable, the red ribbon on it almost as big as Jasper's head.

She cried as she cradled the pictures and then she set them up on the small table, carefully placed so she could look at them throughout the long night ahead.

Chapter 11

⬦ ◆ ⬦

Five months later…

Grace adjusted the pictures of Jasper before turning on the desktop computer sitting in front of her. She smiled sadly at the framed photographs, remembering the last days they shared together. Her decision to stay at Lexie's and make Jasper comfortable in his last weeks was definitely the right one. She missed talking to him. She missed Jasper more than she missed Josh. It was impossible to remember the Josh she had fallen in love with so many years ago, and it was Jasper who had stayed by her side during the awful months following her separation from her husband. It was only right that she was at his side until the end.

She kissed the tip of her finger and placed it gently on the picture nearest her.

A familiar voice pulled her from her musings. "Hey hotshot. Busy day?"

"Dad!" She came from behind her desk to hug him. "Why didn't you tell me you'd be here today?" She stepped back to take a long look at him. "You look great. Were you at the gym?"

He laughed. "Who needs a gym? I get plenty of exercise chasing your mom. Someday she'll let me catch her." It was one of his oldest jokes.

Her return to Chicago in early July, several weeks later than she originally planned, and without Jasper, had been far more difficult than she imagined. Still lost in her grief for the first couple weeks after her arrival, she did little more than sleep on the twin bed in the guest room of her parents' condo. Her mom did her best to comfort her with home-cooked meals, but it was her dad who gave her a push to move forward. His pep talk came just in time, reminding her of her many strengths and gifts. He even offered to help her start a job search. That had been the kick in the pants she needed. As much as she wanted to be the little girl who turned to her dad for every need as a child, she promised him she was ready to get up and get moving again—first out of his house and then into a new career.

And that is what she did. She was proud of herself. Every day she found her confidence growing. The timing was perfect because she was in the final month of her severance money so if she didn't find a job, she would have to start taking money out of her savings.

"Your mom made blueberry muffins this morning so I brought you some. If you were still at our place you would have devoured at least three." He handed her the plastic wrapped muffins he was holding.

"That's not true. Two at the most. Usually." Her sheepish grin spoke volumes as she placed them off to the side of her desk for later, already tempted by the aroma. They would make a great mid-morning snack. "I'm surprised you didn't have everyone in the building following you. It smells like a bakery in here. How come I have a funny feeling you're not just the fresh baked goods delivery man?" Grace already had her suspicions that his visit was somehow connected to her rapidly approaching birthday.

"You're onto me. Your mom sent me here to deliver more than just muffins. It seems to me, young lady, you have a birthday to celebrate. She made plans for the night and she said she absolutely won't take no for an answer. Ready?" He puffed out his chest as though issuing a formal proclamation. "Your mother is hosting a dinner for you at Chisolm's with your sisters and the guys. Remember, you can't say no. Mom's orders." Her brothers-in-law, of course, were "the guys." There was a momentary twinge, realizing she would be the only single one in the group.

The last thing Grace wanted was to make a big deal out of turning 36, but she also knew better than to decline her mother's invitation. When their mom made up her mind to do something special for any of them, they put on a smile and enjoyed it. It didn't take a whole lot for her to get her way.

"Ok, Ok. Tell mom she wins. I'll put on a pretty dress and some make-up and smile my way through a family dinner. I'm sure there are worse things in life." She was determined to keep moving forward. Dwelling on the past had swallowed too much of her energy already. "Tell me how you like my new digs."

Her dad looked around the spacious office on the 40th floor of the Willis Towers, home of the offices of the city's Center for the Arts Foundation. She didn't have a great deal of time to be choosy about a job, but she definitely wasn't interested in jumping into the same type of job she left behind in Arizona. There had already been a lot of changes in her life so it made perfect sense to steer in a different direction for work as well.

Grace sent out resumes in response to a few promising leads and some job postings, and was thrilled when she landed this particular one. Assistant Director of Community Giving was the title on her office door. Ironically, her father volunteered on the Board of Directors of the center's Foundation when Grace was in high school. She felt a special connection to him because of this. She teased him, however, that it was a whole lot better doing work she was getting paid for.

"This was a great choice for you. And on top of that, I think you have the best view of the city from here." She stood next to him, enjoying the scene before her. "The Foundation has been doing great work for a lot of years. I always said we have to keep tourists coming here, of course, but I think Chicagoans love the arts more than they do in just about any other city." He stepped back, sitting on the edge of her desk, admiring the view of the cityscape. "You must be happy to be back here after so many years away. We missed having you around."

"Oh dad, don't go getting sappy on me. You'll make me cry. I don't want to walk around here all day with puffy eyes and a red nose. You know I missed all of you like crazy. Come on. Let me show you around." She gave him a brief tour of the offices, introducing him to some of the other staff. When they returned to her office, she had a sense he wanted to say more.

"What's up dad? You are dying to say something."

George laughed, "Your mom said you should bring someone along on Saturday. You know, a date. I told her you wouldn't want to hear that, but she insisted. I'm just the messenger, remember."

Grace was shaking her head from side to side so hard she could feel her hair clip coming loose. Dating hadn't exactly been a priority in the short time she'd been back in Chicago. "Absolutely not, dad." She flopped down onto her chair and blew a stray hair out of her face, a petulant child with arms crossed on her chest. "I have had exactly two nights of going out with a group of people for drinks. I haven't had time to even think about dating—even if I wanted to. And I don't want to right now." She stood again. "Come on dad! She really can't expect me to do that!" It was a cross between a question and a statement ending someplace around a wail and making her dad laugh.

"You win this one. I'll tell her all of your male friends are busy that night. Of course, that'll be an open invitation for her to find someone highly appropriate for you. I think she started a list." He was walking toward the door, still laughing, and as he turned to give her one last wave, she saw the telltale twinkle in his eye.

"She never said any of that, dad. You're making all of it up, aren't you?"

He shrugged his shoulders, all innocent of any wrongdoing. "Just making sure you aren't sitting all alone in that apartment every night. Glad to hear you've had two dates." He waggled his fingers to air quote the last part of the sentence. "Thought maybe we'd have to invite you over for movies and popcorn so you could remember what a fun night really is."

She listened to his tuneless, albeit cheery whistle, as he made his way down the hall until the sound got lost as he stepped into the elevator. *What a goofball*, she thought. Coming home to her parents had been easier than she imagined. Any concerns that they might be judgmental toward her were completely unfounded. They had generously let her stay with them until she found an apartment.

Her sisters would have willingly helped out, too, but intruding on their busy family lives would have been extremely awkward. Crashing with your parents at 35 was awkward enough.

Her parents would be leaving for Florida after Christmas and she'd miss them terribly. Of course, it would also be a great excuse to take a couple of short vacations if she could get away. She'd come a long way from the despair of losing everything in Arizona. She was starting to feel centered again.

Grace turned her attention back to her computer. She had time to log in, check her electronic calendar, and jot down a couple of notes before she was interrupted once again. This wasn't her dad coming in to joke around with her; her boss stood in the doorway. She rose, extending her arm across the desk to shake the hand of James McWitner.

He smiled, nodding toward the muffins. "I thought I smelled fresh baked goods." Tall, almost painfully thin, his grip was firm but he spoke in a quiet voice.

In a déjà vu moment, Grace was right back to her very first day on the job just two months earlier. *"It's good to have you here Grace. I just wanted to stop by and say hello and let you know you'll have a couple of days to acquaint yourself with the processes. I had Marina put together some binders to get you up to date. The electronic files will also be available to you no later than tomorrow. You know how IT issues can be. HR had to take care of some details and then you'll be all set. I don't especially like working from paper copies, but you'll find the last two campaigns, sample letters to potential donors, and the list of our major donors. Start by familiarizing yourself with the names. That'll come in handy when you are knocking on doors and shaking hands in the coming months."*

As a first day greeting it had felt a bit overwhelming, but now she knew that is exactly how her boss operated. McWitner was certainly all business, but the underlying warmth made Grace feel comfortable and welcomed. His message was clear: She may be new, but she was a valued member of their ongoing operation. Accepting this position had been the right decision.

Now, Grace smiled at the director and settled back into her chair. "My mom baked them fresh this morning. There's more than enough here. Please, help yourself."

"I am actually going to take you up on that offer. If my mom were here to bake like this, I'd probably weigh 300 pounds." Grace laughed at the thought, carefully unwrapping the fresh muffins and handing one to him. She took one out for herself as well.

"I noticed some updates on our electronic calendars. We have some big projects coming up."

He nodded, leaning back in the chair across from Grace and gracefully crossing his leg. He broke off a piece of the muffin, chewing it slowly. James McWitner was always impeccably dressed, the picture of professionalism and high style each and every day. She followed his gaze as he looked out of her office window. There were no mountains, but the beautiful Chicago skyline and Lake Michigan views were certainly not an eyesore. "Looks like it might rain." He turned his attention back to Grace. "Later today I'd like to sit down with you and make final edits on the fall campaign letter. The first wave has to go out no later than next Wednesday. We'll have a little bit of time to breathe between then and the second wave going out."

"I have it all teed up. I'm excited to get started on my first campaign. This is what I've been waiting for. And believe me, I have plenty of time to focus on the campaign. It's not like I have a social life to distract me." Grace felt heat rush to her face, not sure why she had said that, but unable to take it back. She attempted to hide her red face and was thankful he was standing up to leave.

If he was caught off guard in any way by her awkward comment, he didn't let it show. He was almost out of the door, the last of the muffin still in his hand, but turned back to add, "Griff and I will have to have you over for dinner one of these nights. That'll give you something to put on your social calendar at least. Tell your mom I really enjoyed the muffin." He smiled and left as her cheeks turned a darker crimson. She tried to forget her embarrassment by getting lost in the work before her.

That night she returned to her apartment, poured herself a glass of wine and listened to her answering machine. Of course, her mom left a message verifying plans for Saturday night at Chisolm's.

"Oh honey, I'm so glad this will work into your schedule. Can you believe everyone is going to make it? It's been so long. I'll talk to you later. No, she's not answering so I'm leaving her a message. Bye honey. I hope the new job is going well. Dad said your office is beautiful. Bye." The machine beeped, letting her know that not another single soul had anything really worthwhile to call her about.

She sipped her wine, smiling at the answering machine. She knew that part of the message was meant for her and part of it was a conversation her mom was having with her dad midway through leaving the message. Her mom tended to do that a lot, carrying on multiple conversations at the same time.

It was easy to feel guilty for staying away so long. Of course, she had visited as frequently as she could, but she was the only daughter who moved away and she knew they all missed her terribly. Life with Josh had kept her in Arizona and she could finally admit to herself she never thought of Arizona as home. Should she admit that being there had been a waste of too many years she could have been around her family? The wine suddenly tasted bitter in her throat and she swallowed with difficulty. Tears started falling, and she didn't try to stop them. She was accustomed to these bouts and knew she would just have to ride it out. "A good cry never hurt anyone," she said aloud, echoing words her mom had often spoken to her three daughters.

Although trying not to dwell on her sadness, she felt an even deeper sense of…what? Loss? She wasn't sure how to label it. Her inability to have a baby with Josh had been devastating enough and then, just as she was anxious to try again, the opportunity was taken away.

Was it better or worse that she had no child? That was a difficult one for her to determine. A child with her at this moment would be a comfort. She would at least have someone to love. Then again, no parent wants to drag a child through a divorce. She blew her nose, wiped her eyes and reached for the wine glass. She had been through this mental ping pong game too many times in the past months. Her heart ached for all she'd lost.

"I miss you Jasper," she whispered, as she looked at a picture of him as a puppy, a quizzical look on his face. The sharp pain of his loss left her weak with emotion. The flood of tears fell without any attempt to stop them. She would have one really good cry tonight and then face the world tomorrow. "I miss you a lot," she told the dog in the photo.

Not for the first time, she admitted she maybe missed Jasper more than she missed all of the other losses combined: Josh, her marriage, her job and her life in Tucson.

***

The work week flew by and when Saturday morning arrived, she slept in, awakening slowly to the sounds of the city outside that were a muffled hum inside her apartment. After making a pot of coffee and pouring a steaming cup, she returned to her bed to snuggle under the warm comforter and sip. Her parents called to sing "Happy Birthday" to her, as usual. Her sisters would call at some point during the day. Tonight, she would celebrate with her family at one of their favorite steak places. It felt good to have nothing to rush off to this morning. Like a little birthday gift to herself, she decided.

Eventually she pulled out her laptop, not worried about getting any work done, but just to see who had decided to send her greetings today. As soon as she logged on to her email, she saw them, birthday messages from some of her family and friends. She knew which one she wanted to read first. She clicked on Lexie's name, and smiled as she read the message that had been sent at 12:01 a.m. Lexie was always the first one to wish her a happy birthday, guaranteeing it by setting an alarm to make it happen. This had been their routine ever since they met their freshman year, and Grace would do the same for her friend on April 26th.

Good morning sunshine. By my clock, it is officially October 14th! Happy happy happy birthday!! I hope it isn't too cold there in the windy city. I miss my BFF lots and lots. I've been thinking… If you want and if you have time, I might come out for a few days during the holidays. It looks like Thanksgiving will be completely uneventful here so it would be perfect timing for me. I'll call you in a couple of days to make sure that'll work out for you. Hope you have a hot date for tonight. Don't do anything I wouldn't do.

Hot date. Good one Lexie, Grace thought. Lexie of all people knew that it would be a long time before Grace would let anyone into her life in that way. Josh had taken everything she had to give, leaving her empty and unsure of herself. She needed time to re-discover who she was on her own and then maybe she could get serious about a man in her life again. She typed a response to her friend.

Thank you, Lexie! Yes, I have a hot date tonight. Actually, I couldn't decide which guy so I said yes to two. Looks like there's a threesome in my future. Happy birthday to me! I promise to do everything that you would do—and then some. I would love to have you visit. I'll keep my Thanksgiving open just for you. (And those two hot guys too, if they're not busy). Love ya! Hey… I might have to cancel the hot date thing. Mom and dad seem to think I need a birthday dinner with the fam instead. Poor guys. They'll never know what they missed.

She hoped that nobody ever hacked her emails. She'd hate to think what impression they would have of her if they did.

***

Chisolm's was busy, but the table for seven was ready. Grace arrived shortly after her parents, and was immediately folded into a hug from her mom. "Happy birthday baby girl. You look so pretty. Doesn't she look pretty, George?" Her dad nodded and winked, pulling her into his arms and planting a soft kiss on the top of her head. He pretended to search behind and around her.

"Where's your date? You told me you were bringing a date."

Her sisters and their husbands arrived moments after, and soon they were settled around the table, all talking at once. It felt strange to Grace to be surrounded by so many married couples. She forced herself not to dwell on it but to focus on the wonderful evening her mom so carefully planned on her behalf.

She couldn't remember the last time their schedules allowed them to gather for a nice dinner together. She reminded herself again and again that she had plenty to feel good about this evening, but she still felt pangs as her sisters talked about how their kids were doing in school, what activities they were involved in and what all of them were doing for family fun time. She watched the looks Jeremy and Ellen exchanged as they told stories about their "crazy" pre-teen and teenager, Lizzie and Tyler. She saw John reach over and squeeze Geneva's hand as they shared a scary memory about their twin sons' birth nine years earlier. Ryan and Jacob had done nothing but thrive since then, but the fear of that "what if" moment in time would probably never leave them.

The conversations, touches, and glances felt especially magnified tonight, and Grace ached, wondering if she would ever have that intimate connection to someone else again. How could she have ever thought the lives her sisters chose was boring? Was she craving this now? Deep in her own thoughts, she didn't immediately realize her sister was talking to her.

"Grace, do you remember Tom Robertson? Grace? Did you hear me?" Gen tapped a spoon against her water glass to make sure her sister was paying attention. "Do you remember Tom Robertson? He graduated two or three years before you?"

Gen was trying to make her voice heard above the din at the table and everyone suddenly seemed focused on this conversation. The unexpected interest threw Grace a bit off guard. She carefully chewed the bite of salad in her mouth and then set her fork down, aware of the silence and all eyes on her.

"Uhm...Tom Robertson? It doesn't ring a bell." She was cautious in her answer, not quite sure where her sister was going with this out-of-the-blue question. She reached for her water glass, watching her sister over the rim as she feigned a sudden thirst.

"Well, he certainly remembers you. I've known his sister Gayle since middle school. Of all things, we ended up in the same yoga class last spring. A couple weeks ago we were chatting about you being back home. Gayle said her brother recently moved back here from the east coast. He's some kind of an engineer—chemical, I think. Anyway, she asked if she could get your number for him. I didn't give it to her yet, but I think it would be a great idea. So, it's Ok, right?" Gen took a spoonful of her soup, pretending this conversation was nothing more than a casual dinner topic they would have any place or any time.

"You may certainly *not* do that." Grace hadn't meant for the answer to come out quite so forcefully, but she was incredibly uncomfortable, aware that everyone was watching the exchange between the two sisters, heads turning from side to side as though engrossed in a riveting tennis match.

Gen, always cool as a cucumber, didn't react to Grace's tone. Instead, she continued her probing. "She mentioned that he wants to get to a Bears game sometime this season. He used to go to almost every home game Gayle said. I told her you would probably like to do something like that. I think it would be a lot of fun for both of you. But we could all go out for dinner together, if that would be better for you. I'm sure Gayle and Alex would love to." The tennis match continued.

"I don't have any interest in a blind date, Gen. When I'm ready, I'll go ahead and plan a date with someone—without your assistance." Grace desperately hoped everyone would return to their soup and salad and forget about the conversation that had now taken over the table.

"It wouldn't really be a blind date, because you *did* go to the same school. From everything his sister has said, he seems really nice. I just think you two might hit it off really well. It's always good to have something in common when you start dating someone, and going to the same school is certainly something in common. That's a great icebreaker."

Grace couldn't control her emotions, her voice even louder than before. "And if I ever need great icebreaker ideas, you'll be the first person I ask, Gen. Until then, butt out!" Grace abruptly slid her chair back from the table, set her napkin next to her salad plate and mumbled an "excuse me" before leaving the table.

She stood in front of the mirror in the bathroom, looking at the face staring back at her. What was her sister thinking? How could she be so inconsiderate? Another thought came just as rapidly. What's wrong with me? Why did I get so upset about this? I don't exactly have men knocking down the door to date me. But is that what she wanted? She didn't have time to give herself an answer to any of the jumbled questions she was silently posing. Her mom poked her head in cautiously, concerned about Grace.

"I'm so sorry, mom. I shouldn't have blown up at Gen like that." She fought back tears as her mom walked to the sink and pulled a tissue from the box on the counter. She handed it to Grace, who dabbed at the tears and blew her nose. "What's wrong with me? I didn't mean to ruin everyone's night."

"Grace Isabelle, you haven't ruined anything. You are entitled to feel whatever you are feeling. If you want to date, you'll date. If you want your sisters to help you, you'll ask them to help you. If you want Gen to 'butt out,' she'll just have to do that. Now do your mother a favor. Put a smile on that beautiful face and get back out there and enjoy your birthday dinner." Grace smiled and reached for one more tissue. Hugging her mom, she was reminded yet again of how much she had missed out on all her years so far away from the ones she loved most in this world—even when they were the ones driving her crazy.

"I can do that, mom." With that, the two returned to the table and Grace forced herself to stay engaged in the stories, smile over the generous gifts and pretend that her life was on the correct course.

As she blew out the candles on the lovely cake the waiter set before her, she paused, letting a wish form in her mind. *Please let me be whole once again.* Even as she said the words to herself, she knew they sounded more like a desperate prayer than a birthday wish, but it would have to do. She blew them all out, 36 little lights snuffed out, and she hoped against all hope for her simple wish to come true.

Chapter 12

———◆—◆—◆———

Settling into a routine at the Foundation was a pleasant diversion from everything else in Grace's world. She relished opportunities to meet with some of Chicago's most highly regarded citizens, individuals who willingly gave in support of the arts in their community. For Grace, accompanying James on his visits to donors was all in a day's work, yet she couldn't help but be impressed by the lifestyles some of them must have when they so willingly wrote out checks for tens of thousands of dollars. Her family always lived very comfortably but she was definitely a stranger to this standard of living.

She devoted long hours to the Foundation, putting all of her effort, energy and time into her job, mainly so she wouldn't have the effort, energy or time to devote to feeling sorry for herself. No matter how busy she kept herself by day, she still could not escape the lonely nights or the bouts of insomnia.

Insomnia, she decided, was better than the nightmares that had become a frequent occurrence lately. One, especially vivid and frightening a couple of nights ago, kept Grace awake for hours after.

In her dream, she was alone in an unfamiliar house, wandering from room to room trying to make sense of how she got there. A baby started crying so she moved from room to room, searching for it, the cries getting more intense by the moment. As she made her way up the stairs, knowing she had to help the baby whose cries were becoming more strident by the moment, the house was becoming darker and darker, until she couldn't see in front of her at all. She forced herself to continue toward the sound, aware she must be getting closer, but filled with dread. A glow appeared in the darkness in front of her and she inched toward it. Once she was directly in front of the mysterious light, she reached out to touch it, recognizing the shiny object as the necklace Josh had given her while she was pregnant.

She was confused. Was the baby hers? Why couldn't she remember having the baby? As her fingers closed around the pendant dangling from a chain she couldn't see, Katherine's face appeared. Her hand closed over Grace's to keep her from snatching the necklace. *"It's mine. It's mine,"* she shrieked. In the next moment, in that strange way dreams skip time, Katherine was standing at a window in what was clearly a nursery, the crying baby in her hands. Grace was rooted in place, unable to move or scream as she watched Katherine open the window and toss the baby into the darkness below, the cries turning to an adult's screams. Katherine laughed the entire time, turning evil eyes to Grace as she said, *"Nothing belongs to you."*

Grace awoke, her heart racing. For several nights after, she dreaded closing her eyes, the memory of the dream haunting her.

***

Anticipation of Lexie's visit kept her going through this period. She couldn't wait to enjoy the long weekend visit over Thanksgiving. By the time she met her friend at the airport on Wednesday afternoon, Grace was beyond herself with excitement and when Lexie emerged from the baggage claim area, Grace threw herself at her, almost knocking both of them off their feet.

"Lexie, you look so good!" A head of deep maroon hair with streaks of black poked itself above the arms thrown around her neck.

"OK, OK. Uncle! I get it. You missed me." Lexie was laughing, Grace was crying and the two of them realized they were making quite the spectacle of themselves in front of the hundreds of other busy holiday travelers, but neither of them cared. Lexie took a moment to pull on the coat Grace had brought along for her. "It's freezing here, Grace. You're in luck, though. It just so happens I know exactly how I can warm up. I think you need to take us someplace for a hot toddy, or whatever it is you cold-weather dwellers drink when the north winds blow."

"You poor thing. I think you're right." Grace wasn't going to argue with the idea so she helped Lexie get her luggage into the car and they made their way to a bar around the corner from the apartment where they could settle in, have a drink or two and start catching up on all that had happened in the many months since Grace left Arizona.

"The first thing you are absolutely positively going to do is give me some decorating ideas. My apartment is cute but it has *nothing* on the walls, and *nothing* to give it any charm. It just doesn't quite feel like 'home' yet. That's your job. I need to change the aura or something so I can sleep better. If that doesn't work, I might need a priest's blessing or something."

"That bad, huh?"

"I'm finally getting through my days but some nights are impossible. I don't remember ever having nightmares like this before. Anyway, maybe some fresh decorating ideas will be the answer. The place probably needs some of that feng shui stuff."

Lexie clinked her glass against Grace's and rolled her eyes. "No time to just rest. Right away you put me to work. I hope you know I'm officially on the clock and I'll be sending you a bill when I get back home. To think I had visions of shopping and spa days and instead you're putting me to work. For shame, Grace. For shame. Now let's get down to what I really want to talk about." She turned to face Grace, locking eyes. "Have you met anyone yet? I want to hear about all those men throwing themselves at you."

This time it was Grace who rolled her eyes. "Really? Really, Lexie? Come on. You know I'm swearing off men. Want nothing to do with the male species anymore. They might be good for a couple things, but when they go bad, they really go bad."

"It's a big city, Grace, and it's filled with potential boyfriends. Sooner or later, you're going to run into someone you just won't be able to resist. I guarantee it."

Grace wasn't sure Lexie was right, but she was so thrilled to have her visiting she would let her get away with saying just about anything. Thankfully, Lexie changed directions quickly.

"Who's going to be at the big Thanksgiving feed tomorrow?"

It was fine with Grace that the conversation turned away from her lack of dating, so she set about giving the family tree updates. Grace's parents and sisters had seen Lexie only once since the wedding so there was a lot of catching up to do on that front. The thought of her wedding set a dark cloud over her head momentarily, but she shook it away. This was not going to be a wallowing weekend. She needed to break out of that slump.

"My parents are so excited to see you again. Of course, they probably won't recognize you. I don't even remember what color your hair was the last time you were here." She squinted, staring at the top of Lexie's head. "Was that your baby blue stage? I can't remember, but I'm sure they'll love this color you did for the holidays. It's almost…festive."

Feigning surprise, Lexie exclaimed, "What do you mean? I actually toned it down for this visit. I wouldn't want any of those hoity-toity types you hang out with to think you have a weird friend."

"Some of them are hoity-toity. I'll give you that, but if this is your idea of toning it down, Lex, I'm afraid to think about what it looked like before you got here."

Lexie raised her glass to toast. "Well, here's to friends…one may look normal, but she's a real headcase. The other may look a wee bit odd, to some people, but she's got her head screwed on perfectly straight."

Grace laughed, remembering how much fun they always had together. She raised her glass to tap against her friend's. "To friends. One is rather delusional, but I still love her to death."

"Come on. Finish the guest list."

"Gen and John will be there with the boys, Ryan and Jacob. They're nine and will spend most of the day with their faces in their video games, when they aren't arguing with each other, of course. Jeremy, Ellen, Lizzie and Tyler. Lizzie is 12 and Tyler is 15. I'm sure they will pretend they would rather be anyplace other than Grandma and Grandpa's house, but they're really good kids, and they really do love being with all of us. My mom's sister, Aunt Livia, will be there. You probably don't remember her. She's a stitch. She can't hear a thing without her hearing aids but she always manages to 'forget' them." She used air quotes to emphasize the word. "I think she likes to be in her own little world."

Lexie laughed. "Speaking of being in their own little world, Sean is sorry he couldn't be here. He promised his mom he'd spend the weekend with her in Las Vegas. Can you believe it? Thanksgiving in Vegas? She's too funny. I think that's why Sean tolerates me. He's used to living with someone who's more than just a little crazy. His kids are with their mom so it worked for him. Thank goodness he didn't expect me to hang out at the slot machines with them. You're stuck with me and me alone for the whole weekend."

"Don't think for a minute this is the drink talking Lex. I can't think of anything I'd want to be doing besides this. I have to admit. I haven't felt this happy in…well, in a really long time. Bad things piled on bad things and that made it easy to forget what happy could feel like. Thanks."

"Aw shucks. Just call me the joy fairy. I sprinkle it wherever I go."

By the time they reached Grace's apartment they had managed to get a great start on catching up on their three months apart. Lexie was relieved to see firsthand how well Grace was doing. The Grace who left Arizona right after Jasper died was beaten to a pulp, and Lexie had been worried sick about her friend, the grief difficult to watch. Even more difficult was watching her pack up to drive back to what Lexie knew had always really been "home" to her. Not wanting to put even more pressure on Grace, Lexie made every effort to hide her own great sadness at losing her best friend, even if she was a plane ride away.

She tried to explain that as they drove the short distance to the apartment.

"You know how hard it was to watch you leave, don't you?"

Grace glanced away from the road for a split-second, surprised Lexie was admitting this.

"Are you getting emotional on me, Lex? Where'd that come from?"

"OK, never mind, dumbass. I wouldn't want you to think I cared or anything. But we've been best friends since we were 18. It's hard to be there without you."

***

They stepped into the apartment, Lexie pausing to take it all in, using her artistic eye to evaluate what was still needed to make Grace's space more "Grace-like" than it currently was.

"This doesn't feel quite like you, yet. Of course, that's why I'm here." The apartment was craving some of her creative touch and she wasted no time helping Grace get started. It was well past midnight when the two decided they should probably get some sleep. Neither wanted to waste a moment of their time together, but Grace also knew her mom would not appreciate them yawning through Thanksgiving dinner.

Grace slept better than she had in weeks.

***

Thanksgiving turned out to be a festive day. The parade, football games, Aunt Livia's innocently placed comments that had nothing to do with the conversations taking place all mixed together to create a Norman Rockwell-like Thanksgiving experience for everyone—even the sometimes difficult to entertain older kids. And the food was fabulous. George and Sylvia knew how to put on a Thanksgiving feast that left everyone wanting to nap in front of the television. But that would not be the case. Championship-level rounds of Scrabble, Uno and, of course, charades rounded out the evening just before the pies came out. Most of them couldn't decide between pumpkin, pecan, or Dutch apple, instead opting for a "sliver" of each.

Grace smiled happily at her family gathered around her and knew she had made the right decision to leave Arizona. At one point she had made an excuse to leave the table momentarily as tears gathered behind her eyes, a mixture of emotions that included her joy in being surrounded by family as well as the pain associated with this, her first Thanksgiving alone. Knowing the upcoming weeks would include more of these emotional moments did nothing to help, but she was determined to fight through it.

While everyone welcomed Lexie as if she actually were a member of the family, Lizzie was especially fascinated with her aunt's friend, probably taking notes on how she could start expressing her wild and crazy pre-teen self. Grace was amused, knowing there were far worse role models for Lizzie. Lexie was the kindest, sweetest, most open person she knew, and she smiled at the two as Lexie said goodbye to her niece at the end of the night. Lizzie found a new role model and there was a good chance she'd show up to the next family event with an interesting hair color. Grace couldn't wait to see her sister's reaction.

Her dad was the last to say goodbye. As Grace watched him draw Lexie into a hug she swelled with emotion. Her family's love and acceptance of Lexie was evident long ago and had only strengthened, despite not seeing her for several years.

"Lexie, you should plan to visit us in Florida this winter. You and Gracie would have a great time together down there. The beaches are beautiful, you know. If those views don't inspire your artistic side, nothing will." Her dad loved having company down in Venice, always excited to play tour guide for visitors. "I bet you would really appreciate the art fairs in Boca Grande. Heck, you could set up a table to sell your artwork."

"That sounds like fun. I'll have to see if I can squeeze in a little jaunt down there. I won't pack up a truckload of my work to cart down there just yet. I need vacations from it now and then."

Later, sitting together in her apartment reflecting on the day, Grace confessed her moments of sadness. "It was strange because I felt happier than I've felt in months but at the same time it's like I felt sadder than I've felt in months."

"You've come a long way. My guess is that it is perfectly normal to feel sad, angry, whatever. I keep wondering what I'd do if I happen to bump into Josh and Kat-woman one day. I don't think any of us wants to really find out!"

Grace smiled gratefully at Lexie. She tried not to think about the new family life Josh was enjoying so the reminder gave her another round of sharp pangs. She was getting better at pushing them aside.

"Don't get yourself thrown in jail. He's not worth it."

Lexie gave her friend a high-five. "You're right about that!"

***

The weekend flew by far too rapidly for them, mainly because they packed every moment of each day with a ton of activity. Although the office was closed for the weekend, Lexie insisted on seeing where Grace spent her days and find out more about her new job. The artist in Lexie was enthralled with the work Grace was doing for the Foundation.

Getting a start on Christmas shopping, laughing over holiday classics, fixing up the once drab apartment and visiting with Grace's parents made for a whirlwind weekend and their goodbyes at the airport were more difficult than either wanted to admit.

Grace bit her lip as she pulled into the airport entrance, awaiting her turn at the drop-off in front of the main terminal.

"We'll just have to call more often, I guess." Grace was holding back tears, far more overwhelmed by Lexie's departure than she thought she would be. "I wish I could visit you in Arizona, but I…" She stopped and tried again. "There are just too many ghosts there."

Lexie reached across to squeeze her hand. "I understand completely." It was entirely possible Grace would never return to Arizona. "We have your parents' offer to visit them in Florida. We'll have to figure out how to make that happen."

Grace nodded, not trusting herself to speak. She maneuvered the car to the curb and stepped out to help Lexie get her bag from the back.

"Think about what we talked about the other night. I meant what I said. It's time for you to start dating. Promise me you won't rule it out."

A post-holiday travel crowd surged around them, making further conversation impossible.

"You need to move your vehicle ma'am. This is a drop-off zone only. No parking. Move along." The security guard, already low on patience, signaled for Grace to get back in the car and on her way.

One quick hug and Lexie was swallowed up, part of the crowd moving toward check-in. Grace nodded to the security guard, letting him know she was doing what he asked.

Settling into her seat on the plane, Lexie fastened her seatbelt, realizing Grace had not actually made any promises.

Chapter 13

———— ◆━◆━◆ ————

An intense loneliness settled over Grace in the weeks between Thanksgiving and Christmas, sapping her of energy, and causing her to question every decision, which made what happened more surprising to Grace than she could have imagined.

It was both a blessing and a curse that they were busier than ever at the Foundation. James McWitner did his best to be fair as he divided the responsibilities for holiday events at which he and his Assistant Director would be expected to make at least a cursory appearance, although some of the more important events would require the presence of both of them. Working during the holidays didn't bother Grace, but trying to get into the holiday spirit was especially difficult.

The one year she wanted nothing more than to crawl into a cave until Christmas was over was the year she had to be on top of her game. She was unaccustomed to the endless evenings of holiday gatherings the Foundation administrators were invited to and she would just as soon have turned down every single invitation to sit at home on cold, blustery December nights. That, however, was not going to endear her to her boss, so she forced a smile when he handed her the event invitations at which she would represent the Chicago Center for the Arts Foundation.

At first to her amusement and later to her dismay, she learned shortly into the holiday bookings that it might as well have been the same cocktail party cloned several times over as she attended event after event, each one very similar to the previous ones. *Groundhog Day all over again,* she thought, as evening after evening she found herself balancing a tiny plate of hors d'oeuvres and a wine glass while still managing to shake hands and join in a variety of conversations. It was exhausting, however, and by the fifth or sixth one she found herself arriving a little later and leaving a little earlier each time. She was on the verge of concocting an excuse to not attend one evening, but mustered the strength and showed up anyway.

The JW Marriott Grand Ballroom was a winter wonderland, sparkling with a magical fairytale shimmer that the raw cold of Chicago winters rarely resembled. She might have been impressed had it been her first, or even second event there. Making her appearance well after the usual crowd had arrived, Grace meandered through the various groups, greeting those she recognized and taking time to learn the names of those she did not know. *"Foundation work,"* James frequently reminded the team, *"is a constant meet and greet, so that as our new campaigns get started, potential donors are like old friends to us. It's difficult to say no when an old friend asks for a donation to a good cause."* Grace did her job, smiling her way through an hour of "making friends" and then deciding to call it quits.

Handing her claim ticket to the young woman waiting to help her, she set her purse on the narrow counter at the coat check station. Distractedly checking her phone for any messages, she reached for her coat and almost spilled the contents of her purse. She grabbed it as it was about to tip off the edge, her elbow hitting the person waiting in line behind her.

"Let me help you with that." She was apologizing to him even as he was pushing her purse back from the edge, out of danger of falling, and reaching above her head to take her coat from the attendant. He deftly swung it around, holding it for Grace to shrug into. She allowed him to assist and then turned to smile at him, hoping to recognize the gentleman from a previous event and acknowledge him by name. A quick assessment told her she had not met him before because she definitely would have remembered.

"That was very kind of you. Thank you." He had his overcoat draped across his wrist, ready to hand it over to the worker. The young woman took it from him, giving him a warm smile.

"Good evening Dr. Hayward. Here's your claim ticket. Enjoy your evening." Watching in amusement, Grace noticed the woman blush, the brief exchange with the tall, handsome man flustering her.

"Thank you. I will certainly try." Benjamin Hayward was accustomed to such reactions, but it wasn't the coat check worker that was catching his eye right now. Although he hated these events, coming only because the hospital expected him to be here, he was suddenly very happy to be standing right where he was.

Dr. Hayward was a dashing figure, probably mid to late 50's, very distinguished looking, with carefully styled dark brown hair and warm brown eyes. Although clean shaven, Grace imagined it wouldn't take long for a growth of beard to appear on his handsome face.

She finished buttoning her coat and reached for her purse, looking up to see those brown eyes watching her.

"I hate to think you're already leaving and I just got here. Benjamin Hayward." He reached his hand out to shake hers, and she took his warm hand in hers. She felt a surge of electricity passed between them.

Good lord, Grace, she thought. *Maybe you'd better lay off all the old romantic movies for a while.*

Pulling herself together, she released his hand. "Grace Warrens. Thank you again, Dr. Hayward." She had readily picked up on the title when the coat-check worker greeted him and wondered exactly what kind of doctor he was.

"Benjamin. Please call me Benjamin. Are you sure you have to leave already? It's always awkward walking into these things alone. I never seem to get used to that."

Grace smiled, familiar with that feeling. "It just so happens I warmed up the crowd for you so you'll be fine. I do have to go, but it was a pleasure meeting you."

As she walked out of the hotel to catch a cab home, she was surprised to realize she was still smiling. It really had been a pleasure meeting him. She forgot how nice it was to have the attention of a handsome man, even if it was for just a matter of a minute or two. For one brief moment, the endless nights of holiday cocktail parties didn't seem quite so tedious.

***

A week later, as chance would have it, Grace and her boss attended an event together at the Marriott. As she looked around the ballroom, still a winter wonderland but with a different color scheme for tonight's event, Grace allowed herself a moment to remember the prior week's meeting. The smile was impossible to stop as she recollected the warmth of Benjamin Hayward's hand in her own and the imagined current of energy that passed between them. It was imagined, wasn't it?

She found herself scanning the crowd, hoping she might see him again.

The evening wore on without any glimpse of the handsome doctor and as soon as she felt it would be acceptable, she said goodnight to her boss, making her way to the coat check. As Grace shrugged into her winter coat, without anyone's assistance this time, she felt pangs of disappointment. *You can't blame me,* she told herself. *Who wouldn't want that handsome man at her side?*

Her thoughts confused her. She couldn't pretend she was a fairytale princess, or one of those lovelorn ladies in a made-for-television movie, destined to run into the man who would sweep her off her feet and become her prince. The reality was starkly different. She was a thirty-something divorced woman who snuggled a pillow every night. Period.

As she stepped through the main doors to wait in the short taxi line, the blustery night met her with a force so she turned her head to prevent the cold blasts of wind from hitting her directly in the face. Grace was unaware that someone had stopped directly behind her.

"We really are pretty bad at this timing thing, aren't we?" Grace knew as she spun around, the deep voice belonged to the man she had been hoping to see all evening. The flush that warmed her neck and rose up her face was unstoppable, and if she were lucky, the doctor might assume it was a result of the cold winds and not her excitement at seeing him again.

"Dr. Hayward. You like to arrive late to events, don't you?"

"Do you always answer a question with a question?" His brown eyes sparkled and she felt herself excited by his nearness. "Let's try this a different way. If I were to ask you to meet me someplace where we would actually be walking in at the same time, would you maybe agree to do that?

The words tumbled out before she could stop them. "So, are you asking me on a date?" Her embarrassment was immediate when she realized what she had just said. That might not have been what he meant at all. In fact, for all she knew, he was a married man. Her face burned as she tried to hide her humiliation, but she couldn't figure out a single thing to say that would alleviate her discomfort. "I'm sorry. I didn't mean to say that. I...uh... I hope you enjoy your evening."

Without any real plan for where she was going, Grace turned on her heel and walked away before he could say anything in response to her question. She would catch a cab someplace nearby. Despite her attempts to make a quick departure, there was no ignoring his voice.

"Grace!"

Turning back toward him, she could see him standing in exactly the same place, looking even more handsome with the wind rustling his hair. He smiled, waiting for her to say something.

She didn't respond.

He raised his palms. "Yes. The answer is yes. Any more questions?"

She knew he was having fun at her expense and it suddenly brought back memories of her unusual meeting with Josh those many years ago. Why couldn't she just meet a guy in a normal, non-embarrassing way? Why did it have to be such a humiliating experience for her? She simply shook her head and waved, this time walking away as quickly as she could with absolutely no intention of looking back, telling herself her watering eyes were because of the cold wind—not her bitter disappointment in herself.

Benjamin didn't care that others might be staring as he stood rooted to his spot, watching her until she was lost in small groups of people scurrying along the sidewalk in the cold. Something about her was absolutely intriguing. He was oblivious to anyone around him in that moment. One person, however, was intently aware of him and his actions. In the alleyway between the hotel and the parking ramp swarming with people coming and going in the busy city, a figure stood watching the doctor intently, a hood covering most of the face.

When Benjamin finally turned to go into the hotel, the figure stepped out of the shadows to blend into the crowd. She had seen what she needed to see.

***

Getting ready for bed that night, Grace made up her mind that she really was not in the market for a man in her life right now. Shame on her for getting so excited just because some guy spoke to her—twice. She would continue to focus on work and leave it at that. McWitner would be very happy to know that she continued to have no social life to distract her from her job.

As if her boss somehow knew about her renewed commitment to work, he showed up at her door the next morning, two steaming cups of coffee in his hand.

"Light roast, one sugar, and no cream, right?" She nodded, taking the cup.

Following closely behind him was his assistant, Marina, carrying two binders. He gestured for Marina to set the binders down on Grace's desk.

"Can I get either of you anything else?"

"We should be good. Thank you, Marina." He waited until she'd walked out before continuing. "Did you have a good time last night?"

Grace set aside the work she was about to start and turned her attention to him. "How did you know I was craving this?" She was referring to the drink in her hand, but suddenly felt herself blushing as she realized she had done it again. She did indeed seem to have a habit of answering a question with a question. Perhaps it was a habit she should try to break, starting right now. "Thank you for the coffee. Yes, this is exactly how I like my coffee and yes, it was a nice event. I have to be honest, though, James. I'm really looking forward to the end of this stream of holiday parties. Is it just me, or do they all feel the same after a while? It's kind of like that movie about Groundhog's Day." She smiled at her boss and sipped her coffee.

"Absolutely right. Griff never comes with me anymore because he says the same thing. But I'm glad you enjoyed it. Any meet and greet gives us a chance to create a personal connection. These are the people who support our efforts so we do what we have to do, no matter how repetitive."

"I've certainly been shaking a lot of hands, and eating a lot of stuffed mushrooms." They both laughed. "To what do I owe your visit? I'm assuming it's more than just a coffee break."

"You've become an integral member of our team." He sat down in the chair across from her, pulling a binder toward him. "It's time for you to start working with some of the big donors, Grace. It's time for you to get to know our whales."

"I'm ready," she said, pleased that her work ethic had been noticed and appreciated.

He paged through the binder's laminated pages, stopping now and then to peer closely at a picture. "I know it's a little old-fashioned to have paper copies, but some things are best not kept as electronic files. These are the prime donors, the individuals who commit a quarter of a million or more to a single campaign."

Since her first day on the job, Grace had looked forward with great anticipation to this day, so she did her best to maintain her composure even as her heart was racing at the prospect of moving into this new phase. McWitner would never trust her to work with their most important donors if he didn't believe she was ready. "Let's get started. What would you like me to do?" She felt a surge of energy, knowing she had been right. Focusing on work instead of her love life—or lack thereof—was a wise decision.

He handed Grace the second binder. "I'd like you to start by simply acquainting yourself with these past donors. Read their bios, look at their pictures. Get to know them on paper." Grace paged through the laminated pages, none of the faces jumping out as being personally familiar, but some recognizable because she knew them to be local celebrities, political figures, entertainers, and business executives.

She stopped on one page, peering closely at the photo. "I met him at one of the parties. I don't remember her. I think he was with a different woman that night."

McWitner laughed. "We do our best to keep up with divorces and deaths, but it's complicated sometimes. I'll have Marina do some investigating." He paused to job himself a note. "I usually do one-on-ones with whales. They deserve our personal attention. They give a lot of money. Over the next several days I'll be setting up meetings with them because if they're thinking about making a donation, they'll want to do it before the end of the year. Tax break, you know."

"That makes sense."

He pointed to the binder as she started to slowly turn its pages. "These are current donors. They have all given within the past two years or for special campaigns we've run." He handed her the binder he had been looking through. "Those may be the whales, but these are more or less the folks we consider 'Lost at Sea.' For whatever reason, they were once whales who haven't made any donations in the past three or more years." He tapped the top of the binder with his long slender finger. "*These* are the ones we'd love to get back, but we know it's not easy. Once they lose interest, they're usually gone for good. It seems to get easier for them to say 'not this year' if they've already stopped giving for a couple of years in a row. And of course, we never know why they stopped donating. For all we know, they're flat broke now. Those things happen. Sometimes it's the market, sometimes a divorce or death. Some just decide they don't want to give the Foundation another cent of their money." He took a long drink of his coffee and then tossed the empty cup into the nearby trashcan, giving Grace a final smile as he stood, ready to leave. "You're doing great work, Grace. We're very lucky to have you on our team."

She was filled with a heady sense of pride, and allowed herself a moment to glow in the warmth of his compliment before directing her attention to the pages in the binder, turning each slowly, eager to learn everything she could from the documents in front of her. Her boss was clearly pleased with her work and she wanted nothing more than to keep him happy with her contributions to the team.

After spending time on the first binder, jotting some notes to help her remember some of the details of each donor, she turned her attention to the second binder. It was probably a stretch, but she wanted to make it her personal challenge to get some of the "Lost at Sea" donors to return. Nothing would please James more and really solidify her place at the Foundation.

The first pages represented the lower amount of donations from past events. She noticed they were arranged in increasing order of past contributions. Derek Sampson last gave $250,000. Nicolette and John Graves last gave $275,000. Some of the gifts had been given just a few years back, but most were significantly farther back in time. Marcus and Renita Thome gave $400,000 but it was almost a decade ago. Some gifts were in memory of someone, she noticed. Those would be especially difficult donors to get back. If there was a one-time gift from an estate, that might be the only money the family had access to. She decided not to focus much on those.

Her coffee cup was empty and the morning rapidly disappearing as she paged through the last of the entries in the book, looking at the pictures, the dollar amounts, the years, and carefully studying the important details as her boss had instructed her to do. And then he was there, staring back at her from one of the final pages. Actually, it wasn't him—it was "them." Benjamin and Keera Hayward. He was obviously younger than the man she'd seen twice now at the JW Marriott but she'd recognize that handsome face, brown eyes and amazing smile even if his name wasn't right there in black and white.

What she couldn't stop staring at, however, was the mesmerizingly beautiful woman sharing the moment with him. Her long black hair curled around her face like a perfect frame. Her dark eyes were deep, and her mouth curved into a soft, subtle smile, making her appear to be hiding some secret from the world.

There was no secret to hide. It was right there, in front of her face. Grace had a hard time swallowing the lump in her throat. She felt betrayed. That was crazy in many ways, but she was sure he'd been flirting with her, and maybe was even a little interested in her. What she was learning now was that he was a wealthy married man who was obviously enjoying a flirtatious moment with her.

She felt the blood rush to her face, remembering her boldness in front of him. She asked a married man if he was asking her out on a date. It left her feeling nothing short of humiliated. She didn't know what she'd do, how she could possibly explain it if her boss ever found out about the encounter, albeit brief, with the handsome man in front of her—the handsome *married* man in front of her.

Grace closed the binder, already too confused by the feelings she had every time she thought about Benjamin Hayward and not sure she trusted herself not to act on those feelings when the eyes in the picture seemed to be staring so intently into her own. But she also couldn't stop thinking about the woman—the woman who happened to be his wife. *He's a married man.* The thought repeated itself again and again. Images of Katherine flashed through her mind and Grace wondered if Katherine had felt any guilt whatsoever in being with a married man—sleeping with a married man and getting pregnant with his baby. She suddenly felt sick to her stomach and barely made it to the bathroom. For the rest of the day, she worked from her notes—not opening the binder again and less eager to make it her personal goal to find anyone who had been "lost at sea."

***

"He is probably the most beautiful man I've ever seen, Lexie. He's almost too perfect." She sighed, remembering how she felt when she looked at the handsome doctor. "The thing is, even if the guy was single, he's obviously way out of my league." She could feel the effects of the wine she poured herself before calling Lexie, hoping to numb some of her emotions. The wine wasn't helping. Sighing again, she added, "Like, somewhere in the stratosphere, a galaxy far out of my league. Oh, but a girl can dream, right? You should see his bio. He's been a director of pediatric medicine at three different hospitals around the country, he gives lectures, he's a well-known philanthropist in the Chicago area. He's just too amazing…and married!" She finally stopped to take a breath—and another sip of wine. The pause allowed Lexie to respond.

"Never assume a guy is out of your league, Grace. That's just stupid. It's possible he isn't married anymore." She decided to lighten things up. "Maybe it's time to see if the good doctor has any kind of bedside manner." She was thrilled to be having a conversation with Grace about a man. It was time for Grace to get back to dating. Most likely, this wasn't her Mr. Right, but Chicago was brimming with guys who would be perfectly eligible. There was no reason for Grace to be alone. "It's a real shame. You could have had some fun with this. I could see you as the naughty nurse."

"*Ugh!* You had to go there, didn't you? But I must admit, my temperature did rise every time I thought about him." She giggled, took another sip of her wine and wished Lexie was sitting next to her for this kind of girl talk. "I probably won't ever run into him again. Unless, of course, McWitner makes me contact him for the next Foundation campaign." She groaned, thinking about the possibility. "I can only hope he doesn't remember me."

"He might be divorced. Hell, you're divorced. It's where half of all couples wind up and you said yourself you never saw him with a woman. I think you are officially ready to start dating. You haven't been excited about any guy since Josh. Give someone else a chance. How about I help you set up one of those online dating things? We can write a great profile about how you like long walks on those cold Chicago beaches. And that you'll do anything to warm up your man after those long, cold walks."

"Hmmm. Tempting, Lexie, but I don't think I'm ready for something like that just yet."

"There's another option, you know. Your sister said she'd set you up with that one guy she knows. That doesn't sound completely awful"

"Maybe not *completely* awful, but still awful, Lex. I just don't think I'm ready to…to do this yet," Grace groaned in response. She ended the call shortly after, giving herself a moment to imagine being in a relationship again. It was a scary thought. Too scary. She wasn't ready. Yet when she closed her eyes to allow herself to imagine the possibility, it was the handsome face of the doctor she was seeing.

The phone rang, startling her out of the daydream. As if on cue, her mother got right to the heart of the matter, making Grace wonder if she was in cahoots with Lexie. "Have you met anyone interesting yet, Grace?"

Everyone seemed to think Grace should be dating again. Could they actually be right?

"Not yet mom. Not yet."

***

As she suspected, the holidays were a mixed bag of emotions. She was again reminded of how wonderful it is to be surrounded by family. She was also reminded how difficult it is to be alone—spending the first Christmas without someone since she was in her early twenties.

Two days before Christmas, Grace and her sisters scheduled a day of pampering at a spa, which they hadn't done together in years. Grace felt herself reconnecting with them as they indulged in mimosas between treatments. It also made Grace miss Lexie more than ever, realizing how much like a sister her friend had truly been for so many years.

"Gayle said that Tom is all settled into his new place. Have you given any thought to giving him your number?" It took Grace a moment to realize Gen had directed the question to her and it took yet another moment to remember what she was talking about. The blind date guy. This time she decided not to bite off her sister's head—but she also was not committing to a blind date right now. Diplomacy, she decided. Tact and diplomacy.

"I actually have been thinking about it." Gen's excited smile made her quickly add, "But please don't do anything until I ask you to, Gen, *if* I ask you."

"OK. OK. But if it happens to slip out in casual conversation, I'm not going to be held responsible." She ducked just in time to avoid the playful punch thrown her way.

"I need to see how I feel after the holidays, once I'm not such an emotional basket case. Everything makes me cry right now." She couldn't deny she had been feeling overly emotional lately. "I'm so pathetic. You should see me. I even cry over those silly holiday commercials on TV—the ones that show a man handing a jewelry box to a woman, letting her know how much he cherishes and adores her and needs to give her a token of his everlasting and undying love. And she is sucker enough to fall for it."

Gen laughed, while Ellen reached out to provide a sympathetic pat on her arm. Grace didn't tell them it went even beyond that. She had set her items down on the counter and walked out of Macy's a couple days ago simply because the man and woman waiting in the check-out lane next to her, holding hands and smiling at each other, had been too much for her to bear. It wasn't just the obvious—a couple in love—but the words he'd spoken as he reached down to rub what Grace could see was her obviously swollen belly. "We're going to have the best Christmas ever." She couldn't stand the thought that it could have been Josh and Katherine right there in the store next to her. She escaped before the tears started.

"Can I ask you something, Grace?" This time it was Ellen risking setting off a spark in her sister, and she didn't wait for an answer. "Do you ever wonder about the baby? You know, who does it look like? Is it a boy or girl? I think I'd be really curious."

How did Ellen know how much she had been focused on the thought of the family Josh now had—not just on the affair that led to it.

Grace fought the prickly feeling behind her eyes. She took her time answering, wondering herself what she truly was feeling. A couple of deep breaths later, she responded.

"I guess there are moments that I get curious. I get these flashes, like visions, you know, like seeing this happy little family, all three of them snuggled together on the sofa. Then I feel like throwing up or maybe throwing something." Pausing to take a deep breath, hoping she could say what she wanted to say without crying, she decided to keep it light. "You know, Lexie did such an amazing job decorating my apartment, I don't want to break anything I just bought, so I force myself to think about something else—something less sappy, like Josh driving off a cliff or being attacked by a passel of rattlesnakes."

She smiled through the tears, knowing she couldn't have been more honest with her sisters and herself about her feelings. It felt good to finally say it out loud. Her sisters were trying to hide the moisture forming behind their eyes, which made Grace laugh. "Oh great! Now I've made everyone cry."

They had time to exchange a few more potential ideas regarding the demise of Josh before the aestheticians called them in for their facials. Grace felt just a little of the heaviness lift from her heart as she gave a quick thank you once again for the blessing of sisters who really cared. And maybe Gen was right. Maybe she would give serious thought to the idea of that blind date.

Chapter 14

"We are all set at The Towers for the Gala. The lighting there is absolutely incomparable, as you know." He glanced down at the notes he was holding, the checklist clearly detailed, as was his nature. "We are in the final stages of selecting the art pieces and the actual set-up we want for the display. I've decided to do a blend of some new artists' pieces, mostly local up-and-comings mixed in with some of the regular favorites, to shake things up a bit." James McWitner paused to make sure there were no questions before moving on to the next agenda item. "As we already discussed, I want Grace and Marina to review the RSVPs and take a look at any last-minute invitations we might still have to send out. You know my expectations—we have to find that perfect balance between too many guests and too few guests."

There was laughter around the table at this comment.

"You're preaching to the choir, James." Everyone around the table nodded along with Lisa.

"I know. Going on. Lisa will work with me on the art selections and displays. The pieces are prepped for delivery the morning of the event so we won't have a lot of time for set-up. We have our usual crew from Martin's coming in to do that for us and then I will do a final walk-through. OK. We'll meet again next Tuesday at 9:00 for our pre-show review. Let's make sure we have no loose ends, people. Go make it happen."

They stood to pack up their notes, ready to head back to their individual offices to 'make it happen.'

Grace was anxious to finally get a look at the RSVP list. Everyone in the office had been buried in the work of setting up the biggest fundraising event the Foundation would host this year. She hated to admit it, but she also knew what name she was hoping to see on that list. Her internal argument had been going on for several days now, telling herself that flirting had occurred and then countering with "are you nuts?" as she analyzed their two brief conversations again and again.

And all the time, the beautiful face of the man's wife was a constant reminder of just how unavailable this particular man happened to be—if they were, indeed, still a couple. She figured if he was at the Foundation Gala, she might have her answer. His invitation, however, was never acknowledged and Dr. Benjamin Hayward was a no-show at the big event.

Grace's disappointment was deeper than she cared to admit. It did, however, make her realize that it might be time to open herself up to meeting someone. Even better, someone who was actually eligible. She wasn't exactly comfortable with the idea of dating again, but because she was thinking about it more and more all the time it probably meant she was emotionally ready. A movie, a dinner or drink…how hard could it really be? Unfortunately, her suspicions were that it would be really hard, but she pushed those thoughts aside, anxious to keep her life moving in the right direction. To her surprise, the opportunity came even sooner than anticipated—and it didn't include the awkwardness of a blind date.

"Hey Grace. I have a couple of tickets for a standup comedy show downtown Saturday night. I was just thinking, well, would you like to go?" Jeff, a local gallery manager, was in and out of the office in recent weeks dropping off flyers or touching base with James, and as always, he poked his head in her door to say hello. On Thursday, he dropped by as she made her way back to her office from the breakroom with a cup of coffee, falling into step next to her, making small talk. Now that the question was out of his mouth he stood awkwardly, half in the hallway, half in her office door, trying unsuccessfully to hide his embarrassment. While her first instinct was to say no, Grace surprised even herself.

"I'd really like that, Jeff. I haven't been to a good comedy show in ages."

Jeff smiled broadly, embarrassment replaced with excitement. "Well, I can't guarantee the comedy will be good, but we'll have fun." They made all the necessary arrangements before Jeff said goodbye, leaving her to the realization that she was going on her first real date with someone other than her ex-husband. It was a somewhat unsettling sensation that she'd taken this small step.

Lexie, of course, was beside herself with excitement, ready for Grace to move in leaps and bounds instead of baby steps. "You have to tell me everything."

"Don't I always, silly? I'm not telling my mom about this. You know her. She'll have a wedding planned before I can even end the conversation."

"I'm so happy you're doing this, Grace. I told you a long time ago, you aren't broken. You were just a little cracked for a while."

***

As it turned out, there was no reason for Sylvia to plan a wedding. On Saturday, she and Jeff sipped their cocktails after the show, an awkward silence setting in, making it uncomfortable for both of them. They'd already talked about how much they enjoyed the act, and the usual small talk concerning their recent histories had been covered. The lounge was busy, couples and small groups gathered at the bar and at tables scattered around the room. The cold weather wasn't a deterrent for any of them.

They found themselves in a lull in conversation and Grace wondered how to tactfully end the evening without being rude. Maybe a drink after the show hadn't been the best idea. Both of them were clearly out of practice when it came to dating, but Grace thought there was something more to it. She couldn't put her finger on it, but somehow knew he wasn't "the one." She scolded herself for the thought. The one for what? It wasn't as if she were looking for a husband tonight.

Jeff excused himself to use the bathroom. She watched him walk away, wondering if perhaps it wasn't Jeff at all. It could very well be that she wasn't an interesting enough person for a guy to date. Maybe that was the problem. After all, Jeff was nice looking, kind, courteous…all the things a woman was supposed to look for in a man.

Deep in thoughts of how undesirable she must certainly be, she almost fell off her barstool when she recognized the deep voice near her ear. "I suppose you're just about to leave." She turned to look into the handsome face that she'd tried really hard to stop thinking about over the past weeks. "Hello Grace." His smile was absolutely captivating.

Benjamin was pleased he was getting the exact reaction he had hoped to get. She was definitely surprised but happy to see him.

"Oh," she managed, a little more rattled than she should have been and almost spilling her drink as her elbow bumped against it. He reached out to slide it away from her arm and she breathed in the scent of his cologne. "Hello Benjamin."

They were smiling at each other, and she found herself getting lost in the depths of his brown eyes. "I hate to break it to you, but I'm getting pretty close to calling it a night. My friend and I were just wrapping up our date." She found herself blushing at the word "date," not exactly sure why. "I mean, it wasn't really a date, we're just having a drink." Was she really making sure Benjamin didn't think she was in a relationship? What was wrong with her?

"I noticed you were here with someone. I certainly don't want to interrupt your date." The look he gave her seemed to indicate quite the opposite. "Unlike you, I'm not quite ready to call it a night." He leaned closer, conspiratorially, and her heart skipped at least two beats. She reminded herself to keep breathing. "Before your 'date' comes back, I have an idea. I think it's about time we actually show up in the same room at the same time. If you decide you might want to do that, I'll be sitting right over there. It's your call. Of course, I'm used to just watching you leave."

The twinkle in his eye revealed just how amused he seemed to be by their simultaneous entrances and exits at each chance meeting. Before she could respond, he was gone, making his way to a table in the corner of the lounge. Grace let out her breath, unaware she'd been holding it. That man did something to her whenever he was near, and she willed her heart to stop racing.

When Jeff returned moments later, she had already made up her mind to do the unthinkable. She was going to make an excuse to end her evening with Jeff so she could explore whatever it was that was happening with Benjamin Hayward. It was time to find out if he was married and if there was anything to what she now knew beyond a shadow of a doubt was flirting.

Her heart racing even faster, she heard herself say, "Jeff, I'm not feeling well. I should probably get going." His look of concern made her feel guilty and she wished she hadn't feigned illness. Maybe she should have said she was just tired or that she'd received a phone call that her mom was ill. She wasn't good at these covert activities. "I'm sure it's nothing. I probably just need a good night's sleep. I'll grab a cab."

"Maybe I should give you a ride home. Your cheeks are really pink." His worried expression was starting to make her actually feel sick to her stomach. It probably served her right. Karma.

"There's no point in you going out of your way. Honestly, I'll be fine taking a cab."

"Grace, it's no big deal. I'd be happy to drive you home." She felt another pang of guilt and for just a moment she almost changed her mind. Instead, she shook her head, insisting that the short ride home in the cab was no problem for her.

He closed out the tab, helped her into her coat and a few moments later he was holding the door of the cab he'd hailed. "I had a really good time. Maybe we can do this again sometime." He leaned in awkwardly, planting a kiss on the cheek she'd turned toward him and then closed the door. As the cab pulled away from the curb, she watched Jeff run across the street, on his way to the parking garage where he'd left his car.

She waited until the cab was less than a full block away and then announced to the driver that she had to return to retrieve her phone. "I must have left it on the bar." She was searching through her purse, ignoring the phone in it, and hoping it wouldn't suddenly ring, chime, or beep and mess up her whole charade. "That's just like me. If you could just circle around the block and drop me at the front door again that would be great." The driver did as instructed, returning to the front of the bar a few minutes after having left it. "I'll grab a different cab in case this takes a while. Thank you."

She paid the fare and slid out, pleased with her own acting skills, but not sure why she felt a need to make up this story for a perfect stranger. This was all very new, very unfamiliar territory for her. Almost an out-of-body experience, she felt as though she were watching herself from a distance, but her still-racing heart was evidence that this was truly happening to her, and she again tried to control her nerves as she walked back through the door she had just walked out of a few minutes before.

Standing near the door, she took a couple deep breaths then walked directly to Benjamin. He stood as she approached, helping her out of her coat. "It's about time we are actually in the same place at the same time." His smile was sweet and genuine and she felt his warmth wrap around her. The guilt she'd felt moments before over ditching Jeff was suddenly gone. But guilt was soon replaced by feelings of awkwardness.

Before she could stop herself, she blurted, "Are you married?" She knew the answer to this question would impact everything that happened next and hoped against hope she was going to hear that he wasn't.

"Grace, there's no way I would be sitting here with you right now if I were a married man. Maybe I need to ask you the same question. Are you married?" She almost cringed at how forward her question was.

"I was. I'm divorced."

He hardly missed a beat, but she couldn't miss a new look in his eyes. "My wife died."

He glanced away, hating those words, hating that she was gone, and hating how others treated him once they knew. Sympathy in the eyes of others wasn't necessarily a bad thing, but having that sympathy change the way others treated him made him forget who he was as a person. Was he a successful medical professional or just another lonely man with a sad story? He prepared himself for the reaction he knew was coming.

"Oh, Benjamin, I'm so sorry to hear that." The moment was suddenly made one hundred times more awkward for Grace and she couldn't help but feel unsure of herself, and completely out of her element. She wasn't sure if she should ask him more about her—the beautiful Keera she remembered from the picture—or if that would make him uncomfortable. She was already uncomfortable enough for both of them.

"Thank you. My wife was an amazing woman. I miss Keera every single day."

Grace again faced confusion over what to say in response. After a brief pause, she found herself blurting, "Why am I here?" Of course, she regretted the words as soon as they left her mouth. She wasn't sure what a normal conversation should be in this situation, but mostly because nothing was normal about any of this. What had she done? For a moment, she wished she could turn back time and simply finish her date with Jeff like a rational, normal human being. "I mean, well, why did you ask me to come back here?"

He laughed. "I think you're here because you decided you wanted to be here. That, by the way, was a really good choice." She was drawn to him for so many reasons. Yes, he was handsome, but more than that, there was a dignity, a maturity about him that was very new to her. She felt like a silly schoolgirl in some ways, too young and too unworldly to be of any real interest to someone like Dr. Benjamin Hayward.

A cocktail waitress made her way to the table, momentarily drawing his attention away and giving her opportunity to look at him again. She liked what she saw. He was a very distinguished looking man. The server clearly thought so, too, as she took a little longer than needed to get his order, bending over to better display her ample cleavage. Women couldn't help but be drawn to this man, and it wasn't just his good looks. Charisma, Grace decided. There was definitely a charisma about him, and maybe just a little mystery, too.

"I'll take another glass of the Insignia. Bring two, actually, as long as that's satisfactory to this young lady." He turned back to Grace, awaiting her approval of his selection. The waitress gave her a cursory glance, keeping her focus on Benjamin. The name of the wine wasn't familiar to Grace, but she assumed it must be good. He didn't strike her as the kind of person who wasted his time on anything but the best. She was drawn to his confident, take-charge approach, which she found strangely exciting. As the server finally walked away, he returned his full attention to Grace, who was struggling to find some sense of equilibrium.

"I'm sorry. That was a stupid thing to say. This probably will come as a surprise to you, but I'm usually not so stupid sounding."

"You realize you've just apologized twice in the last few minutes, don't you?

Grace shook her head, thinking back over the last words she'd spoken, then realizing he was right. "I'm sorry, I…" She stopped herself, covering her mouth with her hand as he laughed at her awkwardness in a way that was too charming to be insulting to her. He gently pulled her hand away from her mouth, and again she felt that same electric tingle pass between them, even with this brief touch. She *hadn't* imagined it the last time.

It struck her that she'd been dreaming of a moment like this, playing it over and over in her mind, ever since she saw him at the holiday party.

"Let's start all over, shall we? Pretend we are meeting for the first time." He shifted slightly in his chair, turning away from her momentarily and then back again, a look of surprise on his face at seeing her seated next to him. "Good evening, miss. I'm Benjamin." He took her hand in his to shake it and the now familiar surge of energy was there again. "I'm 56 years old, chief of pediatrics at Chicago University Hospital, and I love good wine, spectacular sunsets and nice vacations."

She laughed and played along, relieved to have the awkwardness of the past moments disappear with their 'starting over.' "I'm pleased to meet you Benjamin. I'm Grace. I'm 36, I work in fundraising and I wouldn't know good wine if I were swimming in it. Sunsets are wonderful, but I don't have a view of them from my apartment, and I haven't had much time to take any vacations—nice or otherwise."

She let his hand hold hers longer than was probably necessary, enjoying the feeling more than she liked to admit. The server arrived so she had no choice but to let her hand slip from his as he handed her a glass and took the other for himself.

"You won't have to swim in this. I can assure you it's a good wine." He held his glass up and she followed suit. "To a future filled with good wines, spectacular sunsets and nice vacations." He carefully clinked his glass to hers and smiled before tasting the contents of the glass then nodding his approval.

The wine felt like silk in her mouth. "Oh my! I guess *this* is what you mean by a good wine." She took another taste, letting the liquid sit on her tongue before swallowing. "I think you've officially ruined me for life. My usual wines will never be good enough now." The warmth of the rich red wine moved down her throat and into her stomach, helping her relax just a little. She had to show this man she wasn't always a bumbling, fumbling idiot. After all, she was a well-raised, well-mannered, well-educated woman. As handsome and intriguing as this man before her was, he was still a man who put his pants on one leg at a time, as her dad would have said. "Tell me about one of those nice vacations you like to take. I'm used to living vicariously through others."

"My wife and I absolutely loved Spain, but Italy was a close second for us. We thought about buying a villa in Spain at one point, but we had other places we enjoyed visiting so we didn't want to tie ourselves to one location. We figured it would be the perfect place to retire." A look crossed his face and he took another sip of wine, giving himself a moment to compose himself.

He spent the next half hour telling her stories about the food and wine he and his wife had enjoyed and the amazing places they stayed. "I haven't done any traveling in the last couple of years, besides for work, of course. Since Keera died, I've stayed close to home." There was something so open, exposed and raw about him that she found herself wanting to hold him close and tell him everything would be okay. She had no idea why she felt compelled to help him through the grief. "She was my soulmate. I can't imagine traveling would ever feel the same. Everything was an adventure to her. I miss that the most, I think."

His last words gave Grace an immediate pang, or maybe it was more a punch in the gut. She couldn't specifically define it, but it was somehow connected to the idea that he would never find anyone as meaningful to him as his now deceased wife. A bubble within her burst. A moment before she was sure she was going to take away his sadness. It was crazy for her to think this way. Was she hoping he would fall madly in love with her and completely forget anyone else had ever existed in his life? That was the problem. She did feel that way. And try as she might, she couldn't stop the whirlwind of thoughts spinning wildly out of control in her head.

They didn't even know each other...but...maybe, just maybe, he was feeling some butterflies, too. It was entirely possible he was experiencing the excitement of meeting someone new and maybe, just maybe, someday falling in love. It *was* possible. Or...not. He'd lost his soulmate and might never find what he'd lost with another woman. There wasn't room in his life for anyone else. After all, once you've had the best...

Suddenly the wine didn't taste quite as good and Grace realized returning to the lounge was not the best idea after all. In the awkward silence surrounding them, she stole a glance at Benjamin who was far away, thinking about something completely unrelated to her, this place, or this time. She wasn't sure what to do or say. As she leaned forward to set her glass down, the movement made him look up, returning to the moment. He seemed to be waiting for her to say something, so she said, "You were very lucky to have each other."

"We were." As he took another drink of his wine, he was fighting back tears, making her all the more uncomfortable. Not sure what to do, she reached over and squeezed his arm, afraid she might be making the moment worse for him. Benjamin acknowledged her touch with a brief smile. "She was larger than life in some ways. And such a gifted artist. A painter." He looked at Grace. "I'd love to show you some of her work sometime."

"That would be lovely. I'd love to see them." The words came out of her mouth before she could think about what she'd just agreed to. She wasn't certain she wanted to see his dead wife's artwork. She wasn't sure she wanted to see him again. This wasn't going the way she had expected and it was time for the evening to end. The magic had evaporated. "Benjamin, I really should get home."

For the second time that evening she was in a cab waiting to ease away from the curb and into traffic, and for the second time that evening, she was a mess of mixed emotions.

Benjamin remained on the sidewalk, watching the car, his coat collar pulled up in an attempt to ward off the cold.

Grace attempted to process the evening as the cab maneuvered through the still-busy streets. How had her date with Jeff ended with saying goodnight to Benjamin? Was this her life, or had she stepped through an invisible portal into someone else's? If dating again made her feel this strange, she would rethink it.

She buried her face into her gloved hands, trying to cool the shame of giving in to Benjamin's request to meet her. Jeff was a nice guy who deserved better. The night she earlier thought of as magical was nothing close to that. She thought getting past some of the mystery of Dr. Benjamin Hayward would help, but it only made matters worse. This was not magical. Maybe there was no more magic left for her.

Benjamin turned to walk away as the cab disappeared into traffic.

In the dark shadows of a nearby doorway, a figure huddled against the cold, but her dark brown eyes were alert. She lingered briefly, watching the man say goodbye to the same woman he'd spoken to before.

Chapter 15

❝**A**re you kidding me?" Grace pulled her phone away from her ear, not expecting the decibel level that Lexie emitted when she learned about Grace having a drink with the handsome doctor. "What happened to your date with Jeff? This is going to be good. Spill it. How did that happen? And don't you dare leave anything out."

Grace could picture her friend settling into her sofa cushions for an entertaining story, but Grace knew it really wasn't as exciting as Lexie was anticipating. She told her about the previous evening, stopping to answer the occasional interjected question.

"It was just kind of odd. I can honestly say I've never been on a date that had conversation centered more around a dead wife than on either one of us. You know, the typical first date kinds of things." She found herself stammering, "Not that it was a date, but you know what I mean. We were just getting acquainted but the only thing I really know about him is that he had a wife, he loved her a lot, she died and now he's sad. Is that weird to you?"

"I guess, a little. But maybe he's just getting back into the dating business and you need to cut him some slack. He probably doesn't know what to say on a date any more than you do. I still can't believe you had two dates in one night. Oh my gosh, Grace. I'm stunned. I thought you'd be easing into this whole dating thing instead of double-booking on your first night. What are you turning into?" She couldn't contain her laughter. "The next thing I know you'll be calling to brag about a threesome for real."

"We have to stop calling it a date. It wasn't even close to a date. I mean, yes, the first part of the night was a date. The second was…just a chance meeting. We happened to run into each other. That's it. Nothing more." She hadn't exactly been "in the dating business" for a long time either, but she certainly recognized the excitement of a first date, complete with sweaty palms and a certain giddy euphoria. Unfortunately, it hadn't been Jeff providing those giddy feelings.

Lexie seemed to read her mind. "So, what about Jeff?"

"Jeff is really nice. I don't know. I guess it was just kind of ho-hum. It wasn't anything like being with Benjamin. I have to confess. I had all those first date kinds of feelings when I was with him. You know—butterflies in the stomach, fluttering heart sort of stuff. And that wine he ordered us, oh my goodness, Lexie. It melted in my mouth. But the rest of the…uhm… the 'non-date' was just weird."

"I take it you won't be seeing Jeff again so that leaves you with Dr. Handsome. I guess that works. Focus on the good doctor. Let him take you on a couple more dates and buy you expensive wine and then you can decide if you like him."

Grace groaned. "It wasn't a date. Stop saying that, please?"

Lexie laughed. "You said it first. Did you give him your number so he *can* ask you out on a real, honest-to-goodness, I'm-going-to-bang-you date?"

"Lexie! My gosh! What is *wrong* with you?" But this time, even Grace giggled. "I'll bet he's a great banger, actually. And yes, he has my number. I doubt he'll call. It was just so awkward. I had two guys interested in me in one night and I don't think anything more will come of either one." She sighed. "I'm pathetic, Lexie. Absolutely pathetic! I think I should have stuck with swearing off men like I originally planned. It would be so much easier, you know."

She continued to think about the previous night long after her conversation with Lexie ended, deciding she definitely wanted Benjamin to call her. She was intrigued by him, but she wasn't sure if there was anything more than that. Well, that and the physical attraction. Maybe it would be for the best if he didn't call her. She'd leave it at that. She didn't want Benjamin to call her back. Her life would clearly be much simpler if she didn't hear from him again. And, she reminded herself, they had nothing in common. There were far more differences than similarities between the two of them.

Despite convincing herself of what she wanted, Grace's heart jumped almost out of her chest when her phone rang. It was very sweet of Jeff to make sure she was feeling better. The call also made her feel terrible about herself all over again, though. Jeff just didn't give her butterflies. The second time the phone rang she knew it had to be Benjamin. She was again mistaken. The furniture store worker informing her the chair she ordered was available for pick-up or delivery at her convenience any day the following week was not who she had hoped to hear on the other end of the line. She sighed. At least her apartment was coming together with all of the great decorating tips from Lexie. She should stop thinking about men altogether and focus on that, she told herself.

***

On Monday night, shortly after texting Lexie that there had been no phone call—from Benjamin—she was surprised by the sound of her phone ringing. Her heart raced as she anticipated the unmistakably deep voice of Benjamin. She hoped her disappointment wasn't completely noticeable as the realization registered that the voice was not that of Benjamin, but Jeff once again. "Some friends invited me to a playoff game party next weekend at their house. Sadly, the Bears won't be playing, but I thought maybe, if you aren't busy, you might like to come."

"Oh, Jeff, that's so nice of you, but…well, I promised my parents I'd watch the game with them." She felt terrible for making up an excuse, but what else could she do? Come right out and tell Jeff he didn't make her hear race? It was stupid to let this really nice guy slip away when she had no idea if there was anything else out there for her.

***

It wasn't until the following Saturday that Grace had a voicemail from Benjamin. His message told her he'd been called for a consultation that took him out of state unexpectedly. She listened to his words carefully, the sound of his voice almost mesmerizing to her.

"I'm sorry I didn't have a chance to call you sooner. I've been on a crazy schedule. I'll make it up to you as soon as I can. I'm hoping you'll have dinner with me. I haven't even told you about my daughter. I'm really looking forward to seeing you again, Grace."

Her heart, soaring at the sound of his voice, dropped as suddenly. Daughter? There had been no mention of a daughter. She had visions of a sweet-faced little girl with Keera's beautiful eyes and hair, and Benjamin's charming smile. A daughter? What was she getting herself into? She played the message again and then a third time, expecting to learn more about this once again mysterious man if she just listened carefully. Each time she heard the same thing. She was allowing herself to fall for a man who she knew two things about: He'd lost the love of his life and he had a daughter. Of course, she also knew he worked as a director of pediatric medicine. Once she added a couple more things to her very short list of "Everything I know about Benjamin," she'd feel better. Or would she?

Was she ready to go down this path—even if it meant she might be disappointed when all was said and done? Her confusion mounted and she wanted nothing more than to bury her face in Jasper's neck and tell him everything. He would listen, without judgement or feedback. There could be a raised eyebrow or even a well-placed lick, but no judgement.

Lost in these thoughts quite some time later, a text message alert startled her. When she saw the sender was Benjamin, her heart did a back flip. She opened the message with shaking hands, reminding herself of how silly she was being.

Just thinking about you.

She stared at the message for just a moment before typing back: *Really? What are you thinking?*

Very warm thoughts. Making me smile.

She couldn't help but smile herself. She liked the thought of making him smile. She needed him to know, however, that there was a lot she didn't know about him yet, and she had to somehow start them down that path.

You have a daughter. That came as a surprise.

Caroline. I'll tell you all about her soon. Now about those warm thoughts.

You must be drinking. Are those warm thoughts the alcohol talking?

A glass of wine, yes. It's always a shame to drink wine alone.

So, those warm thoughts… It IS the wine talking!

Not a chance. This is me talking. I like you, Grace.

Grace didn't respond immediately, not sure exactly what was happening, yet not wanting it to stop. She jumped when her phone chimed, heralding yet another text. He hadn't even waited for her to reply to the last one.

Song lyrics rattling around in my head. "Something in the way she moves..."

Grace was even more uncertain about where to go with this. Her internal struggle the last couple of days was leaving her more than just a little confused and suddenly very tired. She wasn't sure she was ready to move into the intimate territory he seemed to be leading them. Not yet, anyway.

That's nice. Enjoy your wine. It feels good to have someone thinking about me. Grace deleted the last sentence and added a *Goodnight* before hitting send. Her heart was racing and she needed to get control of herself. "You don't even know him," she said aloud, wishing someone were there to reassure her she was not doing anything wrong. Jasper would have helped her through this, her confidante through thick and thin. "And you don't even know me," she said to her phone, as if Benjamin might somehow hear her.

Despite her attempts to move slowly, she was excited by his words and the fact that he not only was thinking about her but she had inspired music in his head. She groaned at her own corniness, read his final *Goodnight* and then turned off her cell phone. There was just so much to learn about this man. She reminded herself again to be cautious, despite the way her heart continued its racing as she stared down at her now silent phone. She'd been down a similar path before, and look where that got her. An image of Josh snuggling Katherine flashed through her mind, and she knew how important it was to protect her heart this time.

Chapter 16

——◆—◆—◆——

"**S**ong lyrics? That's so romantic, but seriously, you need to get the scoop on the daughter. Those poor little rich girls can be really nasty to a step-mommy. They make horror films about that sort of thing."

"Lex, we haven't even been on a date yet." Grace groaned. "Well, not officially anyway. I don't think his daughter has to worry about an evil stepmom at this point. Is that why you haven't married Sean? I think I finally get it. You're afraid his kids will see you as the evil stepmom if you two get married." Grace did her best evil villain laugh.

"I get along swimmingly with them because I'm just that cool and they know it."

Lexie could make Grace laugh about all of it, but she knew she had to protect her heart, too. She was still fragile in so many ways.

It was easy to forget all of her arguments for steering clear of him when Benjamin asked her out for dinner the following week. He was sweet, almost shy when he asked and she immediately realized his vulnerable side was just as attractive as his suave, confident side.

Finding the perfect outfit became her biggest problem. After careful consultation with Lexie, a long-sleeved black dress with a little bit of her back showing was the winner. She twirled in front of the mirror, hoping to rediscover some of the magic she'd initially felt.

As it turned out, she did. Benjamin seemed to know everyone, all of them greeting him as Dr. Hayward. The waiters anticipated his every need, and she started to imagine herself as the guest of royalty. When a colleague from the hospital approached, he introduced her as his friend, and she found herself hoping that descriptor would change. She really wanted to be more than Benjamin Hayward's friend.

Once the wine was poured, he lifted his glass to toast. "To a beautiful woman. Thank you for joining me tonight, Grace." He held her gaze for several seconds, even as he took a drink of his wine. "I didn't think I'd ever feel like this again. I couldn't imagine being with someone after Keera died."

She struggled with an appropriate response, wondering if the evening was going to be about Keera once again. "I'm glad you asked me out."

They enjoyed dinner, a bottle of wine and even shared a dessert. When the conversation centered around her life, and what brought her to Chicago, she felt her earlier worries disappear.

She told him about her marriage that ended in shambles with relatively little emotion, but when she got to the part about Jasper, she felt the start of tears and pressed her fingers against her eyes to stave them off.

He took her hand, a gesture she appreciated as she struggled to regain her composure.

"I'm sure it was terrible, but you have to put it into perspective. He was a dog."

His hand in hers felt less comforting and she was thankful the food arrived when it did. Before long, the sting wore off and she forced herself to consider his words. She was crying for a dog...not a lost spouse. She vowed to choose her words more carefully going forward.

They left the restaurant, Benjamin holding her hand until the valet brought his car and opened her door. At her apartment building, he walked her to the front entrance. Out of nowhere, her nerves began to jangle. So many walls still had to come down before she could be with someone. What if he was ready and she wasn't? What if he wanted to kiss her? Should she invite him in? Her face turned pink. Maybe he wasn't interested in anything further with her.

They stood in silence, lost in each other's eyes, and then he leaned down to kiss her. Her first thought was that his mouth felt strange to her as their lips met, but she knew it was because it wasn't Josh. She hadn't felt another man's mouth on her own in so many years she wasn't sure how she should feel. And then her brain switched to auto-pilot and she kissed him back. She imagined fireworks exploding above them, in brilliant flashes of color. This was every bit the fairytale she'd hoped for.

He hugged her close for a moment and then placed one last soft kiss on her forehead before saying goodbye. Grace let herself into her apartment, which looked oddly the same even though she felt like a different person returning to it.

All caution was thrown to the wind. She could easily fall for this man.

Thinking back over every moment of the evening, and hoping against hope there would be plenty more just like this one, Grace got ready for bed. It took a long time to feel the hazy cloud of sleep drifting over her. She was startled out of her near-sleep state by the sound of a new text message. She'd intentionally left the phone on the nightstand nearby in case Benjamin was inspired by lyrics again.

I feel like a new man with you. I hope you enjoyed tonight as much as I did.

I did. Thank you.

She kept her response simple. It wasn't quite time to fully open her heart, even though the evening had been absolutely perfect. She had done that once before and look what it got her. They still hadn't talked about his daughter. She could have brought up the topic, but she'd chosen not to for a reason. At some point she decided she didn't want this night to be about his wife or daughter.

She needed there to be some magic that was meant only for her.

***

Arriving at work on Monday, she literally stopped in her tracks at her office door. A vase filled with long stem red roses sat on the center of her desk. She stepped forward, eyes glued to the card. Marina's voice behind her made her jump, her heart racing even harder than it had just a moment before.

"Did I startle you? Sorry dear." Marina touched her arm. "What a gorgeous arrangement. I've never gotten a delivery quite like this before. You are one lucky girl. He must be a keeper." She walked away as quickly as she had arrived and Grace again focused her attention on the card.

Extracting the envelope from its plastic forked holder, Grace read the message, savoring each word.

Beautiful flowers for my beautiful lady—Benjamin.

She dropped into her chair, the card still clutched in her fingers, staring at the incredible arrangement of two dozen roses taking up a quarter of her desktop. She reached one finger out and tentatively touched a partially opened flower, the petal silky and delicate. She let out a sigh, hearing a crumbling and crashing sound in her head. The walls she so carefully and purposefully built up were falling in pieces around her, leaving her heart open to anything, good or bad.

Benjamin was doing this—breaking down her walls of distrust and uncertainty. She was letting him into her heart and into her life. As she moved her finger away from the petal, afraid even her gentlest touch might somehow bruise its beauty, she touched a thorn, startling her. A tiny dot of blood appeared where the thorn had easily broken the skin on the back of her hand.

The daydreams scattered, replaced by her reality. Staring at the scarlet droplets, she could sense the walls going back up, brick by emotional brick.

"Slow down, Grace. You don't need to be hurt again." The sound of her own voice brought her back to the moment. She stood, picked up the heavy vase, and moved it from the center of her desk to the side table under the window. As beautiful as they were, they would *not* be her focus today. Benjamin would *not* be her focus today. *Move slowly, Grace.* She didn't say it out loud this time, but the voice in her head was loud enough for her to take notice.

Turning away to start her day's work, the petal she touched moments earlier fell from the flower, landing directly on the toe of her shoe. Grace stared down at it for a moment then bent down to pick it up, dropping it in the trashcan on her way back to her desk.

Chapter 17

⬥

race reached over to the passenger seat, keeping her
eyes on the road while maneuvering the paper so she
could quickly glance down at it while driving.
Although she memorized the directions in advance, in her
nervousness she needed the security of that piece of paper
telling her exactly where to go, when to turn, and how long it
would take her to reach her destination. Wishing she had that
kind of guidance for her love life—heck, her entire life—Grace
continued driving toward Benjamin's house.

*"I'd like you to come to my place. We can have a glass of wine, and
then we'll go to the Club for dinner."* Grace realized she was gripping
her phone like a lifeline as she spoke with him the night before.
She wanted to say yes before he even finished asking the
question. In fact, she wanted to jump in her car right then and
dash to him, her resolve already being tested. The earlier
warnings to herself for a slow start melted away as soon as she
heard his voice. *"Write this down. My house can be a little tricky to
find."*

She'd done exactly that, making note of every exit, right
turn, left turn, landmark he told her she'd come upon on her
journey to him. Now, she knew she had just one left turn, a
short stretch on Bayberry Avenue, and then the entrance to his
driveway.

His voice echoed in her head as she drove. *"I'll leave the gate
open for you so you can drive right up and park in front of the garage. I'll
be watching for you."* She wondered if the gate was to keep
someone in or someone out. Now, as she made the final turn
into the driveway, she could see the wrought iron gate standing

wide open for her. In the rearview mirror, she could see it close once she was through.

Must be to keep me in, she decided, smiling to herself as she maneuvered the curve to the right and the house appeared. She sucked in her breath, taken aback by the sheer size of the building that seemed to rise out of nowhere.

She glanced at the note again, realizing that "park in front of the garage" wasn't exactly helpful when there were four garage doors to her right. She straddled two of them, pulling up near his Escalade, which was parked in front of the first garage door. She took a deep breath, and opened her car door, hardly noticing the blast of winter wind.

"You made it." Benjamin stepped out of the front door. Doors, actually. They were enormous, heavy, made of some kind of wood she figured didn't grow naturally around here. "Come on in. It looks like it's going to start snowing any second."

She smiled back at him, any resolve she might have still held onto gone, as he drew her into a warm hug right there on his front steps. "It's so pretty here," she said, as she pulled back from him.

"Let's get you inside. I have a fire that'll warm you up."

He led her inside.

Grace gasped. This wasn't really a house at all. It was a veritable palace. Above her head, a magnificent chandelier glowed and sparkled, welcoming her into the foyer. She wanted to simply stand in that spot and take it all in, from the wrought iron staircase she could see from the entrance, to the rustic wood beams—probably made of that same beautiful wood as the front doors—and the...what was she standing on? Marble floors? All of it was a sensory overload to her.

Benjamin filled her in as he helped her out of her coat. "It's a typical Mediterranean design with a whole lot of Keera touches everywhere. My wife knew exactly what she wanted." He listed them off, all of the little touches she was seeing now. "Italian white Carrara marble floors, touches of wrought iron and rustic wood strategically placed throughout. I swear that was her mantra while we were building, even saying it in her sleep by the time we finished--'marble, wrought iron and wood.'" The memory amused him. "Wait until you see the kitchen. She went all out in there."

It was interesting how he talked about her. Grace almost expected to walk into the kitchen and find a smiling Keera preparing a cocktail for them, wiping her hands on an apron as she reached out a delicate hand to welcome this new woman in Benjamin's life into this home she had so lovingly and carefully designed. The thought sent a shiver through her but she quickly recovered. "Well, I'm excited to see every inch of this place."

Benjamin laughed. "It's just over 6200 square feet, Grace. You might be here for a while. Of course, that's perfectly fine with me, but I did promise you dinner."

Finding appropriate words seemed almost impossible. She smoothed her hands down her skirt, partially an excuse to dry her suddenly sweaty palms, and partially because she was hoping he would acknowledge what she was wearing. After his invitation the night before, she rummaged through her wardrobe, knowing her closet would have trouble keeping up with Benjamin's lifestyle. She wasn't entirely sure what one should wear to "the Club" for a dinner date so she hoped against hope she had chosen something Benjamin liked.

He finished hanging her coat and then took her hand to lead her on the tour. There was no mention of her outfit, which was disappointing, as any little reassurance would have gone a long way.

"We'll start in the kitchen—the heart of the home, as Keera says." They walked from the entry into a sitting room on their left, its welcoming, overstuffed chairs facing an unlit fireplace. "This is the perfect place to enjoy the morning sun," he told her. They continued past the next room, its large paneled doors closed, as Benjamin casually gestured. "That's my office." His hand on the small of her back kept them moving further into the house. A few steps more, and the hallway opened onto a spacious, ultra-modern kitchen, unlike anything Grace had ever seen, but more impressive than the kitchen itself was the way the kitchen opened onto a great room. Beyond it, she could see a spectacular view of Lake Michigan.

Grace had never been in a house as grand as this one, and she had to fight back an urge to giggle, convinced she'd stepped into an episode of that show her mom watched when Grace was little, "Lifestyles of the Rich and Famous." She expected that Robin Leach guy to walk in and start narrating the scene.

The kitchen could have come directly from a celebrity's home. The white marble countertops stood in sharp contrast to the dark, almost black cabinets. Eight padded barstools stood in front of the largest island she had ever seen in a house. Benjamin continued his narrative, as he showed her the wood-burning pizza oven and two separate convection ovens. The range hood was rich copper with intricate designs etched into it. Grace didn't have time to look at any one thing as he continued his narration.

Pointing to the backsplash, he laughed. "Keera made them re-do this twice because she wanted it to be perfect. It's Carrara marble with a subway brick mosaic. She saw it when we were in Italy and knew she was going to have it in her kitchen." He shook his head, still smiling at the memory. "I don't think she ever imagined how frustrating it would be to get it exactly like the one she saw, but she wasn't going to give up. The first contractor quit. He said Keera was just too picky."

The smile remained on his face as he moved them along, leading her out of the kitchen and into the great room. To their left stood a full-sized grand piano, its shiny black surface almost a mirror. Several steps more and they stood in front of French doors looking out on the backyard and an icy, windswept Lake Michigan just beyond.

"It's beautiful in the summer, but I enjoy it in the winter, too. There's a different beauty to it now. I know most people don't think so, but I like the solitude of winter." He looked at her, waiting for a response, but she offered only a nod, seeing the beauty of winter before her but finding the scene exceedingly lonely. "I uncorked a bottle for us. I just need to grab it from the butler's pantry." He finally let go of her hand so he could get the wine.

Butler's pantry? She stood in the middle of the room, turning in a slow circle to take it all in. *Butler's pantry?* She laughed, quickly covering her mouth so he wouldn't hear.

Grace took a deep breath, hoping her heart would stop racing. She had never felt more out of her league. What was she doing here? She looked down at her sweater and skirt and then around at the high-ceilinged room. Perhaps she should have opted for a ball gown to feel less out of place here. But despite these thoughts, she had an overwhelming desire to be here, to fit in, to embrace all of this. Crazy, she told herself. Bat-shit crazy, as Lexie would say. Still, she rubbed her hand across the marble, wondering how something that looked so warm, rich and creamy could feel so cold.

Benjamin returned with two wine glasses, smiling and offering one to her.

"Do you play?" she asked, nodding toward the piano, as much an exquisite piece of furniture as a beautiful instrument.

Although not a piano player herself, Grace wanted to touch its keys, certain the piano would produce lovely sounds regardless of how little talent she might have.

"My daughter is the piano player in the family. She's very talented. Keera hoped she would be serious about her music, but that was never her interest."

Shocked momentarily at the mention of his daughter, Grace waited to hear more about her, but he offered nothing.

"Let's go up to the loft. The view is nice here, but wait until you see it from up there."

Grace had a hard time imagining it could get better, but she followed him up the steep winding staircase, taking in the richness of its marble steps and wrought iron railing. Fortunately, she was holding onto the railing as she reached the top of the stairs because she couldn't possibly be prepared for the expansive view opening before her, the house seemingly *on* the water instead of near it.

This single room was larger than her entire apartment...plus the two apartments next door to her own. Three separate seating areas were each carefully arranged so those using it could see out the floor to ceiling windows—she guessed they soared close to 25 feet overhead—at Lake Michigan. Although snow covered now, she imagined the enormous balconied patio was a favorite entertainment place during the other three seasons of the year.

"Our goal was to optimize the view. I think we succeeded."

"This is beyond breathtaking, Benjamin." She winced a bit at her own alliteration, hoping he hadn't noticed. "I would have a hard time leaving this room." She meant it, too. Looking around, she imagined sitting in front of a crackling fire, reading a book or just staring out at the lake—regardless of the season.

"Keera was always most inspired when she spent time in here. I'm sure that's obvious."

He was gesturing to the oversized framed paintings covering every wall that wasn't windowed. The paintings were bold, dark and dramatic, abstract in design, yet hinting of some concrete inspiration at the center of each. She turned slowly, taking in each picture.

"They're incredible," she whispered.

"These are her favorites. She wouldn't part with any of these, no matter what anyone offered."

"She was very talented. You must have been very proud of her." Benjamin smiled a sad smile, giving her a look that she was not able to interpret. Still looking at the pieces of art, she wondered what Lexie would say about them, this house, and most of all, Benjamin.

"Everyone loved her, but what they didn't know is that in her most inspired moments she was difficult to be around. She existed only for her art and she very capably shut out everyone and everything else during those times. Even us. Her Irish side really came out then. Her name means 'dark.'" He was talking more to himself than to her now. "She seemed to get lost in some kind of darkness when she painted and I think even she was relieved when the inspiration would eventually pass."

He stood lost in thought for a moment then abruptly set his glass down on a small table next to one of the sofas, gesturing for her to have a seat. She was at a loss how to respond to his comments, once again, so relief flooded her when he moved on to a new topic.

"I'm really glad you could be here. The house feels so empty when it's just me around. You light it up, Grace." He retrieved his glass and held it up to her as she made herself comfortable on the sofa, keeping a short distance between them, and modestly arranging her skirt around her legs.

Somehow this place required a primness that she would have to figure out. She was, after all, a t-shirt and jeans kind of girl and didn't want Benjamin to think she was raised without any class at all. She gently touched her glass to his as he said, "To beginnings. It's time for something new, Grace." Their glasses made a soft clanging sound and then they both took a drink. "Ah, one of Napa Valley's best. I hope you like it."

Grace let the burgundy-colored liquid sit for a moment in her mouth, savoring the taste and feel on her tongue, and then focusing on the not entirely unpleasant burn of it moving down her throat. She resisted an urge to cough, not accustomed to the high-quality world of good red wines. She nodded, hoping he didn't notice her momentary inability to talk or her watery eyes. An image of Lexie came to mind again as she wondered what Lexie would make of any of this splendor. If Grace described herself as a simple t-shirt and jeans girl, Lexie was a self-proclaimed modern-day hippie. She would see this as garish and pretentious. Grace decided then and there it might be best to underplay some of this grandeur the next time they spoke.

"The tannins are exceptional. That's what gives it that burn. Red wines have so much character. Are you getting the anise up front and then a hint of tobacco at the end?" He closed his eyes as he swallowed the next taste. Grace took another sip, hoping she would recognize the taste of anise this time, because she certainly had tasted nothing but—well, wine—the first time. "I honestly don't know how people can drink white wines. They are so pedestrian, so uninspired."

Grace made a mental note to nevermore order a white wine as long as she lived. The thought of drinking something uninspired suddenly important to her.

"You know a lot about wines. Is that a hobby of yours?"

"I wouldn't necessarily call it a hobby. I don't drink liquor as a general rule so I am always on the search for good wines. Keera and I loved discovering new ones. We always made opening a nice bottle an event and we promised ourselves that if we opened a wine we didn't like, we'd throw it out and open something else. Life is too short to waste on bad wines." He seemed to catch himself for a moment, realizing the gravity of his words. "We learned the hard way just how short life is."

She put her hand on his arm, hoping he would know how much she wanted to be a comfort to him. She also hoped the evening would hold more than just discussion of Keera, a topic she wasn't sure how to talk about without feeling awkward, so she changed the subject. "How many bedrooms does this house have? I know they must be hidden around here someplace but so far I haven't seen any."

Laughing, Benjamin took her hand and helped her up as he stood. "I did promise you a tour, didn't I?"

He steered her back down the grand staircase, stopping in the butler's pantry where the wine bottle was sitting on the counter. He poured a bit more in each of their glasses. "There's a lot of house to see yet so we better make sure we have enough wine for the whole tour. Someone I know wants to see every square inch of this place." Not completely minding that he was enjoying a laugh at her expense, Grace started to give him a playful punch on the arm, but stopped herself. There was something about Benjamin that didn't exactly scream "playful." A part of her wondered if she liked that idea or not, but she quickly dismissed it as they continued the tour.

They turned down a hallway that ran along the back of the kitchen. "There are four bedrooms on this floor, but the master suite is upstairs, on the opposite wing of the great room you were just in. I'm saving that for last."

He winked at her and she felt her face getting red. Perhaps he was playful after all. He showed her a room with a king-sized bed, dressing tables, and a small sitting area. It was difficult for her to imagine this as a "guest" room, thinking about the simple comforts of the space her parents kept as a guest room. This was more like an expensive hotel room, and she wondered why guests would ever want to leave once they arrived.

"We used to have a lot of visitors. I haven't had anyone else here besides Caroline, of course, since the funeral. Shirley still cleans every other week, but otherwise, it's just me." Grace couldn't imagine being all alone in this huge house.

There were two more rooms similar to the first, each with its own large bathroom and a view of the wooded lot. While not as spectacular as the water views, they were just as pretty, especially with the snow-covered branches. The hallway opened up in dramatic fashion to reveal another wing marked by a decorative double door. Benjamin took both handles and pushed. "This is Caroline's suite."

Grace hesitated, not entirely sure she would want anyone walking uninvited into her bedroom, but her curiosity got the best of her. This wasn't really a bedroom, it was more like an apartment, and a very large one at that. She stepped across the threshold, noticing how neat and clean the room was, with absolutely nothing out of place. The king-sized bed, covered in a light pink bedspread, held about a half dozen pillows of varying sizes and shades of pink. On the shelves were books, trophies, and a couple of framed pictures.

Grace walked to the bookshelf and carefully picked up a silver frame. In the photo, the girl's dark hair was pulled into a ponytail and her smile revealed a mouth full of braces. Probably 11 or 12, she had her arms around the neck of a horse, a blue ribbon fluttering from the bridle. Grace set it back down, placing it exactly as she had found it. Moving along the shelving unit, she picked up another picture. This one showed the same dark-haired girl standing next to her mother. Caroline, probably about eight or so, wore a white dress with dozens of tiny pink flowers along the skirt and Keera wore a tailored white suit, a sharp contrast to her flowing dark hair. Their hair had been styled the same, soft curls softly caressing their cheeks.

"Caroline is beautiful," she offered, feeling a need to break the silence. Benjamin took the picture out of her hand, staring at it for several seconds before setting it back on the shelf.

"She is just like her mother in so many ways." He cleared his throat, and she looked away as he choked up once again.

Hoping to ease the awkwardness of the moment, she continued talking. "How old is Caroline?"

"She's 20."

Grace wasn't sure if she covered her surprise. "Oh, is she away at college?" For some reason, Grace imagined Caroline to be younger. The pictures and the child-like décor threw her completely.

He looked at her, taking a second to come back to the moment. Benjamin was hesitant, and she was unsure how to take it as he obviously was choosing his words carefully. "Caroline is away right now. She wasn't ready to go to college right after high school so she has taken some 'self-discovery' time, let's call it." He walked toward the first set of double doors in the room and she followed, seeing that they opened into a spacious bathroom, complete with a separate vanity area where Grace could imagine Caroline sitting to brush her hair or apply makeup. A walk-in shower and claw-footed tub took up two sides of the room.

It was impossible for her to picture growing up in a place like this. Sharing a bathroom with her sisters had often led to arguing when they were young, but they survived just fine. She remembered how great it felt once both Gen and Ellen left for college and she had the bathroom all to herself—until they returned for holidays and summers.

Lexie warned her that the daughter was probably spoiled rotten, and looking around, she thought that might be true. What could Caroline possibly complain about? Then it hit Grace. Caroline lost her mother. It didn't matter what luxuries she had or how much she had been pampered. She no longer had a mother. Grace couldn't stop the overwhelming sense of pity washing over her for the young girl in the picture, and then shame for her own judgmental thoughts. She was acting as if the poor little rich girl had it all, when she actually had far from that. Caroline's mom was dead. The pampered girl in the photos had no idea her mom would never see her college graduation, wedding, or babies.

Imagining her own life without her mother was unfathomable. Her mom was always a phone call away at the most. Grace made a mental note to call her parents the next day just to say hello, and to be kind to Caroline whenever it might be they would finally meet.

"I'll bet she misses this like crazy when she's not at home." Grace was gesturing around the expansive bathroom. "I remember how much I hated sharing a bathroom with my sisters when they were home, and then with 20 other girls in my dorm wing."

"We can talk about Caroline some other time." His tone left Grace feeling as if she had said something wrong. She had no idea what it was, but Benjamin made it clear he would share no further details about his daughter right now.

They moved on to another set of doors opening into a room-sized closet. By now she knew what to expect, and wasn't disappointed. Far more than a simple closet, and larger than her own apartment, Grace took it all in. Two sides had full-length mirrors, one wall was a shoe rack and everywhere else was space for hanging clothes. Grace couldn't imagine owning enough to fill this entire closet, but Caroline had managed to do just that.

Something struck her as odd, and it took her a moment to determine the cause. Grace thought back to when she was packing to leave for college. Almost nothing had been left behind, other than some of her winter clothes she'd be far more likely to need when she came home for Christmas than she would in Arizona. Caroline must have simply bought herself a whole new wardrobe wherever it was she was living right now, if this full closet was any indication. And why wouldn't she? They certainly had the means. Her parents were probably more than indulgent of their little girl. With a start, she realized she hadn't managed to hang on to the sympathy very long and she gave herself another silent reprimand. Clothes would never replace a mother. She said it over again, just to remind herself to stop being so judgmental.

Benjamin ran his hand across some of the shoes placed on the shelves, like soldiers all lined up waiting for a command. "She was always exceedingly neat, even as a little girl. She couldn't stand to have anything out of place. Every toy was put away after playing with it. She always held everyone to a high standard around here." He was chuckling to himself, and she marveled at the rapid change in mood. Still, she decided to stay on the safest ground possible.

"I think my mom spent most of her days picking up after the three of us. We weren't like Caroline. Now I feel like I should call my mom and apologize." Grace smiled, hoping the sad moments had passed for Benjamin and they could continue the evening in a more light-hearted atmosphere.

"Maybe you should. Send her flowers, too. Women like that." He winked at her yet again, remembering how she had thanked him profusely for the exceptionally beautiful roses. "Let's go upstairs. I still have to show you my bedroom. Maybe we'll just stay there instead of going out for dinner," he teased.

Prepared now for the spectacular views and spacious living areas, Grace followed Benjamin into the largest master bedroom imaginable. She realized the fireplace in this room was the third she had seen so far. French patio doors opened onto a private balcony. Grace sighed, imagining a morning cup of coffee on the patio with the beautiful views as a backdrop. Of course, she didn't mean now, in the dead of winter, but she could easily imagine the sun sparkling on the water and the soothing sound of lapping on the shoreline.

"This is so pretty," was all she managed, too overwhelmed to put the views into any other words. They stood side-by-side looking out onto the veranda, sipping their wine.

Benjamin put an arm around her waist and she smiled up at him, her heart melting as he leaned down to kiss her. How easily she could fall for this man. Why was she working so hard to keep him out of her heart? If she would just allow herself to open her heart a tiny bit, she knew he would be in it.

"We should probably get to the club now or we'll never get out of here." His voice was husky, and she guessed he was as excited by their kiss as she was.

They left their glasses on the counter and he retrieved her coat from the closet, helping her into it. She watched him put on a wool overcoat and wondered if the scarf under his collar was as soft as it looked. She had to keep herself from reaching up to touch it, sure it must be cashmere. They left the house through a service door into the garage, where only the first stall was empty. Next to the space for his Escalade was a two-door Lexus, another space held a cherry red Mustang and yet another a sharp looking sports car. He followed her glance. "The Jaguar was Keera's car. She loved that beast."

Like everything else she'd seen on the property, no expense was spared in the garage. Everything in the space was highly polished. The red paint gleamed on the Mustang, and Grace wondered if that car belonged to Caroline. She decided it couldn't possibly. Why would she ever leave a car like that at home if she wasn't living here right now? So many questions about Caroline were begging for answers, but she would wait until another time. Learning what he was willing to talk about and what topics seemed too difficult for him would take time.

They drove less than two miles to reach the country club, nestled, of course, in the perfect setting to show off the spectacular lake views, not unlike what she had seen moments before at Benjamin's house. Stopping under the porte-cochere, a valet immediately appeared to greet Dr. Hayward and take the keys. Benjamin walked to her side to open her door and reached for her hand to help her out. His hand moved down to the small of her back, guiding her through the large front doors into the high-ceilinged main room of the club.

Grace had been to a couple of country clubs for wedding receptions over the years, but none of them compared to the opulence of the North Shore Golf and Country Club. A man in a suit and tie appeared from around a corner. "Good evening, Dr. Hayward."

"Good evening, Michael. This is my friend, Grace. We decided to dine in the Garden Room instead of the main dining room tonight. We'll be in the lounge for a glass of wine first." Grace wondered when "they" decided to dine in a different room. He probably wanted more privacy for the two of them, she determined, especially after the kiss they'd shared.

He steered her through a grand ballroom, set up with several clusters of comfortable seating areas so small groups of members could enjoy some private space, all with the great views of the lake and property. The old-world charm awed Grace as they walked through the next archway. She thought about the Foundation donors, recognizing the kind of wealth that had similarly astonished her when looking through the binders. People like that were members at this club.

There were several couples in the spacious bar area, most of them older than Benjamin. Actually, she realized the men were indeed older, but several of the women appeared much younger than the men, or more accurately, were making an effort to look significantly younger than the men. She imagined Lexie next to her whispering snarky comments about Botox, facelifts, and personal trainers. Again, she scolded herself for being judgmental. Anyone could see there was a significant age difference between the two of them. Maybe they were also thinking catty remarks about her. Lexie's voice continued in her ear. *Cradle robbers! Arm candy!*

These people were all about appearances. And looking around, she was woefully ill-prepared for a dining experience in their company. Why hadn't she asked Benjamin for specifics of dress at the club? She realized with a start their change in dining plans had nothing to do with intimacy. They would be eating in a different dining area because she was not appropriately dressed for the main room. She felt her cheeks begin to burn, wondering how she would ever feel comfortable in a place like this, and with these people. And she knew the answer could quite possibly be that she never would. Again, she imagined Lexie in her ear, whispering, *"Why would you want to fit in here?"* She whispered an imaginary response. *"Shhh! This is my Disney princess dream. Let me have it."*

On the way to seats at the bar, they stopped at tables so Benjamin could chat with the seated couples. All of them were courteous, greeting Benjamin by name and welcoming her to the club. Benjamin introduced her to the bar manager, Daniel, who brought three bottles for Benjamin to look at, the two of them discussing varietals and growing seasons. The decision made, Daniel opened the bottle with a flourish and served Benjamin a taste. He nodded approval and then guided her to a nearby table, pulling out her chair before sitting in his. Daniel was there immediately, pouring them each a serving before setting the bottle back on the center of the table and walking away. Benjamin swirled his wine, looking into her eyes once again. Grace was taking it all in, feeling as if she was part of some elaborate show, an actress in a play, but not entirely sure of her lines, and wondering why she had been cast for the part.

"To many more evenings with my Grace."

Her heart danced in her chest. She wanted to be his Grace, but wasn't sure she could fit into this world. And if she couldn't fit in with them, did that mean she couldn't fit into his life? And what about Benjamin fitting into hers? Could she picture him at the Thanksgiving table or playing a wild game of charades after dinner? She was afraid she might know the answer. She pressed her imaginary brakes once again, willing her brain to slow down so her heart could just enjoy this moment.

Dinner was nothing short of an event. Benjamin ordered for them, selecting tempura shrimp as an appetizer, fresh wedge salads to follow and then scallops with asparagus and risotto for the main course. He encouraged her to have a dessert but she was simply too full to even think about it. The attentive but never obtrusive waiters whisked away dishes and brushed crumbs from the tablecloth with an impressive finesse, leaving her feel completely spoiled.

"Where would you want to live if you could pick up and go anywhere in the world?" He was looking at her with such intensity she felt a need to glance away. She used the moment to furrow her brow, to let him think she was considering his question carefully. In actuality, she needed the moment to again compose herself as he made her feel a bit off balance, like she was on the edge of a cliff, walking carefully so as not to fall into whatever might be hidden below, yet finding it impossible to step away from the danger.

"Hmmm…that's a tough one. Unlike you, I haven't traveled much so I'd be choosing a place for all the wrong reasons probably. I've always loved pictures of Ireland. The French Riviera would be totally decadent. Oh, I've got it! The Greek Isles. I could live the life of a Greek goddess." She smiled, thinking about the amazing places all over the world that dating someone like Benjamin could make possible. "But I have to admit. I'm a homebody. I love the Midwest so I guess I'd just stay here." She never should have spent all those years away from here, making her add with conviction, "This is the best place in the world. Hands down."

"If you'd like, we can take this to the ballroom and sit in front of the fire for a while." He was referring to the last of the wine in their glasses.

"That sounds really nice."

The roaring fire in the massive stone fireplace was warm and inviting. They sat on a loveseat, staring into the flames, content to sit quietly. She watched as the wood shifted and changed color, flames dancing over, around, and through the pieces of wood, darkening them in brilliant flashes—an art show performed just for the two of them. As far as Grace was concerned, this was one of her favorite moments with Benjamin, and she wanted more.

He helped her into her coat and they said goodnight to Michael, who took Grace's hand. "We hope to see you again soon, Grace."

I hope so, too, she thought.

162

The Escalade was waiting for them, the smiling valet standing at her door to assist. She was absolutely amazed. When had Benjamin asked for his car to be brought around? Who orchestrated these things? She was duly impressed, feeling like royalty. Again, images of fairytale princesses danced through her head. The next time she would have to wear a ball gown. She twirled in pink taffeta and rhinestones in her dream world.

The snow had stopped falling, leaving a fresh blanket on the ground and a sparkling layer on the tree branches, a literal twinkle added to the already magical evening. She could even imagine the traces of snow falling from the branches were fairy dust. Back at the house, Benjamin asked if she wanted more wine. "Heavens no. I'll never be able to drive all the way back to the city if I have anything else to drink." The glass of wine before they left the house and two glasses at dinner were certainly her limit. A part of her wished Benjamin would invite her to stay, but she knew that was ridiculous to even think about and quite honestly, something she certainly wasn't ready to do.

"That's true. I'll just get us some water." Grace followed him into the great room to settle onto a sofa. They sat close to each other this time, Benjamin pulling her close. "I still can't believe we met, Grace." He ran his thumb across her cheek and she closed her eyes, melting into his touch. "We can be pretty special together," he said before letting his mouth find hers.

The kiss lasted a long time, his tongue gently moving in her mouth, causing sensations difficult to resist. When their mouths finally pulled slowly apart, he lifted her chin to again look into her eyes, saying nothing, yet speaking volumes. They snuggled close, and as she rested her hand on his chest, she found herself breathing in rhythm to him. It had been a long time since she'd felt this with anyone, and she ran the emotional gamut, hovering someplace between fear and excitement, but underneath were currents of contentment. Benjamin held her close.

While Grace could have spent hours doing more of this, she knew if she didn't leave right now, she would have a difficult time leaving at all. She waited a few more seconds and then shifted a bit, reaching for her glass of water. She took her time sipping, trying to figure out an appropriate way to end the evening. It had easily been one of the most romantic dates of her life. How could one possibly find an appropriate ending to that? She sighed in resignation. It was time to go home.

"I really should get going. I still have a long drive home."

Benjamin nodded, running his hand down her arm one more time before taking her hand, helping her to her feet. He wrapped his arms around her again, nestling his mouth against her ear. "You are going to be good for me, Grace," he whispered, and she felt her heart soar. She wanted to believe she could be good for him. She wanted nothing more right now than to be something special for him.

Although she didn't necessarily like the long drive back home, there was a lot for her to relive as she drove. Fortunately, traffic was light and she made it back to the city in good time but she was thoroughly exhausted when she dropped into bed. Her eyes closed the minute her head hit the pillow, but her sleep became filled with strange dreams, finding herself alone in a long hallway that somehow turned into a labyrinth from which she was unable to find her way out. The floors and walls of the labyrinth were made of marble but they kept shifting under her feet. When she reached out to touch a wall in an attempt to balance herself, she discovered it was freezing cold and started to crack where her hand had been. She pulled her hand back but understood, too late, that all of the walls and the ceiling were starting to crack and crumble. Panicked, she raced to find a way out or be crushed by the marble.

Her heart was racing when she woke, but try as she might, she couldn't come up with any real meaning behind the dream. There was another vague thought tapping away so deep in the recesses of her mind that she was having a difficult time knowing what it might be. *Too much wine and rich food for you,* she thought. It took her a long time to drift back into nothingness, something still niggling in the back of her mind.

Sometime before dawn she fell into a restless sleep, this time dreaming about walking along a winding mountain road. Aware of a noise behind her. She turned, a car heading directly toward her, forcing her farther and farther to the side of the road. Glancing down, she saw the sharp drop, jagged rocks ready to catch her should she fall. She recognized the car. The Jaguar kept coming, too fast and too close as she struggled to find footing. The car was on top of her now and she was astonished to see Benjamin behind the wheel. He laughed, waving as she tumbled over the ledge, and as he passed, Keera's long dark hair was streaming out behind, leaving a fog that covered everything so as she fell, Grace couldn't tell when and where she would land. She braced herself for the sharp rocks that would pierce her body at any moment.

This time she awoke and gave up completely, not able to close her eyes and relax again. She made coffee, drinking a cup as the city slowly came to life in the streets below. The charm of last night's drive home was long gone and she no longer felt any of the magic of the previous night in this pre-dawn hour. Shaken by the dreams, and trying to make some sense of the senseless, she realized she didn't even know how Keera died. She had jumped to the conclusion she died in a car accident. None of the cars in Benjamin's garage looked like they had been in any kind of accident. What had Benjamin told her about Keera's death? She thought back to the night at the lounge, trying to remember his exact words that had led her to believe Keera's death was the result of a car accident. She could hear his voice in her head as the words he had spoken not all that long ago came back to her: "There was an accident."

Chapter 18

————◆—◆—◆————

"**S**o, when will you finally meet the mystery daughter, Grace? Don't you think it's getting kind of weird…you know…waiting this long?"

It felt like forever since Grace had a chance to catch Lexie up on the latest happenings in the world of Benjamin. By now, Lexie knew that Keera had died almost three years prior, when Caroline was just 17 years old. She also had a description of what Lexie had come to call the "McMansion"—although Grace's descriptions had downplayed much of the actual opulence of the home.

This rare Saturday morning at home provided the opportunity to make a pot of coffee and settle in for one of her much-needed extra-long catch-up sessions with Lexie. In the weeks since her first visit to Benjamin's house, a lot had happened, some of which she had no intention of sharing with her friend, mainly because she was still trying to figure it all out herself. Keeping things from Lexie troubled her a little. She really couldn't pinpoint exactly why there was a need for some secrets. *Not secrets*, she convinced herself. *A lack of full disclosure.* The euphemism sounded so much better in her mind. And how could she share with Lexie the things that she didn't fully understand herself?

"I have no idea. He doesn't seem to want to talk about her. I'm beginning to think there really is some great mystery. Maybe she's in rehab or something and he's just too embarrassed to tell me. People get into drugs for far less than what Caroline has been through so it wouldn't be entirely shocking."

"She's probably a stripper with some crazy stage name like Pussycat Doll. Why don't you just ask him about her?"

Grace hesitated, moving the cordless phone away from her ear for a moment and shifting it to the other side of her head. How could she possibly tell her friend that Benjamin wasn't the type of man who was open about certain things in his life? If Benjamin Hayward said he didn't want to talk about something, it meant he would not talk about it. She wondered if the beautiful girl in the pictures was as headstrong as her father.

"Benjamin will tell me about her when he's ready to tell me about her. Maybe it's a good thing she's not around. She'll probably hate me and then I'll have to dump Benjamin. This is working out just fine right now." Grace was obviously trying to make light of the situation, hoping Lexie would just let it go. The last thing she wanted was a common-sense remark from Lexie, like "no relationship can be built on this kind of foundation. If he won't talk about his daughter, what else is he keeping to himself?" On some level she knew she should be asking herself these very questions, taking a good long look at the relationship, but it was easier to just change the subject. "What did you do last night? Anything special?"

"I finished the sculpture that was commissioned for the Drake building. I put the finishing touches on it and then sent you a picture. You didn't even comment on it."

"Picture? What picture?" Grace uncurled her legs to grab her purse from the counter. "I got home from Benjamin's pretty late last night and I never checked my phone before I went to bed. Sorry." Her hand was in her purse, feeling around for the cell phone that was supposed to be in it. "Oh crap! I must have left it at his house." She emptied the purse on the sofa, hoping she was wrong, but knowing the phone was not in the mess before her. "Now I have to drive all the way out there today."

She sighed. It was one thing to make the trip if Benjamin would be there waiting for her, but he wasn't home. He would be at the airport right about now, catching an early flight to Miami for a consult.

"Does he ever come to your place?"

Grace wasn't sure how to explain to Lexie how awkward it would feel to have Benjamin Hayward in her tiny apartment. He belonged in his grand home. The long pause must have been answer enough for Lexie.

"You shouldn't always be the one going to him, Grace."

Despite her great care in keeping some details to herself, more than once in her conversations with Lexie over the past weeks Grace noticed some less than warm fuzzy feelings for Benjamin coming from her friend. She even warned Grace on more than one occasion to tread carefully. It was strange, since Lexie was the one encouraging Grace to start dating. Now she was dating and Lexie had a whole different set of concerns. Because of her friend's apparent unease, Grace didn't dare tell her any more details about the relationship—like the fact that they had used the "L" word already and that Benjamin even mentioned marriage once. She knew her friend would have all kinds of stress over that.

Grace steered the conversation to safer ground, and after finally saying goodbye to Lexie, forced herself off the sofa to get ready. Earlier thoughts about a relaxing Saturday at home were a distant memory now.

On her drive to Benjamin's, she thought about how easily they transitioned into a couple. Their routine was comfortable. After her initial visit to his house, he gave her the key code to the gate and garage so she could let herself in even if he wasn't there. He wanted her there, he said.

They spent time together at his house, but on occasion attended events as a couple. Now and then she thought about all the miles she was putting on her car, and also the serious hit on her credit card to stay appropriately dressed for him. Such negative thoughts were easily pushed aside, because she was falling hard for Benjamin Hayward. Arriving at his house was her favorite. He'd meet her at the front door or in the grand foyer, ready to just hold her and kiss her. It took them a while to move inside, both enjoying those first long moments together—and those long, lingering kisses. She felt goosebumps on her arm just thinking about it.

She changed lanes, watching the city disappear in her rearview mirror, and allowed her mind to wander back to another time she visited his house. Although they started out on the sofa with their wine, enjoying a typical winter-trying-hard-to-change-to-spring view, it didn't take long for their passions to take over. When he led her to the bedroom, she willingly followed. He undressed her slowly, touching her face, her breasts, her thighs. His kisses were deep, taking her breath away as he lowered her to the bed, enjoying the look in her eyes as she watched him remove his own clothes.

Their lovemaking that first time was slow and deliberate, each wanting to explore every inch of the other's body. When he was deep inside her, her legs wrapped tightly around him, she believed she had everything she could ever want. They dozed afterwards, and this time Benjamin asked her to stay the night. They slept nestled against each other when they weren't making love. The morning had been awkward as a strange panic overcame her when she realized how little she actually knew about him. But then she also remembered the night before as he pulled her close and whispered into her ear, "I love you."

There'd be no greeting today, she thought sadly as she pulled into the now familiar driveway. Grace let herself in through the garage, as if she belonged here, sharing this home with him. Her phone was on the entry table, exactly where she set it the evening before. The message from Lexie with the attached picture was the only new item on it. Putting the phone in her pocket, she turned to walk back out again, then paused. This was the first time she was alone in the house for any length of time and she was overtaken by an odd desire to look around.

She still hadn't seen Benjamin's study, so she moved down the hall to stand outside the door. Giggling nervously, she pushed down on the handle, surprised to feel it give under her hand. For some reason, she assumed it would be locked. Tiptoeing inside, she felt like she was part of a covert operation in the empty house.

This room, not surprisingly, was as beautifully decorated as every other room in the house, with built in maple bookcases lining two entire walls and more of what she guessed to be Keera's artwork prominently displayed. It was the portrait over the fireplace that took her breath away for a moment—the enormous portrait of Benjamin, Keera and Caroline so lifelike and vibrant it made Grace feel as though she had just walked in on the three of them, startling them in this private moment in their own home.

They were the perfect family, hanging there above the fireplace, their smiling faces captured in that moment. They were dressed alike, in jeans and white shirts. Benjamin was standing behind the chair on which his wife was seated, a hand resting protectively on her shoulder. Caroline, probably around 8 or 9 years old, sat on the floor next to the chair, her arm crooked across her mother's knee, chin resting lightly on her bended wrist. Grace was an intruder in their frozen moment together, and she stood rooted to the spot, ready to apologize for having barged in on them.

She stared at the portrait a long time, mesmerized by Keera's dark eyes. When she finally forced herself to look away, the oversized mahogany desk drew her attention. Stepping around, she eased herself into the chair so as not to disturb anything, not wanting Benjamin to think she was snooping around. Of course, that's exactly what she was doing but she couldn't stop herself.

She took in Benjamin's view each time he sat at this desk. Directly in front of him, he could stare at length at the beautiful family portrait, probably wishing for something he no longer had. If he grew tired of that, he could look at any one of the works of art so carefully crafted by his wife. When that grew wearisome, he had only to look at the five framed pictures placed on his desk—each of them showing Keera, alone or with him. It was clear to Grace he came here each day to be surrounded by his lost wife, to pretend for a while that his world was still whole. She felt tears stinging her eyes, wondering if she would ever be as important to him. His office was a shrine to the memory of the happy family the three of them had been. Not for the first time, she wondered exactly what place she could really hold in this man's heart and life.

She left the study, walking the now familiar path up the stairs, past the grand open loft area and into the master suite. They enjoyed intimate, romantic moments together here, but for the first time it hit Grace that it was the same room he had shared such moments with Keera, also. It left her feeling a bit sick to her stomach, as if she was somehow the other woman and Benjamin was cheating on his wife with her.

Not able to stop now, she opened the bedroom door, looking in at the bed where they made love, at the spot in front of the patio doors where he stood behind her, nibbling her ear until she couldn't take it anymore and they ended up back in the bed. *He was with me in those moments, wasn't he?* She hated to ask herself the question, but now that she witnessed how much of Keera still filled the house, she couldn't help but wonder if Keera filled his head and heart when she was the one with him, talking, kissing, touching, making love... She shook the thoughts away.

As always, the closet door was closed, but she opened it, going in now for the first time. Benjamin's clothes were neatly arranged on the right side of the room, his pants, suits, casual clothes all perfectly pressed and awaiting his selection each day. The room held three dressers, two full-length mirrors and, in the center of the room, a long, cushioned bench. Grace sat, taking in the entire left side of the closet. She wasn't surprised to see that Keera's clothes were still hanging in the closet. Dresses, skirts, sweaters, slacks, pantsuits, all in a distinct order, from casual to dressy, lining the walls.

Grace rose slowly, moving to the see-through dress bags hanging in their own section of the magnificent closet. She counted exactly two dozen bags, each housing a gown. The dresses were sensational, in every color and style imaginable. Grace carefully unzipped one bag, letting her fingers slide over the bodice of the champagne-colored Satin dress inside. She tried to imagine the kinds of events Keera and Benjamin attended that called for something so elegant. Had they danced together? Was it a formal dinner or just hors d'oeuvres? Did he keep his hand on the small of her back, protectively near her throughout the evening? Grace had no idea how to make the vivid images of them together disappear.

She zipped the bag and walked to the door, making sure to turn out the light and leave the space just as she found it. Benjamin felt a need to leave it just as it had been when Keera was alive, so she certainly did not want to be the one to disturb it. What would it take, she wondered, for Benjamin to finally clean out all of her things, to finally make room for someone else in his life?

She looked at her watch yet again, wondering what Benjamin was doing. She hoped his flight was on time and his meetings going well. She wasn't sure when or even if Benjamin would text or call today, knowing he would be focused on work. She tried not to think about it, but she wondered if he ever went a day without touching base with Keera. The fact that she perhaps didn't mean quite enough to him to warrant some kind of communication each and every day was a hard pill to swallow. He easily and readily took up all of the space in her head and heart lately. She wanted desperately to believe she had become the center of his attention these past many weeks, but that didn't seem to be possible when she looked around the house, filled with so many reminders of Keera.

She paused in the loft, the sun glittering on the cold Lake Michigan waters. Sighing, she sank into a chair, trying to remember the magic of being with Benjamin, forcing herself to dwell on some of *their* moments together. One of her favorites was a Saturday just a couple of short weeks ago, on one of those rare March days that was so warm you knew you had to spend it outside or it would be a totally wasted gift from heaven. Winters in Chicago make you live for such days.

Benjamin decided they should go the club and sit on the patio. Of course, the patio wasn't set up for guests this early in the season, but at Benjamin's request the staff scrambled to pull a table from storage for the two of them to enjoy the unexpectedly warm weather. Grace had become accustomed to the special treatment. She also enjoyed having Benjamin introduce her as his girlfriend to the people stopping to greet them at the club—or anyplace else they happened to be together. On this particular Saturday afternoon, as they enjoyed their late lunch, patio set up especially for them, guests were arriving for a wedding reception inside the clubhouse. She and Benjamin watched from their seats outside as the bride and groom made their entrance, greeting guests on their way to the ballroom. Benjamin took her hand, looking into her eyes like only Benjamin could do, seeing, she believed, her very soul. "I could see us getting married here. An outside ceremony would be perfect."

Her heart almost leapt right out of her chest as she imagined marrying Benjamin. Yes, it would certainly be perfect. That night, as they were snuggled close together, drifting off to sleep, she let herself imagine a wedding ceremony, honeymoon, and moving into this home together as husband and wife. For the first time, much to her surprise, when Benjamin said that he loved her, she responded, "I love you, too."

If he was surprised by her words, he didn't let on, other than to say, "You make me happy." Yes, the walls she had carefully built were rapidly crumbling. Crumbling, but not entirely torn down. Something was still holding her back, and as much as she wanted to let go, giving herself to Benjamin completely, she couldn't. In some ways, it was a rollercoaster ride she was not entirely enjoying but she couldn't stand the thought of getting off the ride yet, either. She knew all about rollercoasters...and when she'd had enough.

When she was 11, Grace begged her parents to take her to Six Flags. All of her friends raved about the rollercoasters at the amusement part and she was green with envy every time another one came back from an adventure there. It was all she could think about that entire summer. When her parents finally gave in, she was beside herself, carefully planning everything they would see, eat and do on that glorious day. The first rollercoaster line twisted around and around, and despite her parents' request that they not waste their entire morning standing in it, Grace was determined. She spent too much time planning the day to let a long line deter her now. All of her friends said it was the best, the scariest and the fastest, so she was staying right here in this line to ride *The Intrepid*.

So, after waiting all summer, plus another hour and fifteen minutes, Grace was strapped into the car ready for the thrill she knew was coming. Unlike most rollercoasters, this one didn't start out on a long, slow climb. It traveled what felt like inches and then soared into the sky, making her feel as if she could reach up and grab one of the fluffy clouds out of the perfectly blue summer sky. Then without warning, she was falling, no longer looking at a blue sky, but at the back of the car in front of her as the track dropped steeply and she hoped her stomach would catch up to her soon. That, of course, didn't happen as what followed next was a steep banking to the right and then to the left before flying back up to the sky.

Grace wanted it to slow down. She wanted to get back up to the top, the sun on her face and a magnificent view below, but she knew now what was coming next, and try as she might, she couldn't brace herself for the sickening drop that followed. Once off the ride, she sat on a bench with her parents and re-created her list, removing all of the big rollercoasters. As much as she loved the exhilaration of those moments when she felt as if she could fly up and touch the sun and clouds, she hated the drops. One twisting, turning, stomach-dropping ride had been more than enough for her. Her parents hadn't seemed surprised.

Dating Benjamin felt a lot like that rollercoaster ride. She didn't always have enough time to hold onto the perfect moments they spent together, when he seemed completely and totally focused on her. She could see the sun and feel the warmth of a perfect summer day, but just like that rollercoaster ride, it didn't last very long. A drop of some kind always followed every euphoric moment.

As much as she hated to admit it, for all the amazing moments with Benjamin, there were uncomfortable ones as well in their budding relationship. Those moments always came very unexpectedly. The first one took her completely by surprise. They spent what she believed to be a wonderful evening at his colleague's retirement party. Once back at his house, however, he told her they had to talk. She sat next to him on the sofa, not at all sure what was on his mind. "Your dress is pretty, but I didn't find it appropriate. It's too short. It's not the way you should dress when we go someplace together."

She was offended, knowing that her dress had not actually been any shorter than those worn by other women at the party, but instead she apologized, assuring him it would never happen again. It was humiliating, being scolded in that way, treated like a child who just didn't know any better, but instead of being angry with Benjamin, she was resolved never to disappoint him again. His world was foreign to her and she would have to adapt if she wanted to be part of it and make him happy. Once back at her apartment, she took out dresses she deemed "too short" for Benjamin's liking. They would be donated. Someone else would have to enjoy wearing them.

These were the times she clearly remembered the rollercoaster ride, wondering if she should be bracing herself for a drop that wouldn't allow her stomach to catch up—or in this case, her heart.

Grace was startled out of her reverie by a noise downstairs. Her heart racing, she stood, not sure if she should stay where she was or go downstairs. Maybe Benjamin's flight was canceled and he was back. Time stood still as she waited, expecting to hear the sound again—and hoping there would be some logical explanation for it. Silence roared in her ears, her pulse a drum beat so loud she feared she wouldn't hear someone sneaking up the stairs to attack her.

After what felt like forever, Grace tiptoed to the top of the stairs, looking below for any telltale sign that someone else might be in the house with her. Taking a deep breath, she walked down the stairs, took her keys from the foyer table and walked out without a glance back at the house. *When did you become so skittish, Grace Warrens? Are you afraid there's a ghost in the house?* She pulled away, anxious to get on the road and back to her apartment. Had she looked toward the garage, she would have noticed a pale face as a figure moved out of view at the upstairs window.

Grace fell asleep sometime after midnight without hearing from Benjamin, unaware that her feared drop was coming sooner rather than later.

***

"We should get ready. We have to meet the Pensons at the club for dinner at six. I've been avoiding their invitation for so long I couldn't possibly come up with another excuse when I ran into Bob yesterday. I told him tonight would work out for us. You remember Bob and Diane, I'm sure. I introduced you to them at the Opening Day dinner at the club."

It was a statement, not a question, so she thought back to the couples she had met, not at all sure which one might be Bob and Diane. Grace sighed, disappointed that they weren't spending the evening in, snuggling in front of a fire to keep out the chill of the wind coming off the lake. On her drive out of the city to be with Benjamin for the weekend, that was exactly the evening she imagined for them, with the magic of some of their other dates sprinkled in for good measure.

She thought about the rollercoaster again, realizing she was getting used to taking all the good moments she could get, convincing herself they were enough for now and would only get better with time. Time was all they needed. In the meantime, Benjamin was in charge—of everything from their emotions to how they spent their time together. He managed their calendar. He also managed what she should wear to the events they attended together. When she brought a garment bag filled with a variety of outfits to his house so she wouldn't have to carry so many things back and forth every weekend, he told her to hang the bag in one of the guest room closets. He never suggested using his closet, and of course, she knew why.

Now, as she dressed in the downstairs bedroom, she was determined to put on a happy face in spite of the evening not living up to her daydreamed version. Appearances were important to Benjamin. Honestly, she didn't always mind because it was still exciting for her, taking these baby steps into his world, playing dress-up, rubbing elbows with important people—some of whom she now recognized from the binders—and knowing she was with a handsome, intelligent, respected doctor.

As the Director of Pediatric Medicine at Chicago University Hospital, he was highly regarded and connected to other highly regarded people, and that translated into spending time with those people at a variety of social events she never knew about before meeting Benjamin. Most women would give their right arm to be in her shoes, but she still wished she fit in with the people in his circle. She imagined Keera selecting one of her many gowns for an event and let out a long sigh. She wasn't Keera. Keera probably did a better job of remembering all of Benjamin's friends and colleagues.

She continued wracking her brain, trying her hardest to remember which of the couples she had met in the preceding months might be Bob and Diane. She'd have to be on her toes tonight. She didn't want to do anything that might set him off. He seemed a little "off" to her tonight so she wanted to try especially hard to do all the right things, say all the right things and be all the right things. Lexie would be so disappointed in her if she could see her now. There was nothing strong and independent about the woman looking back at her in the bedroom mirror. *"You've got this, Grace,"* she whispered to her reflection.

Maybe it would be different if she took some initiative in planning evenings for them. If she always allowed him to do it, he'd never see she was perfectly capable of it, too. She tested the waters as she met him in the kitchen moments later.

"My parents are back from Florida. We really need to get together with them. I know they'd love to meet you," she ventured. "My mom could cook or we could meet them out for dinner. Either would work fine with them I'm sure." She glanced at him, trying to gauge his interest level, but it didn't seem to register very high on the meter. Her confidence was already waning despite the brief pep talk in the mirror moments before.

"I'll check my calendar."

"And I told you that Lexie is flying in the beginning of June. There is no way she can visit and not meet you." She was trying to draw him in, trying to lighten the evening that didn't seem to be starting off on the right note.

Benjamin gave the same noncommittal response. "I said I'd check my calendar. Are you wearing those shoes? You should wear your black heels—the ones with the silver strap." His phone rang then. "I need to take this. I'll be ready to go in 15 minutes."

He disappeared, leaving Grace alone to stare down at her footwear. Her shoulders slumped as she returned to the room to dig through the bottom of the garment bag in the hope of finding she had thrown the black pumps in without realizing it, but knowing the answer already. She hadn't. Things were going from bad to worse. Now she could only hope that, God forbid, Bob and Diane didn't look down at her feet. She could picture their looks of horror already.

Bob and Diane, if they did indeed notice her less than desirable footwear, were completely gracious and Grace focused instead on trying to figure out what had put Benjamin in one of his "moods" tonight. The last thing she wanted was for him to be in a funk when she wanted nothing more than to enjoy their moments together.

There was something very special about being Benjamin's date. People took notice of Benjamin Hayward when he was in the room, and Grace took a strange pleasure in being part of that. Lexie would find all of it pretentious, uppity and very un-Grace-like. But Grace was learning about a whole different world when she was with people like Bob and Diane. Diane was, as Grace was rapidly learning, a typical doctor's wife, very busy with bridge club, facials, luncheons with friends, and apparently an occasional stint with volunteering.

Most of the wives at the club didn't know the meaning of work—or better said, having a job. That was something others did. They didn't have to. Grace never commented on her own busy schedule and the fact that after a full day of work she sometimes jumped in the car and drove all the way out to the suburbs to be with Benjamin. During the week she never stayed overnight, too fearful that she'd run into traffic problems on the commute to work the next morning. She always drove, never trusting the train. Unlike the women in Benjamin's world, she needed her job—regardless of how much time she wanted to spend with Benjamin. If he asked her to marry him, she thought, maybe then she could leave her job, could become one of the bridge-playing, spa-day-enjoying wives. The thought was fleeting, though, as no other mention of marriage had been made, and with Benjamin's preoccupation again tonight, she didn't expect it any time soon.

He remained quiet on the drive back to his house, his mind elsewhere, everything seemingly a great effort to him. She hoped it wasn't the shoes. Already, she planned to get another pair of black high-heeled pumps so she could keep one pair here and another at the apartment. It was too easy to forget and it was a pain in the butt to keep packing so much to carry back and forth each weekend.

As they settled in for the night, Grace waited for him to tell her what was bothering him. Nothing was said, however, and he simply kissed her cheek goodnight and rolled over, his back to her. It took her a long time to fall asleep and she awoke on Saturday feeling tired, confused and alone. Benjamin was already out of bed, so she wandered downstairs, still trying to figure out what could possibly be wrong, the steady beat of the music he played while working out coming from his basement gym.

Benjamin hadn't bothered to make a pot of coffee, which he usually did, so she busied herself preparing it, rapidly losing hope that his mood the day before had undergone any kind of improvement. All she could do was wait for him to come back upstairs, which he did about 30 minutes later.

"That smells good. Did you make enough for me?"

Grace poured a cup, watching him closely as he sat down on one of the stools at the kitchen island, sipping the hot coffee. He looked as tired as she felt. But there was more to it. He looked... defeated. As much as she wanted to touch his hand, give him a hug, in any way show how near she was, she could tell it wasn't what he wanted.

"Are you upset with me for some reason?" It was difficult to get the words out around the lump in her throat.

He didn't immediately answer, staring into his cup. When he spoke, she had to strain to hear him. "I'm going to need some time alone for a while. I don't expect you to understand. Hell, I don't understand it. I never know when it's going to hit me, but I guess the answer is now. I'm sorry, Grace. I don't think you should stay tonight. I just need some time."

Grace's heart ached. He was shutting her out once again. She wanted to wrap him in her arms and hold him through whatever emotional rollercoaster he was stuck on right now. She wanted him to stop missing Keera so much that he didn't want to be near her. At the same time, she wanted to shout at him, to tell him Keera was gone and not coming back.

What she did, however, was touch his shoulder as she moved past him to get her overnight bag packed. She couldn't force Benjamin to feel better. He was still sitting at the counter when she came downstairs with her bag. She paused, not sure if he would get up and walk her out or if he would even say goodbye to her.

"I wish I could say something or do something to make you feel better." He could only nod, understanding what she meant but too helplessly lost in his own feelings to make a change. "Just call or text when you want to. I'm here for you, Benjamin. I'm right here for you."

Somewhere in the back of his mind, Benjamin knew he was hurting Grace, but this was out of his control. He heard the front door close and realized she was gone. Had he said goodbye? He couldn't remember. The anniversary of Keera's death was nearing and once again it hit him like a punch in the stomach, taking his breath away, making him trudge through his days with a numbness he hated. He couldn't completely describe that to Grace and expect her to understand, and he didn't have the energy to try. He knew the coming weeks would be his personal storm to ride out and he was tired.

"I'll call you soon," he said, but he was too late. Grace was already gone.

***

The drive back to Chicago felt longer than usual and Grace had no idea where to go or what to do as she approached the city. Without really thinking, Grace found herself driving not to her place, but to her parents' condo. She suddenly wanted nothing more than to walk in and let her mom tell her that everything was going to be just fine.

Grace managed only "hello" before bursting into tears. Sylvia wrapped her arms around her daughter, unaware of what was wrong, but giving her a few moments to compose herself. The sobs quieted, leaving Grace with hiccups and a runny nose. When she could talk, Grace told her mom everything—about meeting Benjamin, his dead wife, Caroline, and most of all, what happened today, and his unwillingness to allow Grace to help him through his pain and grief.

If she was surprised that all of this had happened in the short time they were down in Florida, Sylvia didn't let on. She chose her words carefully, hearing the ache in her daughter's voice. "Do you love him?"

Grace nodded, her eyes brimming with fresh tears. "I do, mom. He's so sweet and gentle and smart and sophisticated..." She stopped herself. Her mom didn't need the entire litany of Benjamin's amazing qualities.

"Then you are going to have to be more patient than you've ever been in your life, baby. He can't control his pain any more than he can control the weather. I don't know what I'd do if your dad decided to up and die on me, but I know it would take me a long time to feel anything close to normal, if there even is such a thing. I'm sure Benjamin is thankful that you're in his life, but you have to remember what he lost. If they were close, he lost his wife and best friend—and the mother of his child. That's a lot to deal with. Just be there for him. When he's ready, he'll let you know." Sylvia felt compelled to add one more thing. "If you can't wait patiently, sweetheart, then you should probably get out of the relationship now."

Her mother was right and she *did* want to be there for Benjamin, but she also wasn't sure how much longer she could be the supportive girlfriend in this hold-me-tight, push-me-away relationship he controlled. She felt helpless.

"It's just so hard, mom." She wanted to explain to her mom so she would understand Grace was not only thinking of herself. "Just when I think we are moving in the right direction he pushes me away. The worst part is that I was the one holding back. I was the one who didn't want to open my heart," Grace took a tissue from a box nearby, blowing her nose noisily into it and reaching for a second one. Finally sharing all of this with her mom was an incredible relief. It struck her that Caroline would never be able to talk with her mother.

"I can understand why you'd want to protect yourself."

"I think it would be easier if he just had an ex-wife I could hate." It wasn't the first time the thought crossed her mind.

"Oh honey, that would just come with its own set of problems. This is what you have to work with. You're the only one who can decide if he's worth waiting for, worth fighting for, Grace."

At that moment her phone alerted her to a new text. Looking at Benjamin's words on the screen, clarity set in for her.

I'm glad you understand. You're so good for me. Thank you.

She had lunch with her parents and when it was time to go, held her mom in a longer than usual hug. How had she lived without this all those years in Arizona?

At the apartment, she looked again at the message. It would be a tough journey for both of them but she was ready. It would be worth it, as long as she would have Benjamin in the end.

I love you, she typed, staring at her phone a long time, waiting for the same words to come back to her, but the screen remained dark.

Chapter 19

Exhausted, Grace drove home and crawled into bed, even though it was the middle of the afternoon. When she woke, she curled up in front of the TV, hoping to find an old movie to watch. Something romantic and sappy would certainly match how she was feeling. When that proved fruitless, she tried reading, but couldn't focus.

She stayed in bed late on Sunday, not sure what to do with herself. It occurred to her that she couldn't remember how to be alone on weekends. Should she go to the office for a while? Maybe she could call one of her sisters for a shopping trip? Both would take an energy she couldn't seem to muster right now.

She missed Benjamin and looked at her phone constantly to make sure she hadn't missed a call or text from him. It was late that night when she looked at her cellphone once again and actually noticed the date on the screen: April 26th. Her heart dropped. Feeling sorry for herself all day, she had completely forgotten Lexie's birthday. That wasn't entirely true. A gift had been shipped almost a week ago, but she completely dropped the ball on sending an early morning first birthday greeting message. Her oldest and dearest friend, and this is how she treated her? Grace felt sick. She was the worst best friend ever.

"I'm so sorry, Lex. I've never missed sending you the midnight plus one message."

"It's OK, Grace. I'm a big girl."

"I know, but it was a really shitty thing to do. You'd never forget my birthday. Don't hate me."

Lexie's sighed. "I could never hate you, Gracie." She hesitated, wanting to add something else. "Just...I don't know...just be careful with Benjamin, Grace. He's changing you."

Taken aback by Lexie's words, Grace was unable to say anything and a silence settled between them. Grace found her voice, finally.

"It's OK, Lexie. I'm a big girl, too."

When she ended the call moments later, Grace knew something had changed between them, and it frightened her. No friend had ever been as important to her as Lexie. If not for her, Grace wondered how she ever could have made it through Josh's affair with Katherine, the divorce, and Jasper's death. It was horrible that she couldn't even remember Lexie's birthday. She would make it up to Lexie, maybe do something special for her when she visited in June. If she still visits, Grace thought.

She tried to shake her friend's words, but they stayed with her. Maybe Lexie was right. Maybe she was changing. Benjamin's world was a far cry from her own, but that didn't mean she was actually changing to fit into his world, did it? She wanted to answer herself with a resounding "no," but the more she thought about it the more unsure she was becoming.

***

Between her bad friend moment and Benjamin's need to be left alone, Grace had two horrible weeks. When Benjamin finally called and asked if she wanted to meet for a coffee, her heart soared. As she slid into the chair across from him at the coffee shop the next afternoon she noticed his eyes looked empty, his face drawn, and she fought the urge to mother him. That was probably the last thing he needed or wanted.

"How are you?"

He gave her a brief smile. "I'll be OK. It kind of hits me right between the eyes. I don't know. Maybe I should go back to my therapist. I didn't think it helped before. Maybe now it would be better."

"I'm here for you. Just tell me what you need from me."

He took her hand for a moment and then let it go. She hoped they would be back to their old closeness sooner versus later.

It turned out to be later. Except for that coffee date and one dinner, they had little contact in the next two weeks. She was starting to get a little impatient, not sure what else she could do to make him understand she could help, if only he'd let her. And to make matters worse, when they ran into a couple he knew from the club when they did finally get together for dinner, he introduced her as his friend. Her patience was being tested, and even remembering her mom's words of wisdom did little to help. Emotions that had been bubbling under the surface for all those days apart were ready to erupt. She pushed the last of her rice around on her plate, afraid to look at him, tears stinging her eyes. "I guess I've been demoted, huh? Now I'm just your 'friend'?" She couldn't say more.

If she expected a reaction of sympathy or contriteness from Benjamin, she was completely off base.

"Maybe I can't be who you need me to be, Grace." He looked into her stunned face and she was surprised by the coldness in his eyes. "You'll just have to let me know."

They finished dinner in an awkward silence and he said a terse goodbye as he opened the cab door for her. He didn't so much as kiss her cheek, leaving Grace deflated and miserable.

She was sure the cabbie thought she had totally lost her mind as she sobbed all the way home, his furtive glances in the rearview mirror showing how much he wished he had picked up just about any fare besides this one.

She couldn't understand what just happened or what she did wrong, but whatever it was, Benjamin was angry with her. She wrestled with this for the next couple of hours. Was she expecting too much of him? Was she being impatient with him? She didn't think so. In fact, disrupting his life was the last thing she wanted to do.

Later that night she sent a brief text to tell him she was sorry. She didn't know what she was sorry for, exactly, but felt as though he expected to hear those words from her. There was no response. Her mom's words rang in her ears. She was the one who had to decide if she could withstand the emotional rollercoaster Benjamin was on—and by default—that she was on, too.

***

Lexie's upcoming visit was the only thing she had to look forward to. It was a strange sort of limbo to be in right now, as she was pretty sure she and Benjamin were through. Grace looked at the calendar. Lexie would arrive in less than two weeks, a Thursday, and stay until late afternoon on Sunday. It wasn't easy, but she forced herself to plan fun activities during the visit, something she certainly owed Lexie. Despite this, she missed Benjamin like crazy, not sure if they were still a couple or not, and afraid to call or text. Sometimes it was better not knowing, in order to keep some hope alive.

Shortly after she arrived at the office on Tuesday, just two days before Lexie was scheduled to arrive, Grace was shocked to see an incoming call from Benjamin. Relieved to hear his voice, she forgot about all of the previous weeks of worrying and wondering.

"Any chance my beautiful girlfriend could come to my house for dinner tonight?" Her heart beat out of her chest and she heard herself laughing.

"I'm not sure if there's anyone beautiful interested, but your girlfriend would love that. Should I head over right after work or do you have a late meeting?"

"The sooner the better. I miss you, Grace." She melted at his words. The long to-do list before Lexie's arrival no longer mattered. She was going to see Benjamin.

"Want me to bring anything? I can pick up some take-out." It felt like old times, as though the last weeks had never even existed.

"Just you. There's nothing else I need."

Grace couldn't remember ever feeling happier. When 4:00 finally arrived, she almost ran out of the building. The drive to his house felt longer than usual but definitely worth it when she saw him standing at the door, just like he had the very first night she came to his house. He held her tightly right there on the step, and she breathed him in, not wanting to let go, not wanting to go through another month like the last one.

"I have a surprise for you, Grace." He led her up the stairs to the master bathroom, proudly opening a vanity drawer on "her" side. The drawer was completely empty. Keera's make-up and brushes were no longer there. "I cleaned this out for you. I wanted you to have a place for your...things." He waved his hand at the empty drawer, indicating with that gesture that he meant all that stuff women seem to need as part of their everyday routine. "And there's more." He led her back into the bedroom where he pulled open the two drawers at the nightstand on "her" side of the bed. "All for you. I want you to be able to leave some things here. I want you to spend as much time here as you can." He wrapped her in a hug and Grace melted into him.

"That means a lot. Thank you."

She really meant it, but she was also just a little ashamed of herself as she wondered if he had done any "cleaning" of the closet. Keera might be absent from a few drawers, but Grace guessed she was still very present in the rest of the house. She kept those thoughts to herself, knowing it had probably taken a great toll emotionally for Benjamin to take this small step.

She never did find out what he had planned for their dinner because they went directly to the bedroom and spent the next few hours re-discovering each other. He ran his finger down her chest, over her stomach and gently touched the warm welcoming place between her legs. She reached down, rubbing, teasing, until he rolled on top of her. He moved in her gently, whispering in her ear that he loved her, and she believed him. It was a lovemaking session unlike any they had shared and they hated to see the sky darken and the stars shining in through the skylights, knowing it was time for Grace to head home.

"I should probably feed you something." He was watching her get dressed, reaching out to pull her panties back down after she had just pulled them up. She slapped his hand away playfully and he reached up and cupped her breast in his hand. "Or we could just do more of this."

"At least this is nonfattening." She moved a few steps away from him, removing the temptation a little bit. "But I really have to go."

"That's OK. We'll have the whole weekend."

Her heart dropped, and she was unable to cover the disappointment written across her face. "Lexie is coming this weekend. I won't be able to make it out here. I'm sorry. I wish it was any other weekend besides this one." She had so looked forward to Lexie's visit before this, and now she would give anything to be with Benjamin instead.

"Oh, then I guess we'll just have to figure out when I can see you again." The playfulness was gone. He was out of bed and getting dressed to walk her out.

She loved Lexie. She really did. But right now, more than anything, she wished her friend wasn't coming for a visit this weekend. She had to make this better, somehow. She wanted—no, she needed him to go back to the feelings of a few moments ago. Hoping to change his mood, she walked to him, wrapping her arms around his waist and giving him her most disarming smile. "But I still want you to meet us for dinner on Saturday night. Or we could do it on Friday if that works better for you."

She and Lexie were scheduled to be with her parents for a cookout on Friday night and she hoped they wouldn't have a problem rescheduling if Benjamin said Friday would be the better night. She would do some scrambling to re-create the plans once Benjamin decided. She waited, terribly disappointed that they couldn't continue over the weekend all they had re-discovered tonight, but still trying to look forward to Lexie's visit. Feeling torn, for one fleeting second, she even found herself imagining a call to Lexie, with an excuse of having to work all weekend, a visit to some sick relative…anything to allow her to be with Benjamin. The moment passed. She could not and would not do that to Lexie, especially after the forgotten birthday incident.

"I'd rather just meet you for a drink. Saturday is fine. Have dinner and then we'll meet up afterwards." That was the answer. She wouldn't have to change her plans with her parents, but she was disappointed that Benjamin was only willing to commit to a drink with them. She felt let down. Just when she was feeling like his girlfriend again, she seemed relegated to a different status once more.

She shook it off. Their first night back together had been too fabulous for her to be disappointed now.

"Then that's the plan," she said brightly, pretending she stopped hugging him first. Never again did she want to hear him say that he might not be able to be who she needed him to be. He was exactly what she needed. Still, a voice in her head added, isn't he?

Chapter 20

⋄━◆━⋄

"I'll bet you dishwashing duties that this is the winning throw right here." It wouldn't be a family cookout without a game of corn hole at George and Sylvia's. The weather was warm for the Friday night get-together, despite an earlier threat of showers. Now, Lexie was challenging her mom in the championship round.

"That's not much of a bet when we're just throwing away the paper plates and plastic forks. The stakes need to be higher. Let's get some skin in this game. I think the loser has to clean the grill, too. What do you think George?"

Grace's dad raised his drink high in the air, a salute of agreement. As long as he didn't have to clean the grill, he would be happy to root for either of the two players still in the running for the bean-bag toss championship title—and the all-important bragging rights that came with it. Lexie's toss didn't do exactly what she intended and Sylvia's toss was met with loud cheers from everyone.

She held her arms high in the air, acknowledging their applause. "Mom wins again," she shouted above the noise and George grabbed her around the waist to twirl her around before planting a kiss firmly on her lips.

"George!" she exclaimed, feigning embarrassment at his public display of affection, but it was all an act. She loved every bit of it. Grace adored that about her parents and wondered if she would ever find that same connection with someone. Grace desperately wanted to believe it was Benjamin but she couldn't picture him doing what her dad had just done. He would be reserved, saving such things as a victory kiss for a private moment between the two of them.

"I think you've already checked it about 50 times." Grace was startled by Gen's voice. Guilty as charged. She had been checking her phone frequently, hoping to hear something from Benjamin.

"Waiting for a call from that mystery man of yours? Mom said he might be here today."

"She did? He had plans from a long time ago that he couldn't get out of so I don't know why mom would have said that."

"I'm just teasing, Grace. Mom never said anything. But he is mysterious. Does he actually exist?"

"He does and I'm working on him for your housewarming party. He's checking his schedule." That wasn't entirely true. So far Grace hadn't mentioned the party to Benjamin, dreading the disappointment if he said no once again. At least he agreed to meet for drinks the next evening. She was both excited and nervous to have Lexie finally meet Benjamin—and for Benjamin to finally meet Lexie.

"You and John must be busy, finishing the house and planning a party right away. I don't know how you do it." Grace chose to turn the conversation to safer ground. Gen loved talking about the house they bought and remodeled. "The twins must be excited. Are they ready to move?"

"They are, but they're nine years old and getting ready to leave the only house they've ever known. They sometimes think it's great and then they think of something they'll 'miss to death.' They're actually in the same school, but it's still going to be a big change for them. Of course, the swimming pool is a huge draw. It's all they talk about. They seem to think they're going to have pool parties every weekend until school starts."

Grace laughed, picturing the always rambunctious Ryan and Jacob entertaining their friends. "I'd love to have pool parties all summer long, too. Make sure they invite me. But seriously, you have just two weeks to get everything ready for the party. Mom said the moving trucks will be at the house at 8:00 Monday morning. You'll have your hands full."

"John has appointments all day so I'll be directing traffic."

Gen was the perfect doctor's wife, a stay-at-home mom who was heavily involved in the boys' school. She stayed busy taking care of her husband, kids and home—not at all like the wives of the doctors Grace met at the club. Pampered, most never working a day in their lives, unless supervising nannies, cooks and housekeepers counted as work. John and Gen's humble beginnings helped them know what they wanted for their boys as well. There would be no pampered doctor's wife role for Gen—and Gen would have nothing to do with that anyway.

"Well, you tell…Benjamin, right? You tell Benjamin we are really looking forward to meeting him. If he really does exist, of course." Gen gave her sister a playful push before going in to help their mom get the food set out. "And if he doesn't call you soon, you better call him. You're driving me crazy checking your phone every two minutes like a teenager. I almost mistook you for Lizzie."

"Very funny," she countered, making a face at her sister, but Grace knew she was right. She put her phone face down on the table next to her, determined to ignore it the rest of the evening. She had a party to enjoy.

Grace looked around at the small common area her parents were lucky to have in this downtown condo. She wished Benjamin was part of the gathering. As usual, she wondered how he would ever fit in here. She wanted to believe he could, but wasn't entirely certain.

"Your mom must spend every day practicing." Lexie plopped down beside her on the chaise, taking a long drink of the beer in her hand. "I could get used to this. Nothing but fun and games. Maybe I'll retire and move in with your parents. They're a helluva lot of fun. You can visit anytime you want"

"What am I? Chopped liver? Why wouldn't you want to move in with me? I'm a lot of fun, too."

"Your head is somewhere else. We'll call that somewhere else 'Benjamin.'" Grace knew Lexie was just giving her a hard time, but she also knew there was plenty of truth behind the ribbing. Everyone was noticing her distraction lately.

"I've never met anyone like him, Lex. He's smart and sweet and sophisticated…I don't know. He's this *real* man who others look up to and he's so successful. I still can't believe I'm with someone like that. It's all very surreal." Grace couldn't find the words to describe exactly how it felt to be with someone like Benjamin. She shrugged, giving up. "You'll just have to see what I mean tomorrow. He's just amazing. There's nothing else I can say."

"I'm going to ask you a strange question and I don't want you to get mad at me. Are you sure you aren't just attracted to the idea of helping him get over his dead wife? I can get where that would be kind of an ego thing."

Grace probably would have been upset had that question come from anyone other than Lexie, but because it was Lexie, she pondered carefully before responding. She said more than once it would be easier to "compete" with an ex-wife, and she certainly wanted Benjamin to love her as much as he had loved his wife.

"No, that's not it. Remember, he asked me out. I didn't pursue him. And it was purely a physical attraction on my part." She laughed at that, and Lexie joined in, but became serious again.

"I just don't think a woman should change to be with a man—unless there was something inherently wrong with the woman in the first place and the man is helping her become a better version of herself. That's not you, Grace. You're wonderful just the way you are. With the exception of your pathetic corn hole skills, of course. Maybe you could ask the great Benjamin to give you some lessons. In fact, I'll be sure to ask him tomorrow. Right now, I want to eat and then I have a grill to clean."

***

Lexie didn't ask Benjamin that question the next night when they met at the Sky Lounge, a spectacular view of Chicago sparkling below them from their seats on the patio, but she certainly had her fair share of other questions to ask him. Grace wondered if he was feeling as if he should have been sworn in before the questioning began. As always, he was the perfect gentleman, making Grace almost burst with pride.

"Grace said you have a daughter. Is she in college?"

"Not right now. She needed a break after high school. That was a traumatic time for her—for us."

"Will Grace get a chance to meet her soon?"

"I'm not sure what Caroline's plans are so I'm not sure. Tell me about your art, Lexie. Grace tells me you're a very talented artist. I'm sure she mentioned that my wife was an artist as well."

Benjamin carefully steered the conversation away from his daughter. Grace wasn't surprised that Lexie was trying to get him to talk about her. That was Lexie's nature. And now she chose to stay on her questioning path, not bothering to get drawn into Benjamin's diversionary tactic.

"She did tell me that. Grace also said you haven't met her family yet. You must be looking forward to the big housewarming party in a couple weeks. I know they're all anxious to meet you."

If Benjamin was surprised by this, he didn't let on at all to Lexie. "I look forward to meeting Grace's family."

He reached over and gave Grace's hand a squeeze but she did notice the momentary raising of an eyebrow for her benefit. Yes, she should have told him about the party but that wasn't a big deal in the grand scheme of things. All in all, Grace was happy with the evening, despite a tense moment or two.

During the cab ride back to Grace's apartment the small talk centered around insignificant topics, neither wanting to get into any real conversation in the less than private setting of the backseat of a cab. Once settled on the sofa, knees touching, Grace couldn't control her anticipation, anxious to get Lexie's thoughts on Benjamin. She was literally bursting with pride all night along as she sat with her two important people and she had a pretty good idea what Lexie would conclude about him.

Benjamin had been, as usual, the quintessential gentleman, self-confident, kind, courteous, and certainly interested in Lexie's stories. Now Grace was excited for Lexie's validation of all of the great qualities she had seen yet again tonight.

"I know you really like him a lot, Grace. And you are certainly right about him being incredibly handsome." She hesitated, searching for the right words. "There's something about him that makes me almost uncomfortable. I can't really put my finger on it, but there's *something*." She looked away momentarily, searching for the right words. "He's quite...well...I guess aloof. I'm wondering if you really know him as well as you think you do. He strikes me as the type of person who doesn't want others to get to know him, like he's holding something back. I mean, what's *really* going on with his daughter? He won't even talk about her. You *have* to admit that's odd."

Shocked, Grace sat up straighter, pulling her knees away from Lexie's. "Were you talking to the same man I was talking to tonight? He was wonderful. I'm not sure what you're trying to get at, Lex." She was hurt. Her best friend couldn't be farther off base. "He was charming even when he was being barraged with your questions. He was probably feeling like he was on trial but he never let on if he was upset. I have no idea what you expected. He is a private man. I haven't told him every last thing about me. Why would he tell me everything?"

Beside herself with hurt, Grace didn't know where to begin, trying to both defend Benjamin and express her disapproval that Lexie would be judgmental of him. The friend she knew and loved was never quick to judge others.

"I'm not trying to hurt your feelings. This is me telling you what I saw and what I felt. Gracie, don't be mad. If he's your everything, then I'm really happy for you. Maybe my intuition is out of whack. It's been known to happen once or twice before."

Thinking about Lexie's words kept Grace awake long into the night as she found herself more confused than ever about her relationship with Benjamin and maybe even more so, her relationship with Lexie. She wasn't sure which one would lose if she had to choose between the two of them.

Would she have to choose between the two of them?

At some point, she fell asleep, drifting into a dream in which she was floating from room to room in Benjamin's house, gathering items into her hands. She marveled, in her dream state, over her ability to fly. She was also impressed with how much she could hold in her hands. Floating to the window, there was enough light coming in for her to see the objects in her hands. She was holding pictures of Caroline. She stared at them for a moment and then let them drop, laughing at the noise of the breaking glass but shocked to see flames fly up from the wreckage, burning the bottom of her feet.

She awoke with a gasp, her heart racing, and the stark realization she had never seen a current picture of Benjamin's daughter. Every photograph in his house was of a young girl, probably no older than 12. Trying to come up with a reason for that, Grace was left even more confounded. Maybe Lexie was right, she allowed herself to think for just a moment.

As she said goodbye to Lexie at the airport, she hugged her close. "I'm sorry I got upset with you."

Lexie returned her hug. "You know I love you and only want you to be happy."

Grace didn't go so far as to tell her she might be right about Benjamin.

***

Grace may have been disappointed in Lexie's reaction to Benjamin, but his reaction to Lexie was downright shocking.

"I know you've been friends for a long time, but it's probably one of those friendships that should be under careful consideration. I don't think she really brings anything special to the table, Grace. She offends people with her appearance. That doesn't reflect well on you. You'd be wise to spend less time cultivating that relationship. She's not like us at all."

Not like us? What did that mean? She knew she should be angry. She knew she should tell him to mind his own business. She knew all of this, yet she found herself saying, "You're probably right. I was kind of thinking the same thing."

"I'm taking off on Thursday for a conference in San Diego so I won't be able to see you for a few days. I'll give you a call as soon as I have time. This week will be busy. I know you understand."

The phone call ended and Grace let the tears slide down her cheeks, no longer sure what to feel. She didn't want to lose Benjamin, and she couldn't picture her life without Lexie. Of course, looking at it practically, with Lexie living so far away it wasn't like they could see each other very often. Maybe she would just touch base with her less frequently, not even enough for Lexie to notice at first. Their friendship would either be just fine or it would die a slow, natural death. She would do anything for Benjamin. Even this.

It occurred to her then that Benjamin would be in San Diego during John and Gen's housewarming party. Everyone would once again be on her for his absence. She sighed, wondering how she could be so in love with someone and still feel so alone.

Chapter 21

———◆◆◆———

"I can't believe we still aren't meeting the mystery man." Gen juggled bowls of chips, making room on the large picnic table in the spacious yard of her new home. "Boys, pick up the beach towels and put them in the laundry room. I need you to give me a hand. Now!" The twins continued chasing each other with squirt guns, oblivious to their mom's shouts. John chose that moment to open the sliding door to step out onto the patio, getting a face full of water. He laughed, grabbing the squirt gun from Ryan and returning fire. Gen shook her head. "I give up. I have three kids and I can't control a single one of them. Don't take any covers off the food yet. Everything will end up waterlogged."

The yard soon filled with family and friends celebrating the completion of Gen and John's home. Grace deflected comments about her "mystery boyfriend," each one leaving her more disappointed than ever that Benjamin was noticeably absent again. Kids were in and out of the pool, and Grace found herself on a lounge chair taking a turn watching them so the moms could take a break. Watching them, she tried to imagine what it would be like to have kids with Benjamin.

"Tell me these aren't all yours!"

Grace shaded her eyes from the bright late June sun to see who was speaking to her. He was smiling broadly, a Cubs cap on his head, and a heaping plate of food in his hands. "I'm just on lifeguard duty here. I'm not claiming any of them—except maybe my nephews, I guess." She determined he must be one of John's friends. A woman was hurrying to join him.

"Gen said we'd find you here. I'm Gayle, this is my brother Thomas. I've heard so much about you. It's wonderful to finally meet you."

It took a second for Grace to put it all together and her cheeks burned with embarrassment, knowing what was happening here. "You're Gen's high school friend. It's nice to meet you, too. Gen said you're in yoga together." Grace did her best to be polite. She'd kill her sister later. "Thomas, I'm happy to meet you."

"Meet me? You don't remember me?" Tom pulled his cap off, awkwardly arranging his blond hair into a less disheveled look with one hand while carefully balancing the plate. "We were in advanced writing together. I wasn't exactly advanced, but I needed another English credit my senior year. You were a freshman. Really smart. Great writer. I remember you." Grace smiled as the man before her tried his hardest to get her to remember him from 20 years prior. "Tom Robertson? Well, everyone actually called me TJ—everyone except that battleax English teacher Barlow. She always called me Thomas John Robertson. Remember?"

His bright blue eyes were staring into hers, willing her to remember him.

"Oh my gosh, Tom, not everyone has your memory." Gayle turned her attention back to Grace. "He never forgets *anything*. Memory of an elephant our dad always said."

Grace laughed, the sibling teasing so familiar to her, and then returned her attention to the pool, making sure there was no trouble in the pool for any of her young charges. Satisfied all were safe, she turned back to Tom. "I'm sorry. I really don't remember."

Gen appeared at the patio door. "I'm heading back in by Gen. It was great meeting you, Grace." She carefully stepped around the deck chairs, just out of the way of splashes from the pool.

"You were in my editing group for one of our assignments. You wrote an essay on love and lust. It was really good. Do you still write?"

"You really *do* have an incredible memory. My goodness. My love essays are a thing of the past, but I do write a mean grocery list." Try as she might, she couldn't place him. She couldn't tell if she was more impressed with Gayle and Gen's well-orchestrated plan to get them to meet or his freakishly amazing memory. She would definitely kill her sister later. "I don't even remember writing that essay. Are you sure it was me?"

"It was definitely you. Man, look at all this food your sister gave me! She probably thinks she has to bribe me to keep working with Tyler. Maybe we'll have a chance to chat later. It was great seeing you again, Grace."

Not only surprised by his sudden exit, Grace was completely confused about what Tyler had to do with any of it. And Ellen? What was that all about? She assumed Tom would find an excuse to stay attached to her hip for the duration of the party. Maybe there hadn't been a grand scheme to make sure they met. Maybe her sister would actually live to see another day.

"Hey, Aunt Grace. Mom said it's my turn to watch the kids so you can get something to eat." Ironically, it was Tyler, Ellen's oldest, standing next to her this time. He finished the last of his burger in one big bite and plopped himself into one of the lounge chairs, fiddling with his iPod. The twins spotted their cousin and waved. They adored Tyler.

"Come swimming with us," Jacob pleaded, hanging onto the side of the pool, feet kicking out behind him.

"Maybe later, goober. Go have fun. Watch out! Ryan's gonna get you." Jacob let out a squeal as his brother jumped on his back to push him under the water. Both swam away, not the least bit concerned Tyler declined their invitation. "You should get one of those burgers, Aunt Grace. They're really good."

"I will, Ty. Hey, do you know Tom Robertson? That guy in the Cubs cap who was down here a little while ago?"

Her nephew nodded, finding a piece of hamburger bun on his t-shirt and popping it into his mouth, before turning his attention to the rousing game of tag in the pool. "Yeah, he's my mentor for the engineering projects class. We all have to have a mentor who's a professional in the field to work with us on our summer projects. Mom got Aunt Gen to ask Mr. Robertson. He's pretty cool." Tyler attended a prestigious charter school for gifted science, technology and engineering high school students. "He promised to take me out on the job so I get like real world experience as an engineer. It's really cool."

Grace was ashamed of herself. Her assumption that some grand scheme had unfolded to get her to meet Tom was completely wrong. Perhaps she needed to do a little vanity check. Tom was there because of her sisters and her nephew— not because she was being set up on a blind date with him. Of course, this could be part of an even grander scheme than first imagined. That sounded ridiculous even to her. "It's great that he's helping you. He seems really nice. I'll send someone else to relieve you of your duties soon."

"OK. Get a burger."

On the patio, her parents were chatting with John and Gen's new next-door neighbors. She patted her dad on the shoulder as she walked past him, wondering if he was enjoying the story Laurie was animatedly sharing about their Great Dane eating their whole dinner when they left the kitchen for just a minute. Grace heard the whole story about an hour earlier when Gen first introduced her to Laurie and Joe. She imagined the story would be told several more times before the party ended.

John was flipping burgers, completely loving his master griller role, and proudly sporting a paper chef's hat atop his head. He wiped beads of sweat from his forehead with the towel he kept nearby for that sole purpose. "Every man needs a backyard like this. The way I see it, the outdoor kitchen is an absolute necessity for those nights I'm in the dog house." He laughed at his own joke. "You should grab a plate and get one of these while they're hot. They seem to disappear as soon as I take a pan of them to the picnic table." He was holding a burger on a spatula, so Grace did as she was instructed, grabbing a plate from the stack sitting on the nearby table and holding it out to John to slide the burger onto.

"How could I resist when they came so highly recommended by Tyler?"

"Was that review after his first burger today or the fourth or fifth? He's a frequent flyer to the food table. To hear Jeremy talk about how much that kid eats, I think it's more about quantity than quality. I wouldn't hold a whole lot of store in that culinary review. Just taste one for yourself. Oh, and do me a favor. Could you grab another ketchup from the kitchen? I think the one on the picnic table is getting pretty low."

With a laugh and a quick wave over her shoulder as she walked away, Grace took her burger to the kitchen to fix it up properly. She was placing the perfect dollop of ketchup on it when Gen returned to refill a bowl of potato chips. "I'll take more ketchup outside in a second. Nice work on getting me to meet Gayle's brother, by the way. You knew you could make it happen somehow, didn't you?"

Gen gave her a playful nudge. "That's what big sisters were put on this earth to do. He's cute. Look at him out there playing with Lambeau." A staunch Green Bay Packers fan, John named the black lab after the famous team founder and coach so he had at least one ally among all the Bears fans in the family.

"He clearly likes dogs. That makes him…nice," Grace offered noncommittally.

"Come on, Grace. I'm sure he has all kinds of great qualities. For one, he's here. Where's your guy? Was he too busy to join us?"

Perhaps Gen hadn't meant it to sound quite as harsh as it did, but the words stung Grace to the core. "He's a busy doctor, Gen. I'm sure he'd love to spend more time at family functions—his own or mine," she jumped to his defense, "but he has responsibilities."

"He's a doctor?" Grace hadn't shared very much about Benjamin with anyone besides her mom so it was no wonder Gen was surprised by this revelation. "Maybe John knows him. Is his practice in the city or is he in the suburbs?"

"Whose practice?" John slipped through the patio door with the plate full of burgers. "I want to take more buns out before I put these down on the picnic table or you'll have twenty people streaming through here to get one. Whose practice?" He was looking from his wife to his sister-in-law, waiting for someone to answer him.

Gen offered, "Her mystery boyfriend. He's a doctor."

"He is? Maybe I know him. Who is it? Where does he practice?"

Overwhelmed by the flurry of questions, Grace hesitated to reveal too much about Benjamin. They, like Lexie, would be concerned that he had too much "baggage." She could hear it now—a deceased wife? A daughter? He's that old? After all, she was still the baby sister who needed protecting in their minds. But she was also thrilled to be part of the sophisticated world Benjamin introduced her to, and that was the part of her that won out.

"Benjamin Hayward. He's in Chicago."

John almost dropped the whole pan of burgers he had in his hands. He carefully set them down and turned slowly to face Grace. "Dr. Hayward? Dr. Benjamin Hayward—the Chief of Pediatrics? *That* Dr. Hayward?"

Grace nodded. "Is something wrong?"

John quickly recovered. "I just had no idea that's the Benjamin we've been hearing so little about. He's a big deal at CUH." He turned to Gen to fill her in on some additional facts. "You know Stan Lord, my former Chief at Martin Luther Hospital? He retired and then two months later Chicago University Hospital asked him to step in to cover for Hayward. His wife died and he took a 6-month bereavement leave of absence but during that time there was the investigation of..." He left his sentence hanging.

Gen nodded, recalling what had been in the news at the time. "That's right. They cleared him of any wrongdoing and he eventually went right back to his position."

"And there were a lot of people, Stan included, who believed it was nothing but a big cover-up because CUH didn't want to lose their big man on campus." Both John and Gen seemed to realize at the same time that Grace was still there, mouth agape, learning all of this for the first time.

She finally found her voice, whispering, "What was he cleared of?"

John hesitated, suddenly intent on getting the buns and burgers outside. Finally, he looked at her. "Any responsibility for the death of his wife."

Chapter 22

———— ◆·◆·◆ ————

S he couldn't hear anything because of the roaring in her ears. Grace shook her head, trying to clear it, but flashes of light appeared where John had been, and everything started going dark around the edges.

Next thing, someone was holding a cold compress on her head. She didn't immediately recognize who it was. Gen was standing nearby, worry etched on her face. John was checking her pulse, and trying to get her attention. "Grace? Hey, Grace. Can you hear me? Grace? You passed out. Just lie back for a few minutes."

She pushed the cold compress away, not understanding why Gayle's brother, Thomas, was holding it against her head.

"I'm fine. I'm fine." She wanted all of them to stop looking at her. Why were they hovering over her? She was trying to remember what happened, but her brain was sluggish. A vision of a painting came to mind, confusing her further. What did a painting have to do with anything?

Like a lightning strike, she remembered. Keera! John was talking about Keera. She felt queasy.

"Have you fainted before, Grace?" She stared blankly at John for a second, not sure why he would be asking that.

"No. Well, yes, once. Did I faint? I got really light headed all of a sudden. I'm fine." She wanted to process the news. It couldn't be possible. She saw the sadness in Benjamin's eyes every time he thought about his wife. There was no way he had any part in her death. That was crazy. She shook her head again, willing her brain to catch up with her.

"Your pulse is rapid, Grace. I want you to just stay here for a bit. Why don't you two get back out to the party. The burgers and buns should go out. We don't want everyone to think there's something wrong in here. I'll sit with Grace for a bit to make sure she's OK." Gen and Thomas left, Gen reluctantly, worried about her little sister. "And stop looking like that Gen. She's fine. You don't want your parents thinking she has to be rushed to the hospital. Let's give her some space."

Grace was desperately trying to piece it all together.

"Is there any possibility that you're pregnant?"

Her jaw dropped, making John laugh. "OK, OK, I'll take that as a no. I didn't want to ask in front of your sister, but I had to ask. We docs like to rule out the obvious."

"It's my fault. I haven't eaten anything since yesterday afternoon," she lied. "I know it's stupid and I promise I'll never do that again. I'm fine." She wasn't fine, though. She was hit by the realization that she knew nothing about the man she had fallen head over heels in love with. Her own family members knew more than she did. It was too disconcerting to wrap her brain around.

"I don't think you hit your head. You slipped down pretty gracefully." He smiled, and Grace knew his patients probably adored their doctor with his gentle bedside manner. "Gayle's brother walked in just as you were about to hit the floor. Gen would probably say he's your knight in shining armor."

Grace glared. "Stop!"

"I'm just kidding. She's really not trying to play matchmaker. And you have the great Dr. Hayward as your boyfriend. Who could ever compete with that?" The twinkle had returned to his eye.

"Can I get up now? I'm fine. I just want to get some ibuprofen."

"Tell you what. You stay here for a few more minutes. I'll get the ibuprofen and then you can get back to the party once you feel up to it." He patted her arm and stood, certainly not about to take no for an answer, but he hesitated long enough to add, "Grace, I'm sorry we were talking about Benjamin that way. We had no business doing that. I can imagine it was very upsetting to you."

Grace was finally alone to sort through what she learned, but there were so many thoughts racing through her brain she didn't know where to start. She closed her eyes, trying to find relief from the pounding that was starting in her head and the ache that was forming in her heart.

"Are you OK? John asked me to bring you this." Thomas was holding a glass of water in his hand, not sure if he should approach her or just stand in the doorway. He looked worried. Grace might have found that endearing if there wasn't so much spinning around in her head right now. And on top of that, Thomas had to be the one to catch her as she fainted? It was humiliating.

"Other than a headache right now, I'm fine. Sorry if I scared you." He moved out of the doorway, handing her the glass, standing awkwardly near her head. "Thanks." She sat up and sipped, hoping Thomas would simply turn around and leave, but he sat in the armchair across from her, watching her carefully in case she should hit the floor again. "And thanks for being in the right place at the right time." Or was it the wrong time? She wasn't sure.

"All I wanted was more ketchup and all of a sudden you were just sort of, I don't know, sinking." He was embarrassed, too, she realized. "I just kinda grabbed you. I hope I didn't hurt you."

Grace started to shake her head, but that made her dizzy. She closed her eyes, willing the pounding to stop and hoping

John would appear with aspirin for her. "You didn't hurt me. I don't think I ever actually fainted before. I almost did once. I was at the veterinary hospital with Jasper, my dog, and I started seeing flashing lights and then sort of a darkness in front of me. But they got me into a chair so I never actually passed out."

"You have a dog?"

"I had a dog. He died before I moved back here."

"I'm sorry to hear that. Losing a pet is the worst! I'm sure you miss him." The sympathy in his face was almost enough to bring tears to her eyes, so she was grateful when he changed the subject. "Why did you move back here? I'm sure Arizona is really nice."

"It's a beautiful place." She wondered what else her sister had shared with this stranger. It wasn't the time or place to share any of her intimate thoughts or feelings about leaving Arizona to return to Illinois, and Thomas wasn't somebody she would share them with anyway.

Thankfully, John returned, holding out his hand to her with three tablets for her to take. "Sorry. Had to doctor a scraped knee along the way. Let me know if you feel dizzy, lightheaded or sick to your stomach. And get some food in you! Doctor's orders." He gave her arm another pat and then gave them both a wave as he walked out, leaving them in embarrassed silence.

Thomas was watching her closely. She closed her eyes again, concentrating on breathing in and out, hoping he would take the hint that she just wanted to be alone for a while. When she opened them, he was still in the same spot.

"I'm not going to faint again. I'm fine. Go enjoy the party. I'll be out in a minute."

"Oh...well...Feel better."

She watched him walk away, thankful to be alone to figure out what she was going to do with this new information about Benjamin. She missed Lexie. Lexie would help her sort through it.

She sat up tentatively, then shuffled down the hall to the bathroom, wanting desperately to call Lexie and tell her everything she just heard, but she couldn't. In fact, she wasn't sure she could ever share any of these revelations with her friend. It wasn't in Lexie's nature to issue an "I told you so," and Grace wasn't worried about that happening. It was hard to admit that once again she didn't have the intuition to know something wasn't quite right. She hadn't figured it out with Josh and now she was caught unaware again. What was wrong with her? Was she missing the woman's intuition gene?

Lexie suspected something was "off" about Benjamin right away. How had she figured it out so quickly? Grace was intimately familiar with this man and didn't have a clue. Her stomach churned and her head ached, but she had to re-join the party. She would not let on that something wasn't quite right in her relationship.

She stared at herself in the mirror, trying hard to see who was looking back at her. *"Do I know you?"* she whispered to the face. There was no answer. The image was a little pale, but otherwise the same face that always looked back at her. Grace took a deep breath, willing strength back into herself. As she walked out of the bathroom, making her way back to the party, her mind flashed back to her birthday party and the wish she'd made as she blew out the candles. *Please let me find myself again.* It was difficult to admit that she still hadn't found herself. Prayer or wish, it hadn't come true.

Outside, Grace gave her sister a thumbs up, hoping that was adequate to let Gen know that she was feeling better.

Her parents were still trapped in a conversation with the next-door neighbors and she wondered if she should try to rescue them. She didn't have a chance to do that as Thomas appeared at her side.

"Did you get a burger yet? The salads are good. Would you like me to get you some?" As he spoke, he reached for a plate.

She spun to face him. "I don't want anything. Please leave me alone."

The second the words were out, she regretted them. He put the plate back. Grace wanted to kick herself. What was wrong with her? Obviously, he was truly concerned about her well-being.

He had taken two steps, doing exactly what she'd asked, when she realized she didn't want to be alone.

"Thomas, wait. Please. I'm so sorry." He turned back to her.

"I didn't mean to bother you. I can take a hint. Don't worry about it."

Tears made their way down her cheeks, taking him by surprise.

"Let's take a little walk over here." He steered her away from the group at the picnic table, his hand under her elbow. "Are you sure you're OK? I can get John for you if you want me to."

She shook her head. It wasn't John she needed. What she really needed right now was Lexie, her confidante. But Lexie wasn't here to help her sort out the mess spinning around in her head. Thomas guided her to a couple of Adirondack chairs under a giant elm tree in the back corner of the yard.

"Is there anything I can do to help?"

"I don't want you to think I'm crazy even if this sounds kind of crazy. First, I'm sorry I snapped at you. And thank you for catching me. You know how people faint in the movies when they hear something shocking? I never knew that could really happen."

"That's what happened? Wow! You must have heard something pretty upsetting. I'm sorry."

"You must think I'm totally crazy."

"You don't look too crazy. I'll assume you're not." He smiled, reaching out to pat her arm.

"I found out the guy I've been dating for about five months has been keeping a really huge secret from me. It shook my world, I guess."

"Oh no! Let me guess. You found out he's married?"

Grace smiled a cheerless smile. It was sweet of him to try to play the role of 'girlfriend' at this moment. "I wish it was that. No, that's not true, but it's actually more complicated, unfortunately." She chewed the inside of her cheek, contemplating how much she was about to share with him. She leaned forward, lowering her voice. "His wife died in an accident a few years ago. He doesn't talk about it at all but it turns out there was some investigation into his possible involvement." She hesitated, wondering if she was betraying Benjamin by sharing these details. She closed her eyes, trying to make up her mind whether to stop talking or just get if off her chest. The latter won. "And he has a daughter I've never met and I don't know where she is or what she's doing, and he hasn't met any of my family, yet, and…oh my gosh. Saying it out loud makes it all sound even worse. I *am* crazy."

"Are you going to talk to him? Maybe there's another side to the story that will put everything into some logical perspective for you. It's probably not a good idea to just jump to conclusions."

Grace shook her head. "No, I can't bring up a topic like that. 'Hey, did you have something to do with your wife's death?' No. I can't say anything. I don't know. I can't believe he would have done something to her. He talks about missing her all the time and he has pictures of her everywhere in his house, like some kind of shrine to her." She shook her head again. "I would never be able to confront him. And they did an investigation that cleared him, so I can't bring it up."

"I think it's really good that you're taking time to think this through instead of jumping all over him and making him feel even crappier. Plenty of women would rather shatter a guy's world, make all kinds of accusations and stuff instead of showing a little bit of compassion."

"I never dated a widower. I don't know what's normal and what's not. He talks about his dead wife as if she's in the next room. I don't know sometimes what role I'm supposed to play. Honestly, I'm not sure he'll ever find room for me in his world because he's still living in his old world." Words spilled out, but now she hesitated, realizing she was sharing far more than she would have imagined being able to share with someone she'd just met—or just became reacquainted with after many years. Thomas was taking it all in stride, acting like women confided their deepest, darkest secrets in him on a regular basis.

Ellen's voice interrupted, calling out to them from the patio. "You two want to play? We have bocci ball or washer toss. Take your pick." It was time to rejoin the party.

"I'll play!" Thomas responded, but he didn't move. Turning his attention back to Grace, he said, "This has to be a lot for you to deal with. I'm not emotionally invested in it and it's overwhelming just to hear about it."

"So, it really *is* crazy. I knew it." She shook her head in an attempt to clear it. "Thank you for listening, Thomas. I haven't been able to say any of this out loud to anyone." She paused, then added, "And I'd appreciate it if you'd keep it to yourself."

"I'll keep your secrets if you promise to stop calling me Thomas. It's TJ. You called me that in high school and you for sure can't be so formal now that I know all about your love life." He threw an imaginary key into his mouth and then pulled his thumb and forefinger across his lips to close the imaginary zipper. He mumbled through his 'zipped' lips something that sounded like "Ikehemsnekt."

"I'm going to assume you just gave me your solemn promise." Grace laughed and they both stood. He took her hand for a moment, giving it a reassuring squeeze.

He ran his fingers over his lips in the opposite direction, this time unzipping them to add, "I hope you figure it out. Maybe you'll be writing about love and lust again after all."

As the pounding in her head finally subsided, some of the anxiety she'd felt earlier subsided as well. It had been a relief sharing the heavy stuff with someone. It was too much to process on her own and Lexie was too distant—in more ways than one. She had a lot of thinking to do before she faced Benjamin again.

She caught Gen looking at her, a knowing grin on her face. Gen believed she was playing matchmaker, but Grace knew the truth. Gen had placed a new friend in her world, and she smiled gratefully back at her sister. Let her believe what she wanted to believe.

Chapter 23

———◆—◆—◆———

"I don't pay you to tell me something's a longshot. Do what I pay you to do!" Benjamin had his phone on speaker, making the words echo around him. He leaned back in his chair, a patient's file opened in front of him, but his attention far from the document.

"Hayward, you *do* realize there are over 200 inhabited islands there, right?"

Benjamin leaned forward, moving so rapidly two wheels of his desk chair lifted off the floor. Placing his face closer to the phone to make sure every word was crystal clear, he snarled, "I don't care if you have to search all 6,000 of them, inhabited or not. Got it?"

The private investigator wasn't about to argue further. The wealthy doctor was footing the bill so he'd just go along with whatever instructions he was given, as futile as all of it seemed to him. "No problem. I'll get a couple of my guys over there to start checking it out. Anything else?"

Benjamin looked down at the note he'd written to himself several weeks ago. *Ireland, French Riviera, Greek Isles.* He had placed an asterisk next to the last one.

"I'll let you know. Start there." He touched the end call button and leaned back again.

He didn't know where to search anymore. Grace had unknowingly given him some ideas and he was going to explore the possibilities. Well, *he* wasn't. That's what he hired someone else to do. The small fortune he'd spent to date on the search didn't faze him in the least. He had to find her. This was all his fault and he had to somehow make it right—even if it took every cent he had and he had to search every corner of the world. He had to make this right.

Chapter 24

Sitting cross-legged on the floor of her apartment, a yearbook opened in her lap, Grace was trying to remember the face staring back at her from the pages of the book. TJ had a very different look back then, sporting a crewcut and glasses, but the smile was definitely the same. She paged back to the freshman class section. Maybe she would do a better job recognizing the face that had her name printed beneath it. Yes, she remembered that version of Grace. Quiet, confident, comfortable with her close group of friends, and determined to take on the world. She missed her almost-15-year-old self a little bit.

She'd had a long and tedious week. When she retrieved her purse from the bed of the guest room where she'd left it during the party, she found a text from Benjamin waiting for her. *The weather has been beautiful. Good conference. I miss you.*

She mulled a long time over how to respond, her newest knowledge about Benjamin making her feel unsettled and uncertain.

I hope you can take some time to enjoy San Diego. Stay safe. I miss you, too.

Grace wanted everything to be the same between them, but that was impossible. She needed to rely on something more than just her intuition—which was in need of some serious upgrades and repairs. She needed facts. It was time to do a little investigating of her own to figure out something about Dr. Benjamin Hayward.

She decided to do a little investigating about someone else first.

The day after the party she went to her parents' house to hunt through their storage room. Her mom kept everything, so she knew she'd find a box labeled "Grace: High School." Sylvia claimed she had to keep all of the memorabilia for each of the girls from those four years because one day they would want to look through it. Grace didn't necessarily want to walk down memory lane, but there was one yearbook she especially wanted to look at now—the one year she would have been in high school with TJ, when he was a senior and she a freshman.

Flipping to the back, the section reserved for seniors to record their high school activities, she read that TJ was a four-year debate team member, a four-year science club member, founder of the engineering club his senior year, and school salutatorian. Also listed was his four years on the tennis team, captain his senior year. It was a shame she couldn't remember him. He was probably a really nice guy back then, too. Investigating TJ was easy. It was Benjamin's past she needed to spend time digging into.

Setting aside the yearbook, Grace reached for the notepad next to her. She'd jotted some notes, documentation of what little information she had about Benjamin. So far it didn't add up to much. John provided some of the details.

She'd found a few minutes to talk to John as they cleaned up after the party, thanking him again for taking care of her and reiterating her promise to develop better eating habits. What she really wanted was to learn more about Benjamin. Her questions had to come across as simple curiosity, because she didn't want to raise any suspicion with her brother-in-law that would immediately be relayed to her sister and possibly her other sister and then from there to her parents... She needed to be discreet.

What would they all think if they knew how little she knew about her boyfriend?

"Did you ever have a chance to work with Benjamin?" She was putting away the utensils she had just dried as John continued washing his grilling tools at the kitchen sink.

"No, I really just know about him. I don't actually *know* him. He's probably the most highly respected pediatrician in the Midwest. He sits in on consults all over the country—and probably the world. We're really fortunate that he's stayed in Chicago all these years."

"Everyone seems to know him when we go out. I would assume he's really well liked."

"I really don't know anything about that, Grace. Like I said, he's really well respected. There have been rumors over the years about a lot of erratic behaviors, but most brilliant people seem to have that attached to them. Could you hand me that towel?"

Wanting to probe a little more before anyone interrupted, she chose her words carefully. "Erratic? So, are you saying my boyfriend is a little nuts?" She laughed, hoping to fool him into believing this was a causal conversation, and not the search for answers it actually was.

"The usual stuff. Yelling at a resident who isn't catching on quickly enough to suit him. Going off on the staff because somebody moved a chart. Like I said, lots of brilliant doctors have a hard time when others around them aren't the perfectionists they are. I guess Hayward has a lot of that. It's too bad he wasn't able to make it today. I would have enjoyed meeting him. He's an amazing doctor, Grace."

Smiling, she thought, *And most of the time he's an amazing boyfriend, too.* Grace didn't ask him any more questions. Benjamin wasn't crazy and he wasn't a murderer. Confident that he was a decent human being, a brilliant doctor, perhaps sometimes misunderstood, she wasn't going to doubt him in any way. Or was she? Deep down, she still felt a twinge of something. What was he hiding from her?

Now, looking through her notes, she hoped something would be revealed to her, but not sure what it might be. When she decided not to rely on her less than trustworthy intuition, opting for some old-fashioned sleuthing of sorts, she started with the obvious. The obituary revealed little, stating that Keera Claire Fitzgerald, wife of Benjamin Edward Hayward, died unexpectedly at home. She was survived by her husband of 26 years and her daughter, Caroline Elizabeth Hayward. Preceding her in death was a list that included her parents and grandparents.

Died unexpectedly at home. What did that mean? Grace thought through scenarios that seemed most obvious— suicide, drowning, a fall—but somehow couldn't picture the beautiful woman in the photos suffering any of those fates.

Further probing online revealed nothing of importance or interest. Grace still had no idea how Keera died and she still had no idea where Caroline might be. If she really wanted to know, of course, she would have to ask Benjamin. The big question, though, was could she really bring herself to do that? Frustrated, she set the notebook aside again.

She would be as patient as humanly possible with him. Maybe one of these days he would share the truth about Keera and Caroline. She hoped it would be soon. She couldn't bring herself to believe their relationship was built on secrets. Benjamin wouldn't intentionally be dishonest or misleading. If she loved him, she had to accept that.

"And I do love you, Benjamin. I do." She said the words aloud, convinced of their validity.

Rummaging through the box, Grace pulled out a folder labeled "12th Grade." It held report cards, returned assignments, a certificate from a writing contest. *"There's no way…"* she said aloud, putting the file to the side and digging even deeper to see if there was one marked "9th Grade." Of course, it was there, and Grace eagerly rifled through its contents until she found what she was looking for: "It isn't Rocket Science: Love and Lust." Why this essay was suddenly so important to her, she wasn't sure, but she had to give her mom credit for saving everything.

She read the essay written so many years ago, groaning as she re-read the final paragraph. *"It is ridiculous to believe a relationship can survive when it is based on lust. True love has to be part of the equation. Any sane human being should be able to tell the difference between the two. One will make you tingle; the other will make you commit heart and soul to another human being for the rest of your life."*

Had she really written those words? She looked at the teacher's comments, not remembering those any more than she had remembered TJ or writing this essay. In her neat cursive writing, Mrs. Barlow had noted: "Well written in terms of the conventions of standard English. Arguments seem unsubstantiated and immature to some degree, if not flawed. Life lessons will help you better understand some of the errors in your reasoning. B+."

Life lessons? Oh, she had plenty of those. There was a failed marriage, to start, and now a relationship that seemed to be built on nothing more than… Grace closed her eyes. No. She couldn't bring herself to say it. Lust? Was her relationship with Benjamin based solely on lust? For that matter, what had her relationship with Josh been built on? She fell for his rugged good looks, yes, but there had been more, right?

Battleax Barlow, as most of the students called her behind her back, required students to submit all drafts, including those that had peer comments from their small group editing sessions. She turned the pages, finding the corrections and comments made by the group members, wondering which ones might have been made by TJ. *"This is really good. I like it,"* written in neat block letters across the top of the last page was her best guess.

She put all of the files and the yearbook back in the box and resealed it, not happy she had unwittingly described herself as less than sane.

Benjamin called that evening. They talked about San Diego and how they would have to travel there together one day. She told him about the housewarming party, letting him know how sorry everyone had been about not getting a chance to meet him yet.

She didn't tell him she knew a little more about him than she had when he left. And that was still troubling. She knew only a little more.

Chapter 25

J une turned into July and before long, the city was hot, humid and uncomfortably sticky. Visits to Benjamin's house meant sitting on the veranda or the main floor patio enjoying the cool breeze blowing off Lake Michigan. They spent as much time as possible outside, taking in the view with a glass of wine. Sitting in her office on weekdays, Grace longed to be with Benjamin. Their routine was easy and comfortable now, but she still awaited the day he would completely open up to her. She didn't push him. They were in a good place and she preferred to keep it that way.

Today was especially hot, and while she wished she could be enjoying those cool breezes, that wasn't going to happen. Benjamin was on one of his trips again so she was finding ways to occupy her time in her stuffy apartment. After a refreshing shower, she poured herself a tall glass of lemonade. Settling in to read a book and enjoy a quiet evening at home, she was surprised when her phone rang, but it wasn't Benjamin.

"Is this Grace?" She didn't recognize the voice.

"Yes, it is."

"It's TJ…Thomas. Gayle's brother?"

She laughed. "Did you really think you had to identify yourself in three different ways for me to remember you?"

"Yes, I did. You're the one with the bad memory."

"Touché. How did you manage to get my number?" She guessed it was her sister, the quintessential matchmaker.

"I'll confess. I told John I'd promised to get you information about a band you wanted to see. He gave me your number. Are you mad?" John would never be considered the matchmaking type so she felt better instantly.

"You could have just asked me for it you know."

"Oh, I don't think so. You were pretty mad at me for a while. Admit it Grace, I annoyed the hell out of you."

She laughed again. "Ok, Ok, you've got me there. I thought you were a little annoying. And now you're sneaking around to get my phone number? I don't know, TJ, you're turning out to be quite the creeper."

"Yikes. Not my plan. But I can see why you'd get that impression. So anyway, I just wanted to check in on you. You doing OK?"

"Yep! No more fainting spells. Haven't even felt a little woozy." She curled her legs under her, completely at ease chatting with her new friend.

"I'm glad to hear that, but it's not really what I meant. Everything copacetic between you and the boyfriend? You were dealing with some pretty heavy-duty crap. I'm here if you need a sounding board."

Grace was silent for a moment.

"Grace? Did I say something wrong? I didn't mean to come across too strong. I guess I might be a creeper *and* a jerk."

"No, you're not. I think it's really sweet of you to call. You took me by surprise."

"Whew. I thought you were going to hang up on me and start screening your calls."

"Well, I might screen calls, but I do that with all the guys in my life." He was so easy to talk to, so she shared more. "So, I got my yearbook out—the year you were a senior. I have to admit, TJ, you were a pretty impressive student, but…I'm sorry…I still don't remember you. Can you forgive me?"

"Ouch! I don't know. It's not very flattering to be told you're totally forgettable. But I did have some serious acne, ugly glasses and a crewcut, so I should probably be grateful that you don't remember me."

"Good point. I'm going to retract my apology."

"I don't think you actually apologized, but I'll accept the retraction anyway—due to my total unattraction."

Grace groaned. "Ok. If your jokes don't get any better, then I'm definitely going to screen my calls. Would you like to retract that last comment? Please?"

"OK.

"Things are going pretty well with Benjamin. I still don't have all the answers, but I will leave it at that right now."

"I'm happy to hear that it's going better."

"Are you still helping Tyler with his project?"

"We have just two more weeks to finish it. He's a great kid."

"He is." She found herself smiling into the phone. "It was really nice of you to call TJ. I promise I'm not even mad at John for handing out my phone number willy-nilly."

"Well, it wasn't exactly nilly or willy. I have a theory. Deep down, John is probably a creeper, too, so he took some perverse pleasure in helping a fellow weirdo."

"I'm sure that's it." Grace couldn't remember the last time she had laughed so much over a conversation, and she realized something else. "You remind me a lot of my friend Lexie."

"I remind you of a girl? Nice, Grace. Really nice. You know how to boost a guy's ego. Was she in your class?"

"Oh no, Lexie is from Arizona. I met her at U of A and we became best friends almost the second we met. *That's* why you remind me of her, silly. Lex and I can talk about anything." She felt a stab of guilt, knowing she had not been the best of friends to someone who had always been nothing but loyal to her.

"You can never have too many good friends. I'm glad you think of me that way."

"I'm not sure I deserve to be called her good friend right now. She doesn't like Benjamin and vice versa. Maybe it isn't that they actually dislike each other, but…He asked me to spend less time on my friendship with her and I agreed to it." Tears stung her eyes. It was hard to hear those words from her own mouth. She sounded like an awful person.

"She's still your friend, Grace. You're just trying to figure out some pretty big things with this guy. Good friends are forever."

Grace wanted to hug him through the phone. "The worst part is that when she met Benjamin, she said something was a little 'off' about him and she wanted me to be careful. She's apparently a lot better than I am at reading people."

"Then I never want to meet her because she'll instantly peg me as the creeper I am." She loved that he knew when to lighten the mood.

"I'm giving you my express permission to call again if you want to. I won't call you a creeper anymore."

"That's good to know. I hope everything stays good with the boyfriend *and* the girlfriend."

"Thanks, TJ. You made my day."

"Seems to me, Grace, that's what friends are for."

Perhaps it was guilt, but more likely it was the confidence TJ had given her. Grace called Lexie and spent the next hour telling her funny stories about her nephews and niece, co-workers, and everything else not directly related to Benjamin. She had to keep Lexie in her life, despite Benjamin's request.

Chapter 26

———◆—◆—◆———

Benjamin was out of sorts. Grace felt herself walking on eggshells, wondering what could have gotten him so on edge. She took her overnight bag to the bedroom, placing some items in the bathroom, as usual, and then returning downstairs to hang some clothes in the guest room. She took her time before wandering out to the deck where Benjamin was sitting. He hadn't bothered to wait for her arrival, but had already opened a bottle of wine and was drinking alone. She noticed he hadn't brought a glass out for her. There had been no mention of dinner plans either.

"Would you like me to order something for our dinner tonight?" She spoke quietly, hoping he would come out of his funk quickly.

He didn't respond, staring out at the water. It had been several weeks since she'd had to deal with one of his moods. She sat still, not sure if he preferred being alone or wanted her company, but opting to just sit quietly next to him,

Some time passed, and she was startled when his voice finally broke the silence. "She shouldn't have died. We did everything right." She couldn't tell if he was talking to her or to himself. She also didn't know who he was talking about. Was he talking about Keera? She didn't respond.

He stood so abruptly he almost knocked over the small table between their chairs. "I'll get you some wine." He left her sitting for a long time. When he returned, he had her wine glass and a plate of cheese and crackers, which he set between them.

They ate and drank in silence, watching the sun make its way down. Finally, she said, "It's a beautiful evening."

Benjamin reached over to take her hand. "Sorry. I didn't mean to take that out on you."

"Do you want to talk about it?" Benjamin had to start trusting her to be there for him. He had to hang on instead of letting go all the time. And if he sent her away again...

"We lost a patient today. She was doing better and we lost her. Twelve years old. It just didn't make sense."

Grace stood, took his hand, and led him to the bedroom. Without a word she unbuttoned his shirt and placed her hands on his hard chest. She softly kissed the area over his heart, willing him to keep it open to her. When he reached over to pull her shirt over her head, she shivered. They were moving in the right direction. They didn't have to talk about it. They could start to feel something together.

When they were done, both exhausted, Grace rolled away. She wiped away a tear, hoping Benjamin wouldn't notice. She wished she was crying because the moment had been special, forging a deeper bond between them. The soft flesh between her legs was on fire, bruised from Benjamin's force. It hadn't felt like lovemaking at all. It felt more like Benjamin needed to take out all of his anger and frustration on something or someone, and unfortunately, it had been her.

She drifted off to sleep, awakened by a noise. She rolled over and touched his back, his sobs frightening her. "Benjamin? Are you OK?"

"Sorry. I didn't mean to wake you." She could see on the red display of the digital clock it was just past midnight

"It's OK. Talk to me. I'm here for you."

Benjamin hiccupped. "It's Caroline. I need to tell you about her, Grace. I wanted to right from the start, but I... I didn't know how."

Grace was wide awake now. She could not imagine the burden of being Benjamin in the past three years, dealing with his own grief while helping Caroline through her loss as well.

"I'm listening, Benjamin."

There was a lengthy silence, and Grace wondered if maybe he changed his mind, but finally, Benjamin sighed and started talking.

"Keera died the spring of Caroline's senior year. One day she was here and the next she was gone. I didn't know what to do. Hell, I couldn't take care of myself and I was supposed to take care of Caroline, too?" He paused, then continued.

"Caroline didn't even go to school the last few weeks of the year. That's the good thing about going to a private academy." His tone changed, disgust evident. "If you pay them enough money, they'll do anything you need them to do. They let her graduate based on the work she'd done up to the time of her mom's death." He was struggling to get the words out and Grace touched his arm, willing him to go on.

"I had no idea how much she was hurting, Grace. I was so caught up in *my* grief that I... We were supposed to celebrate her 18th birthday, just the two of us, but we weren't fooling anyone, there wasn't anything to celebrate. I guess Caroline decided that, too, because she disappeared that day. She cleared every cent out of her bank accounts, took cash I had on hand here, and... disappeared."

A sob escaped him as her own tears slid unnoticed down her cheeks. Anger rose. What was Caroline thinking? How could she be so inconsiderate, so uncaring? "Oh Benjamin."

"I haven't seen her since then, Grace. I have no idea where she is or if she's even...alive. I have private detectives searching, but nothing has worked. She disappeared. I watch for her every day. I keep thinking she'll simply walk through the door. I don't know what else to do."

The desperation in his voice was palpable, and she finally understood much more about the pain he'd kept from her all this time. Grace tried to imagine losing the two people she loved most dearly in life and it almost took her breath away.

"I'm not going anywhere, Benjamin. I'm right here."

They made love again just before dawn.

The more she tried to ignore the pain from earlier, the more an all-too-familiar sensation was growing. She could feel the rollercoaster dropping onto tracks that seemed to disappear below her feet.

Chapter 27

———— ◆ ◆ ◆ ————

The room was exactly as it had always been, the temperature and humidity carefully controlled to protect the pieces of art. That was not true. It wasn't *exactly* as it had been. There was no Keera, lost in her work, struggling to quiet the raging demons by creating her works of art.

He thought about the two versions of Keera he knew. The beautiful, kind, soft-hearted woman who loved being a wife and mother. Nurturing, caring, attentive. The talented artist, who heard voices in her head and then spent days upon days trying to rid herself of them by painting. Angry, tortured, unrelenting. In a strange way, he had been able to love them both, knowing the good side always found its way to the surface. And then one day, it didn't.

Benjamin stood in the middle of the room, breathing in the familiar scents. Everything remained as Keera had left it, neatly stored rows of bristle brushes in the handcrafted holder he helped her design, the color mixing wheel tucked away on its shelf, dozens and dozens of paint tubes, cans of oil she used to clean the brushes.

Canvases were leaning against every wall in the room. Too many to count, they filled the space, leaving little room to walk.

There wasn't a single blank canvas.

When he finally was able to step foot in this room after she died, Keera's art studio above the garage, he wanted to destroy everything. The urge to get rid of all of the art that had stolen her away from him for so many hours at a time was overwhelming and all-consuming. He picked up a piece, ready to shatter it, slice it apart, burn it, anything to stop the taunting. *I was more important to her than you and Caroline. She loved me more than she ever loved you.* But something stopped him. This *was* Keera. She was here in every brush stroke. He couldn't destroy her. She had already done that to herself.

He decided to take out his frustrations on an empty canvas, a blank whiteness that hadn't been touched by her hand. He searched the room, looking for one, becoming frantic as he moved pieces aside, leaned some forward, sure there had to be one empty canvas among all of the pieces sitting in the room. But he was wrong. There was nothing left unfinished.

That day he had slumped to the floor, his legs unable to hold him. He understood. She had finished her work so it was time for her to go. There was not a single blank canvas or even a work in progress. Keera may have left all kinds of unanswered questions for him, but she had not left any unfinished paintings. That story was complete. There was nothing else for her to tell.

He wished he could finish a story. He missed Keera so fiercely it left him physically sick. At least he knew where she was. Caroline's absence left a different kind of hole. It was all his fault she was gone. Until he knew she was safe, until he knew she could forgive him, he wasn't sure he had room for Grace. He needed to finish a story.

Chapter 28

———◆–◆–◆———

It was such an incredible relief to both of them that the silence had been broken and they could talk openly about Caroline.

Benjamin seemed more exhausted than she had ever seen him, and she held him close when they were together, willing him to let her take on some of his pain.

They needed a break, so in early September, he took her on a special weekend getaway. The spa resort was relaxing and romantic, and just what the two of them needed. She sighed as the masseuse found every tense spot in her shoulders.

It wasn't his fault, she told herself, that life had handed him the terrible blow of losing a wife and having a selfish daughter. Benjamin loved her. That's all that mattered.

At dinner that night, both of them relaxed and pampered, Benjamin asked the waiter to take their picture, and later, sitting side-by-side in their suite, they admired the image on his phone, deciding they made a handsome couple. She made him forward a copy to her phone so she could have one, too. Yes, they made a handsome couple.

***

Arriving at Benjamin's house the following weekend, she held up a gift bag with brightly colored tissue paper.

"I have a little surprise for you." She pushed the bag into his hands. "Open your gift."

He pulled out an antique frame holding the picture of them at dinner the previous weekend. He looked at the image for several seconds, his voice husky as he said, "Thank you, Grace. You are so beautiful."

He re-wrapped the frame in the tissue paper and placed it back in the gift bag. Grace watched his movements, confused.

"Is there something wrong with the picture?"

"I told you I like it, Grace."

"Are you going to just keep it in the bag? I thought you'd like to display it, put it on a wall or a shelf? That's what most people do with a framed photo."

His anger was palpable, and Grace took a step backward. "What do you want me to do Grace? Build a shrine in your honor?"

Her stunned silence didn't last long, months of frustration fueling her to find her voice. "No, Benjamin, I don't expect that. You've already done that and there's not room for another one. It's in the closet, it's in your study, it's on every wall in this house. You've built the shrine. There's not one space left for anyone else."

Too late, she realized what she'd revealed. He would know she snooped around his house. Torn between packing up the items she kept at the house or simply making a quick get-away before she said anything else, Grace stood frozen in the moment, staring into the shocked eyes of Benjamin.

A loud thump startled them, a bird hitting the glass of the large patio door with such force it dropped to the deck, neck and legs twitching with spasms. They were rooted to the spot, watching the bird, assuming it was dead or would be soon. It was impossible to know how much time passed, neither able to take their eyes from it, but the bird stopped twitching. Grace realized she was holding her breath, willing the bird to move. To her surprise, it did just that, shaking itself until all the feathers fell neatly back into place. The bird blinked several times and then flew away, leaving them to wonder what had just happened.

Grace shook her head, finally breathing again, feeling a strange connection to that bird.

He didn't break you…

She knew what she had to do.

"Goodbye Benjamin."

***

She never expected to return to Arizona, especially not this soon. Calling her boss to say she needed to take a few personal days had been her first step. McWitner was surprised to hear from her, but since they didn't have any major projects at the moment, he granted the leave without hesitation.

She packed lightly. This wasn't going to be a long trip, but it was one she had to take.

"I'm catching a flight tomorrow to see you, Lexie. Don't change your work schedule or anything. I'll get a cab from the airport."

She'd left the message immediately after leaving Benjamin's. She wasn't surprised when Lexie called shortly after.

"What's wrong Grace? Are you OK?"

"There's no way I can talk about it without completely falling apart. I really need my best friend and a phone call just isn't going to do it this time." It felt so good to say that and mean it. Nobody would ever replace Lexie.

***

They took a bottle of wine out to the art studio, needing a place where they would be completely uninterrupted. They had a lot of ground to cover.

"I can't explain it. I watched that bird shake off the pain, put itself back together and fly off, good as knew." *new*

"You are a lot stronger than you know, Grace."

She wanted to believe that. Facing one demon—returning to Arizona—was an important step. More important, however, was facing Lexie to apologize for being less than the best friend she was supposed to be. Her outpouring of emotions in the casita was different than it had been the last time she was in this space. Today it wasn't about self-pity, Josh, or Jasper. This was a catharsis and a starting point for a new Chapter.

"What are you doing next? Are you staying with him?"

"I honestly have no idea. If Benjamin wants to make some changes, there might be a chance. I really do love him. I just can't always handle the other stuff."

"But you're kind of stuck with the other stuff. It's all part of who he is."

"That's the weird part. I can handle that he misses Keera and Caroline. I really can. That's normal. I can't handle not knowing what he really feels about me. If I knew beyond a shadow of a doubt that he could love me as much as I love him—I'd wait patiently. I just don't know if he's ever going to be able to." She looked down at her hands, not sure how to continue. "You once told me that it's always difficult when one person loves more than the other person is able to love. I think I had that with Josh. I never wanted to admit it, but I think I always loved him more than he loved me. I'm so afraid... I can't do that again." Saying it aloud was difficult, but a sense of peace filled her.

"You're getting really wise in your old age, Grace."

"Some of us just take longer to mature."

A couple days later, as Lexie hugged her friend goodbye at the airport, she was confident Grace was ready to face the challenges back in Chicago. This was not the shattered Grace she said goodbye to last summer. This Grace was going to be just fine. Even as she thought it, Lexie had a strange feeling.

"Grace, wait." She closed the distance between them, hugging her friend closely. "Be careful."

Chapter 29

──── ◄━► ────

Keera is dead. She's dead. Those words played repeatedly in his head, a broken record that wouldn't move past the scratch to play something else. Acceptance was impossible. When he found her, too late to help her in any way, he cradled her in his arms, begging her to wake up, to stop this foolishness. But she didn't. She couldn't. She was already gone.

The prescribed sleeping pills helped him in the first couple of months. He remembered very little, which was the whole point of taking the pills. He couldn't go to work, even if he wanted to. Questions were raised about the drugs found in Keera. Did he give them to her? Where did she get them? He didn't know. He just didn't know. All he wanted was oblivion. The pills did that for at least a short time. When the pills alone weren't enough, the edge still too sharp to handle, he added whiskey to the mix.

He had taken both the night it happened. In his drug-induced sleep, thanks to the combination, he rolled over in bed, and she was there. He knew it couldn't be possible, yet she was there. He pulled Keera close to him, holding her tightly. Running his fingers through her long dark hair, the silkiness of it arousing him. He pulled her close. Keera was back.

"I told you you'd never leave me. All those times you said you would, I knew you couldn't," he whispered into her ear as he held her close.

Then something changed. Time seemed to shift. He heard her. "Daddy, don't. Don't cry. I'm here daddy."

He tried to force himself out of the fog, but he couldn't. Was his daughter crying?

Maybe it hadn't been Keera at all.

Had Caroline, lost in her own grief, crawled into bed with him?

The alcohol and drugs pulled him down into a deep abyss where he couldn't tell what was real and what was not.

Had Caroline been in his room? Had he done something unthinkable to his daughter?

He was sick with worry.

What had he done?

Chapter 30

C aroline gently ran her fingers across the painting, first tracing the shadows and then following the vibrant colors above. This one was her favorite.

Others didn't quite get her mom's paintings the same way she did. She knew that because the look on their faces was always the same. They would comment on the beautiful colors, but then they would notice the darkness of the shadows. They didn't know what they were supposed to feel.

Caroline always knew what to feel when she looked at her mom's art. Sometimes it spoke to her. She heard voices, telling the story behind the colors and the shadows. Sometimes the voices were angry. Those were the bright reds, scarlets, burgundies and crimsons. She knew what they were saying and she sometimes covered her ears, frightened that anything could be so dark and evil. The whispering voices, captured in the shadows, were different. They always told her how to get away from the anger. Sometimes she listened to those voices.

Cassie helped her with that. She was Caroline's best friend since fifth grade. They weren't even friends before that. But when she was in the fifth grade, Caroline walked into the bathroom and found Cassie huddled in a corner crying. She sat next to her and took her hand, not saying anything. Cassie finally wiped the snot from her nose with her sleeve. "I hate my mom."

"That's OK. I hate my mom too, sometimes."

"Sometimes I just wanna die."

"I know. Me too, sometimes."

They became inseparable after that strange moment.

By the time they were in middle school, Cassie started to sneak the sleeping pills for them. Caroline kept them hidden in her dresser, under a pile of clean underwear. Whenever she came over, they carefully opened the Ziploc bag so Cassie could add the pills she had taken. Cassie was careful, taking only what her mom wouldn't notice.

Over the years, they collected dozens and dozens. Every now and then they used a pill or two, but they hated seeing any of them disappear. They needed enough in case they both wanted to die at the same time. The bag remained in its hiding place, filling more and more with each passing week, month and year.

She wondered how long her mom had known about them.

After her mom died, Caroline and Cassie made a pact. Nobody would know about the pills. Even when her dad was in trouble with the hospital and the police were asking all sorts of questions about how her mom got all those pills, they didn't say a word. It wasn't that she wanted her dad to get in trouble, she just didn't want anyone else to know about the voices.

Her mom heard voices, too. She didn't want to take medicine.

This isn't working, Benjamin. You have to let me go." Caroline heard them yelling when they thought she was asleep.

She wanted to go with her mom. She was ready. Maybe the voices would stay behind if she went with her mom.

Instead, her mom went away by herself.

Then her dad started treating her differently. He woke up one morning and couldn't even look at her. He didn't talk to her. He must have figured out that she was the one who had the pills. She was the one who let her mom find them and die. It was all her fault that her mom was dead and now her dad knew it, too, and now he couldn't stand to be around her.

She made her plan to leave so he would never have to look at her face again. He had to despise her face.

She looked like her mom, but she wasn't her mom. He hated her for that.

Before she left the house on her birthday, she gathered all the pictures of herself that looked like her mom. She didn't want her dad to look at them anymore. She threw them out, all reminders of Keera gone.

The angry colors were screaming at her. They had been getting worse and worse for a long time. Covering her ears didn't help. The pills weren't an option now. Her money was gone. She spent the last of it finding relief from the voices and now it was gone.

There was only one way to make them stop for good. She left the studio, cautiously climbing back down the stairs and through the garage to the service door. Following the side path to the edge of the property, she easily scaled the gate where the ground sloped.

It was always easy. She knew all of their schedules—her dad, Shirley, the woman her dad had been with outside of the hotel—so she could come and go as she pleased. One time she made a mistake, but nobody saw her. Pretty soon she would go for good. The colors were screaming too loudly now.

Chapter 31

————◆–◆–◆————

"Will you meet me for coffee, please? We need to talk."

Grace shifted the phone to her other ear, looking through some papers on her desk in search of a misplaced memo. "Benjamin, can I call you back later? I really need to take care of something."

"Just promise you'll call, Grace. I really need to talk to you."

His voice was different. His words were different. But she didn't have time right now to deal with it. Work had once again become her priority, giving her purpose and drive. He wanted to suck her back into a world that wasn't hers, and she wasn't ready to let him.

"I promise I'll call."

***

They were seated across from each other at what had always been a favorite meeting place for them, The Coffee Shoppe. Benjamin was seated at their usual table when she walked in and sat down, her coffee ordered and waiting for her arrival. He reached across the table for her hand and she let him take it. The same surge of electricity she'd felt from the start was there, but this time she pulled her hand back. This time, Grace wasn't going to be fooled by smoking mirrors and fairy dust. She had to figure out once and for all if this was love or lust. A wise teacher told her she would learn through life experiences. She was ready to be a student again.

"I hurt your feelings, Grace. I never meant to do that."

"Benjamin, this isn't just about hurting my feelings. I'm not sure I know who you are at all."

His face sagged. "Unfortunately, Grace, I don't know who I am. I thought I had that all figured out but then my world crashed down around me."

"I'm sorry, Benjamin. It's probably not fair of me to say that." This was going to be harder than she thought, her old feelings for him impossible to ignore. "I guess a better way of saying it is I don't know who I am when I'm with you."

"Is it possible for us to figure this out together?"

"Is it possible for you to open up to me instead of keeping everything bottled up inside and then pushing me away when I least expect it?"

He smiled sadly. "I remember the first time you answered my question with a question. I thought I had all the answers then. I don't." He took her hand again, locking eyes with her. "You've been good for me. I should have told you that more often. I've made an appointment with a therapist, Grace. I'm going to work through some things."

"I'm happy to hear that. You deserve to be happy."

"You do too, and I want to be the one who makes you happy."

Grace could feel her heart start to thaw, but there was still work to be done. "You've kept a lot from me Benjamin. It's time for you to be honest with me—about Keera and Caroline. If you can't, there's no way we can be happy together. I can't live with secrets. I did that once and all I have to show for it is divorce papers. I can't live that way again."

If Benjamin was surprised to see this side of Grace, he didn't let on. He never gave her the chance to be strong around him. Now she was.

"I don't want you to live that way. You aren't going to live that way. Where do I start?" It was difficult for Grace to watch

Benjamin struggle to find the words. As much as she wanted to stop his pain, tell him he didn't have to tell her anything if it was that painful, she forced herself to sit and wait. It was time to hear something—anything—about his past.

"Keera was bipolar. You have no idea how hard it is to say that. She was diagnosed in her mid-thirties and started taking medication. I just wanted her to find some relief from the mood swings, but she hated the drugs. She told me she...she couldn't paint anymore because the pills took away her vision and she couldn't see the colors the right way anymore. She could only see a blank canvas and not what she wanted it to become. It killed her to stop painting." He paused, rubbing his eyes, as if trying to remove the vision of his wife in pain. "I was so torn. I wanted her to be happy, which meant she had to be able to paint, but it was too difficult to watch the torment she was going through when she wasn't on meds."

He paused, a deep breath necessary before he could continue. "We travelled. We built our house. I was doing anything I could think of to take her mind off not being able to paint. I didn't even know she was off the medication until I discovered she was painting again. I couldn't find her one day. Her car was in the garage so I knew she was home, but I couldn't find her." Benjamin paused again, the pain in his eyes made it difficult for Grace. She wanted to tell him to stop talking. She thought maybe that would make the pain stop, but she couldn't do it. They had to get through this.

"I finally figured out where she was and it scared me to death. She used to be so happy when she painted. Her studio above the garage was her favorite place to be. But when I found her that day, she wasn't the same. She was like a woman possessed. It was like she had to get the demons out of her head and onto the canvas. I convinced her to try the pills again, and she did for a little while. Everything seemed fine but I knew when she stopped again. One day was especially bad. When I walked in on her, she looked at me like she didn't even recognize me. She started screaming and throwing things at me, so I left. She didn't even remember doing it. I never made her go back to the meds. I should have but I didn't. I couldn't. She told me she'd leave if I made her."

She put her hand up to stop him. When she made arrangements to meet with him, she thought the coffee shop would be the best option. But now, although the coffee shop wasn't busy, the weighty conversation was too much for this public setting. "Benjamin," she said softly, "would you like to go to my place? You can tell me the rest there."

"Only if that's what you want."

"It is. Meet me there."

This was far more involved than she could have imagined, and she wondered if she really wanted to know everything. Her dad often told her to be careful what she wished for. This might be one of those times. She scolded herself for the thought. Stopping it now would be foolish if she had any chance at all of a relationship with Benjamin.

She walked toward her parked car while Benjamin went the opposite direction to a nearby parking garage for his. As she was about to step off the curb, a crying baby caught her attention. She shuddered, reminded of her nightmare, and glanced to her right to find the source. Instead of seeing a baby, however, her attention was drawn to a person standing in a nearby doorway, half hidden by shadows, hoodie pulled over her head. In the split-second Grace looked at her, their eyes locked.

It wasn't the face or the eyes that Grace focused on, however, it was the tattoo. She couldn't see it clearly, but inked on the woman's neck was the image of clasped fingers, as if hands were reaching around from behind to choke her. Grace shuddered again, more disturbed by the vision than she had been by the nightmare.

It was a relief to put distance between them as she rushed to her car.

Benjamin arrived a few minutes after she let herself in the apartment. They sat in silence, an awkwardness suddenly weighing heavily on them. "If you want to talk about something else for a while, that's alright with me."

"No, I need to say this. It's now or never. The longer she would be in her 'painting moods,' the more creative she was. You wouldn't believe the money people paid for her art. It's so strange that it made her so happy to look at her pieces when they were done. How can someone be that tortured and then feel good about it? I will never understand how her mind worked."

"Her paintings are exquisite. The colors are so shocking at first and then you kind of get lost in them, seeing more deeply into the story. I have been spending a lot of time around great pieces of art lately, Benjamin. Her paintings are amazing."

He nodded in agreement, pausing only a moment before continuing his story. "She was having a lot of trouble that spring. I begged her to go back on the medication for a while and she promised she'd think about it. I was so happy to hear that. You can't even imagine. I thought I was finally going to get my wife back." He paused to collect himself even as his eyes welled with tears. "I found her just a couple days later. She took pills. Dozens and dozens of sleeping pills. I have no idea where she got them. Nobody did. They investigated me, because I had access. I never gave Keera any pills, Grace. The only pills I wanted her to take would have saved her life—not taken it."

She went to him, wrapping him in her arms. As he sobbed, she held him, trying to soothe him like a mother would a crying child.

"I might as well have killed her myself, Grace. I knew she should be on her medication. I knew she needed it. It's all my fault. And then Caroline left and I thought I would be better off dead. I chased her away. I couldn't be the father she needed."

"You did the best you could, Benjamin. You have to believe that."

They sat in silence for a while, the sound of muffled traffic a backdrop to his occasional sniffles.

"I want to show you her studio. I want you to see just how much her painting meant to her and then maybe you'll see why it killed me to take that part of her away. You'll understand. I know you will."

It was late when Benjamin finally prepared to leave, both exhausted from the raw emotions of the night, but also relieved. Finally, they could move forward together. Finally, they could better understand each other.

As she stood with her face against his chest, Benjamin's arms wrapped around her in a tight hug, their breathing in rhythm, Grace finally sensed the ground steadying under her feet. The rollercoaster ride was over. She would be a rock for Benjamin moving forward. And Benjamin would be her rock in return. "I love you, Benjamin Hayward."

"And I love you, Grace Warrens."

It was a new beginning. Their new beginning.

Chapter 32

———◆—◆—◆———

Beginnings sometimes have a strange way of becoming endings.

Pulling into Benjamin's driveway, the gate sitting open for her, Grace smiled to herself. In some ways she was as excited as she had been the very first time she arrived at his house. In many ways, this was the starting point of their new relationship. The bag of groceries in her arm was heavy so she was thankful the door was unlocked for her. Although she expected Benjamin to be waiting for her, as excited as they both were for this evening together, he wasn't.

Everything was different for them—better for them. They were in sync, focused on their relationship—one just as much in love with the other. They decided to mark their new beginning by making dinner together. Imagining the two of them, side by side in the spectacular kitchen, laughing, working together, enjoying being in the moment, felt like a scene from a romantic movie to her and she couldn't wait for it to begin. They had split the duties, Benjamin responsible for selecting the wine and setting the table and Grace responsible for picking up the groceries. The rest they would do together.

She left the bag on the counter and walked to the living room to get a view of the patio, but he wasn't there either. She decided he must be in the upstairs loft waiting for her.

"Hey you. I'm here," she shouted as she climbed.

At the top of the stairs, she stopped dead in her tracks and gasped, almost losing her footing and tumbling backwards, her grip on the wrought iron railing saving her. Standing before her was someone other than Benjamin and it took her just a split second to realize she had seen her before, lurking in a doorway last week, the tattoo of fingers locking around her neck prominently displayed.

"On my way." Benjamin walked toward the great room from the master suite wing, seeing what had stopped Grace in her tracks. All three of them stood frozen.

The tattoo, even more gruesome close up, wasn't the only unusual thing about the figure. The young woman pushed the hood back from her face to reveal a shaved head. Grace couldn't breathe as terror seized her.

How had an intruder gotten into his home? The security system should have alerted someone. Help would be on the way soon.

"Oh my God. Caroline."

Caroline? Grace could not begin to reconcile the ghastly figure before her with the sweet child she had seen in pictures. The eyes bore a resemblance to Keera, but nothing else could be connected to the pretty girl in the pictures. What had happened to her? Grace couldn't move, fear and uncertainty rooting her in place despite a desire to turn and flee. Something was not right.

"Are you OK, baby?" Benjamin took no notice of Grace, intent on the girl before him instead.

The romantic evening was long gone, replaced by a scene from a horror film. Grace watched it unfold before her eyes, still not sure what she was seeing.

"I have to go daddy. I have to go." Even the voice took Grace by surprise. The sweet childlike voice could never match the shaven, tattooed figure speaking.

"No, you don't. Everything's going to be OK. I'm going to take care of you."

"You can't. You can't even look at me anymore."

Grace could not make sense of the words. Still frozen in place, precariously close to the top of stairs, she didn't dare speak, she could only listen and watch.

"You shouldn't have left. I wanted to help you."

"It was all my fault. I killed her. It was all my fault and then you knew and you hated me. I had to go."

"You didn't kill anyone, Caroline. Your mom did that to herself. She took the pills."

"Why did you stop loving me then? Why?" Grace wanted to cover her ears. The tortured sound of the questions unbearable, yet fear kept her motionless.

"I hurt you. I know I hurt you and I'm so sorry. You have to forgive me."

"You knew it was my fault. You knew and you hated me for it." Caroline's hand was in the pocket of her baggie, shapeless sweatshirt. She clumsily pulled her hand out, gripping something heavy. Ugly and black, the gun looked completely out of place in Caroline's small hand. She shakily brought her other hand up to steady it.

It waved precariously, the barrel not pointing at anyone or anything in particular.

Benjamin broke the silence. "I didn't know it was you. I didn't know. I never meant to hurt you."

Caroline looked away from her father momentarily, locking eyes with Grace. Grace thought her heart might leap out of her chest. She was about to die. Her eyes moved down to the gun Caroline was holding. Benjamin took a few steps forward, drawing Caroline's attention back to him.

"Stop daddy." It was impossible to know if she meant stop talking or stop moving, but Benjamin did neither. He moved further into the room, now just an arm's length away from Grace, but still several feet from his daughter.

"I love you, Caroline. I want you to put the gun down. I can help you."

"I don't need help. I don't want help. I'm going away."

As if in a bizarre time warp, Grace saw it all slowly unfold before her eyes. Caroline lifted the gun, pointing it first at Grace and then at her father. At the same time, Benjamin reached his arm out toward Grace. Startled, she realized she was losing her balance, an attempt to grab for the railing futile. The last thing Grace saw, the final image etched on her brain was Caroline lifting the gun to her own head. Benjamin's *"NO-O-O!"* a desperate wail, cut short by the explosive noise of the gun firing.

The blast and fall were simultaneous, and Grace had no awareness other than searing, stabbing pain as her body tumbled down the stairs, her head bashing against the wrought iron, opening a gash, but not stopping her continued fall. Then there was nothing. Total oblivion spared her seeing the ugly scene that continued unfolding above, a deafening silence after the second shot reverberated.

Why did she feel so tired? Opening her eyes was too much work so she kept them closed. It was another nightmare. If she let herself drift back to sleep, she would wake up in her bed with Jasper sleeping on the floor next to the bed and Josh on his side. This wasn't her bed. She shifted her weight and felt pain everywhere. This brought her closer to the surface. Where was she? Why did she hurt all over? She shifted again, afraid of falling, the sensation causing her to grasp for anything that might keep her from hitting whatever was waiting below. She was...on a hillside? She must have fallen. She was cold. Very cold. Then why was she sweating? Her head was pounding and every move she made caused her to sweat more. It was running down her face. She reached her hand up to her face. The sweat continued to pour. She tried to wipe it away, but it felt warm and sticky on her fingers.

She panicked, trying to see into the darkness. She must have fallen. Did Josh know she was here? She went for a walk. But if she went for a walk, she must have her backpack. She'd never go for a walk without her backpack. It had to be nearby. She tried to push back the panic, feeling around her for the backpack she knew would be there, expecting to feel rocks and plant roots. She had to be careful not to touch a cactus. She was already in enough pain. What if there were snakes here? How had she fallen? She didn't remember going for a walk. She didn't remember anything. She reached up again, trying to keep the blood from going into her eye. Her ears were ringing. Why couldn't she hear anything? Somebody had to help her. Maybe Josh was looking for her. She tried to call out, but no sound came out. It was getting hard to breathe. What was wrong with her? She could hear nothing besides her own pulse in her ears. Hurry, Josh. Please hurry.

Chapter 33

aught in a world between wakefulness and sleep, a world of some dreams and some reality, Grace drifted. Searing pain was real. Images of a girl's face that was there one moment and gone the next was a nightmare.

There was no beginning and no ending to the parade of macabre images dancing in her mind's eye. A faceless baby somehow morphed into Jasper leaping off a cliff and lying shattered and broken on the rocks below. A pretty songbird somehow became a vulture flying straight for her, its face human, tattooed and bloodied.

Grace struggled to find a foothold in the drifting existence, but it was useless. Too tired to battle the cerebral war, she gave in to the drifting. She thought she could hear a voice, but she couldn't tell what it was saying. At some point she decided it had to be Benjamin. He was calling her name. He wanted her to stop drifting. She tried to tell him she was on her way, but she couldn't speak. Hopefully he wouldn't give up on her. She was trying.

The hardest part about waking wasn't the roaring in her ears. It wasn't even the unbearable pain she felt in every part of her body.

The hardest part of waking up was finding out what she was waking up to.

That alone would have made her stay asleep.

When you come over on Friday, we need to do something really special. This is our new beginning, Grace. We have to somehow mark it.

"Grace? Can you hear me?" She didn't know the voice, but it wasn't Benjamin.

She drifted again.

"…medically induced coma…bringing her out…"

Blackness eventually turned to patches of light. The patches of light turned to moments of recognition. Coming out of the cloud of pain for brief moments gave her glimpses of the world around her. The starkness of the hospital room. The sounds of the machines attached to different parts of her body. Nurses. Doctors. Her parents. Her sisters. Benjamin's face never appeared. He gave up on her already. She had tried so hard to tell him she was coming, but he already left. She needed him. She tried to ask for him, but sounds didn't come out.

I'm ready to give myself to you, Grace. Keera isn't coming back. I know that. I want you in my life. I want to be in yours.

You can't be in my life if you won't come and see me. His was the only face she looked for every time she forced her eyes to open, her mind to focus, the pain to give her a second to exist again. Caroline was at the house. But she'd used the gun…Caroline must be dead. Benjamin had to be deep in the throes of despair all over again. He couldn't come and see her because he was in pain. Now Benjamin had to start over again finding his way out of the abyss. But he had to come to her. She couldn't get to him. He had to come to her.

This is our new beginning Grace. We have to somehow mark it.

There weren't enough painkillers to take away some aches.

I'm ready to give myself to you, Grace. Keera isn't coming back.

Drifting out of the darkness meant accepting.

You are so good for me. I don't know how I can ever thank you for that.

But she still didn't understand. In that terrible, terrifying moment, a gun pointed at him momentarily, was Benjamin trying to push her out of harm's way or was he trying to pull her toward him.

I love you, Grace Warrens.

Because if he was pulling her toward him, it could only have been for one reason. He needed a shield. Her mind replayed the moment again and again. For the first time in their relationship, she hoped against hope Benjamin had been pushing her away.

She needed to ask him. She needed to hear his answer.

Chapter 34

———◆—◆—◆———

"There's another new reporter lurking in the main entrance. I think that makes a full dozen now. Vultures. I know they think it's their right to be here, but someone should put them in their place!"

It was Ellen coming in this time. They were taking turns, making sure she was never left alone. They sat nearby, sometimes talking to her, sometimes talking to each other, making sure Grace knew she was not alone.

The roar was subsiding more and more every day. Her hearing was improving. She wished it wasn't. She didn't want to hear what the voices were telling her. Doctors, police, nurses, her family. They all had something to say but nothing she wanted to hear.

Her dad was standing at the window. He closed the blinds again, knowing how much the light hurt Grace's eyes and pounding head. "I counted only five news vans in the front, but I think they're starting to hang out in the back now, hoping to catch some nobody who'll make a comment for them. You're right. Vultures."

"Can I have water?" Her voice was barely audible yet both George and Ellen were immediately at her side, there to make sure she had everything she needed. Since waking a day ago, she couldn't be sure if it was a day or more, someone had been ready to rush to her side.

"You look better today. Doesn't she look better? Some of the swelling is down. Do you want a mirror so you can see?" Ellen gently rubbed her head, smoothing back the matted hair, but keeping a safe distance from the bandage covering her cut.

Grace started to shake her head, but that brought a stabbing pain. "No," she mumbled instead.

George gently rubbed her hand, his thumb smoothing the skin in slow circular movements, his voice heavy with emotion. "You are so lucky to be alive. Falling down the stairs probably saved your life, Gracie. I know everything hurts right now, but you're alive. Just keep fighting, little bird."

Little bird. Her dad hadn't called her that in so many years, she'd almost forgotten the pet name. She thought about the bird she and Benjamin watched. She wanted the strength of that little bird. Could she shake it off and fly again? Everything hurt so much, she wasn't sure.

"The police are coming back later today. They said they have to get your statement as soon as you can talk. We can't put them off any longer," Ellen said.

A groan escaped Grace, making both her dad and sister lean in closer, waiting to hear what else they could do to help her right now. There was little to be done for her. She needed time to heal.

"I can't." Tears rolled down her cheeks. Ellen took a tissue from the nearby box to wipe them away as they fell. "Not today." She needed to know. "Is Caroline's dead? Is that why Benjamin isn't here? Why isn't he here?" It had taken so long to get Benjamin to open up to her about Keera. They had made it through the hard times, but now the grieving process would start all over again. How would he ever get over Caroline's death? She didn't know if she would have the strength to go through this with him. She hurt so much.

George spoke softly and soothingly to his youngest, willing her to listen. "They need a statement now—even if you can't remember everything. They'll come back and get another one as soon as you're a little stronger. Any information you can give them to help make sense of all of this mess is going to be really important. You can do it."

Ellen gave her dad a look of despair across the hospital bed, silently asking him to stop. Grace was getting upset and the nurses carefully monitoring her would notice the agitation and once again sedate her. "Try to relax. We'll help you through this."

"Can you call Benjamin?" Her barely audible voice shook with the effort of talking. "I want to see Benjamin."

As Ellen predicted, a nurse arrived, checking monitors, increasing the pain medication flowing from the bag next to the bed, a direct line to Grace. That wouldn't even begin to help when they finally told her the truth, all of them fearful of her fragile state and the impact more bad news would have on her.

"Shhh. You need to just relax, Grace." The nurse was gentle, everything about her a calming presence in the tense room. "This will help. Just close your eyes. You'll be fine."

Grace drifted, all sense of time once again meaningless.

***

George and Sylvia wanted both girls with them, ready to weather this storm as a family. The police officer agreed that it would be better coming from them, but he would be nearby in case Grace had anything else to share that might be important before they closed the case. Revealing the horrible truth to her would be one thing. Helping Grace accept the news would be another. At least they would all be there for her when she learned the rest of the tragic story.

"The sooner she knows Benjamin is dead, the sooner she can start healing," George told them, hoping he sounded more confident than he felt.

Chapter 35

Time was making no sense to Grace.

One voice turned into another without her realizing anyone had come or gone. She remembered a doctor talking to her, but she couldn't focus. Was he talking to her? About her? Medically induced coma. Concussion. Laceration. Broken ribs. Broken leg. Broken heart. Broken life. Everything broken. She didn't realize at first the sound ringing in her ears was her own screams. Slipping back into oblivion was her only relief.

Time heals all wounds.

At first, every move brought excruciating pain. It took weeks and weeks, but the pain was subsiding. Her head wasn't pounding as much when she opened her eyes. She could breathe without as much stabbing pain in her side. The bandage was removed from her head. Pain killers were not being released into her body as steadily as before. She was moved to a different hospital room. She was moved to her parents' guest room.

Time was healing her body.

Time was not healing her heart.

A soft knock signaled another visitor. It was TJ. Ellen stood to hug him and TJ walked around the bed to shake George's hand. He sat in a chair, inching it closer to the bed so he could talk to Grace.

"You're awake. I can finally see your eyes. I won't stay long. I know you're exhausted. You look better today."

"I told her the same thing." Ellen *had* told her that. She remembered hearing it, but it meant nothing to her.

TJ rested his hand tenderly over Grace's, willing some of his own strength into her, giving her hand a gentle squeeze. Grace gave him a weak squeeze in return. "Can I do anything for you?"

"No." There was nothing that could be done. As much as she appreciated TJ's friendship, there was nothing he could do. She needed Benjamin. They were going to start over. She couldn't start over without him. She groaned, wanting to drift away.

Sylvia poked her head in the door. "I've made some sandwiches. All of you should come and eat. You too, TJ. I'll sit with Grace."

"Go ahead and get something to eat. I'll stay here with Grace." TJ was gently running his hand up and down Grace's arm, watching her closely, worry evident on his face.

George patted TJ on the back, a thank you for his presence, his attempts to comfort Grace. She needed all the support she could get.

Grace was drifting off to sleep again, not fully aware of the comings and goings of anyone. She may or may not have remembered TJ sitting next to her, or his leaning down to whisper in her ear, "I wasn't there to catch you this time. I'm sorry I wasn't there." She definitely didn't see the anguished tears running down his face.

Time would keep going, whether she wanted it to or not.

Chapter 36

———— ◆·◆·◆ ————

Seven months later...

Mchchh arch in Chicago is cold, gray and slushy. Grace was thankful that in Venice, Florida, March is sunny and warm. It helped the stiffness in her leg. She shifted on the lounge chair to look at Lexie, wondering if she had put any sunscreen on her face.

"Your nose is getting pink. Do you want this?" Lexie didn't reach for the tube she was holding.

"I live in Arizona. I'm not the winter pale-skinned northerner that you are." Lexie leaned forward in her chair, reaching around the back to adjust it to a sitting-up position. "I can't believe we actually made this work. We needed a vacation."

"It was a scheduling miracle. Of course, McWitner is so happy these days he probably would have given me a month of personal days."

"I guess it's true that something good can come of even the most terrible things."

Grace nodded, her mind momentarily back in the office 40 stories above the streets of Chicago. Her doctors—those healing her body and her mind—encouraged her to get back to work as soon as she felt up to it. James McWitner was more than happy to accommodate her reduced schedule, easing her back into the working world. It was difficult in the first few weeks, using a wheelchair to get around, but she was determined to make it happen. The sight of a small bird hitting its tiny body so hard on a sheet of glass that it surely had to be dead, yet shaking its feathers and flying away, drove her forward. Even on the days she felt dead inside, she put on make-up, combed her hair, and pretended that moving on was helping.

The wheelchair was a short-lived experience. Crutches in the big city were almost as bad for getting around, but her bones mended even if her mind was doing so at a much slower pace.

Her heart was a different matter. It was in a holding pattern, getting neither better nor worse. She pretended it was no big deal. This was her life now. Take it or leave it. Somehow, somewhere in the deepest recesses of her despair, she had chosen to take it. Her family, TJ, and most of all, Lexie, made sure Grace kept her head above water when all she wanted to do was sink into her ocean of despair. She would be forever grateful to all of them. She figured it sounded corny to say it out loud to them, but she knew they had, collectively, saved her life. Even her boss helped her on her road to recovery, whether he fully realized it or not.

"I know how much you love the holiday meet-and-greets but I've decided to give you a pass on them this year."

She had been surprised to see her boss standing in her office first thing that morning, and even more surprised by the "pass" on an important part of her job. *"Don't feel sorry for me. I'll do it. I'm getting around much better now."*

"I actually want you taking care of something else for me, if you think you are up to it." He sat across from her, his face reflecting the difficult words he was about to share. *"We received a donation, a really significant donation, and it's going to need a lot of attention in the coming weeks."* He was holding photos, which he passed across the table to her. Although she had never been in it, she immediately knew she was looking at pictures taken inside Keera's art studio. It wasn't the room she recognized, though,

it was the artwork. The canvases, rows and rows of them lining the room, shot from various angles in the many pictures before her, were clearly Keera's work, the bold colors her trademark, her tormented trademark.

She looked at her boss, confused. *"I don't understand. These are Keera Hayward's pieces."*

"They are. Dr. Hayward, Benjamin, wanted every piece of art in the studio to become our property. They were bequeathed to the Foundation, Grace. I want to offer you the opportunity to take on this project—but only if you think you can. They've been moved to one of our storage facilities and are waiting to be inventoried. We'll have decisions to make in terms of storage, display or auction for each one. I'd like you to oversee that team. It's going to be a lot of work. They need special attention. They need someone special to take care of them, Grace. I don't know if this is something you feel you want to take on, but if it is, I'd like you to do it."

Her first instinct was to say no. She wanted nothing to do with anything associated with the pain of all that had happened. Tears streamed down her face as she looked from the beautiful paintings to the face of her boss. Benjamin wanted her to see the studio, but he never showed her. Thoughts swirled around in her brain, a roulette wheel of indecision. When it stopped, she knew her answer. Could her boss possibly know what he was giving her? This was her chance to say goodbye. This would be the closure she never had. She nodded, needing a moment before responding to his request.

"I would be honored."

He patted her hand and left her to a much-needed cry.

The irony, Grace realized, was that Benjamin Hayward's generous donation meant he was no longer "lost at sea." She was the one who had been left to drift unmoored.

Lexie's voice brought her back to the moment. "Do you want to talk about any of it?"

This was their routine. Lexie could tell her thoughts were far away and always gave her the chance to talk about it or not talk about it. This was Grace's road to healing. She had to be in the driver's seat.

"I'm OK. Let's just enjoy the sun."

They let the warmth of the Florida winter sun caress their skin, no more words needed between them to know the bond they shared was and always would be completely unbreakable. Grace reached her hand across the span between their two chairs and Lexie took it in hers, squeezing it gently and then letting go. She would always be there for Grace and Grace for her.

"Lexie?"

"Hmmm?"

"What did you think of Keera's paintings?"

"They were amazing...but dark. Why?"

"I don't know." Her fingers played with the edge of her beach towel. "Every time I look at one, I have this feeling. I'm not sure I can even describe it, but I feel somehow connected to Keera. I *feel* her paintings. It's like starting a book you never finish, but you know exactly how you want it to end. She never felt whole. I get that. I'll shut up now. That sounds stupid. I told you I couldn't describe it."

"Maybe she did what you did, Grace." Lexie's voice had dropped, making it difficult to hear her. Grace turned toward her. "You changed to fit into Josh's world. Then you changed to fit into Benjamin's. You have a chance to discover yourself. You. Not you in relation to someone else."

Grace thought about it. "You think she wanted to escape but couldn't? Painting let her do that for a while?"

"I don't know. It was just a thought."

"She had *everything*."

"She had everything money can buy. That doesn't make you whole."

They sat in silence for several minutes.

"Lexie?"

"Hmmm?"

"What would you do if you weren't afraid to do it?"

"You mean like jump out of a plane?"

"No, silly, I mean with your life."

Lexie didn't have to think about it. "I'd propose to Sean. I don't think he'll ever ask me to marry him because somewhere along the line he got the impression I don't believe in marriage. As long as it wouldn't send him running for the hills, I'd ask him to marry me."

This was not the answer Grace expected and she leaned forward to get a good look at her friend. "Really?"

"Yes, really. What about you?"

"I think mine is less scary than yours, maybe. I'd start writing. I'd quit my job to become a writer."

Closing her eyes again and drifting into the sweet depths of an almost-asleep state, Grace had a clear vision of herself at 15. She saw a confident young woman handing in an essay to a teacher who usually didn't have a lot of smiles for her students.

"It is ridiculous to believe a relationship can survive when it is based on lust. True love has to be part of the equation. Any sane human being should be able to tell the difference between the two. One will make you tingle; the other will make you commit heart and soul to another human being for the rest of your life."

Grace smiled to herself. That 15-year-old was a wise young woman. Even Battleax Barlow would have to admit that she had enough life experiences at this point to shape her views on love.

Chapter 37

———◆◆◆———

Four years later...

G race set the notepad down on the sand next to her and uncurled her legs, her toes overstretching the blanket to dig into the warm Florida sand. Even after all this time, her right leg was sometimes stiff, one more reminder of that day. She sighed, leaning back to let the sun touch her face like a welcome kiss.

Leaving Chicago had been difficult in some ways, yet very easy in others. As soon as she saw the house in Florida there was no turning back. It was everything she wanted—cozy, comfortable and very near her parents' condo in Venice. Now that George and Sylvia were living in Florida year-round, it would give them plenty of time together. Her father's health was slipping, and she wanted to be near. The stroke six months prior had been mild, but was a wake-up call. Grace never wanted distance between them again. She saw the move as her opportunity to watch over them, returning the favor provided for so many years. Of course, the move was important for other reasons as well.

She opened her eyes, glancing down at the sketches on her notepad. A little remodeling and she knew the place would be exactly what she wanted. The realtor said it had "good bones." Grace liked the sound of that, wanting the support of those good solid bones around her as she ate, slept, and healed. The quaint bungalow was perfect. Updating the plumbing and electric, and opening the kitchen into the living room was the next step. Lexie was visiting for a week and giving her great ideas. In some ways she missed the weird, wacky Lexie. It wasn't something that happened overnight, but now Lexie's shoulder-length hair was almost normal looking—light brown with a single strip of pink. Only a tiny stud was visible in her nose. She may have toned down expressing her individuality in some ways, but her creativity was as masterful as ever. Although Grace started out with some good ideas for the remodel of her home, Lexie worked her magic and now Grace was excited to see the ideas on paper come to life in the coming weeks.

Grace closed her eyes again. So much had happened in the years since Benjamin's death. She allowed herself a moment to let emotions wash over her. As hard as his loss had been, she was finally coming out on the other end and enjoying the life she was creating for herself day by day. Gone were the days of meticulously planning out her every move. That was a difficult lesson to learn. Life is full of surprises—both good and bad. Planning for them is not always possible.

Surprisingly, enough time passed and she could eventually go hours and then finally days without thinking about the horrific scene that unfolded before her eyes all those years ago. The pain of it had been almost too much to bear in the first months. Then the physical pain subsided and the mental toll almost did her in. Her family didn't understand at first how she could be slipping further into depression so long after the bones had healed. Outward signs all but disappeared when new symptoms arose out of nowhere. Diagnosed with Post-Traumatic Stress Disorder, she was left almost debilitated. Loud noises sent her into a near-panic, hyperventilating, shaking, unable to function. In crowds, she saw the face of Caroline. Sleep was impossible. Nightmares were common, each one more violent than the last. Maybe she returned to work too soon. Maybe she should have returned to work sooner. There was no clear answer.

It took a couple of years to find a sense of peace again when she closed her eyes. Her therapist led her through exercises to see the events of the day through a different lens, teaching her to be the director of a movie, some scenes requiring take after take in order to put it all together. It worked wonders, giving her steps to accept her loss, to help re-build the pieces into a whole again.

"One sidewalk square at a time," Dr. Franz told her every time she came in with a setback. Grace awoke to that mantra morning after morning. One sidewalk square at a time.

The notion of being a movie director of the scene had been powerful. She was able to watch the events of that day in her mind, frame by frame, pressing an imaginary pause button sometimes to watch one moment a little longer than others. At first, she did it with a purpose, thinking she might get some answers to her many questions if she just listened closer or analyzed harder. Dr. Franz explained that she might have to accept that no answers existed.

Frame: Caroline pulls a gun out of her pocket. She brought the gun to the house for a specific reason. Was it her plan all along to kill herself?

Frame: *"I didn't know it was you. I didn't know. And I hurt you."* What didn't he know? How had he hurt Caroline?

Frame: Caroline looks directly at Grace. Grace was sure a bullet was meant for her. But Caroline's look didn't match that thought. Was she pleading for help? Was she warning Grace of something? What was she saying with that look?

Frame: Caroline points the gun at her father. If Caroline was blaming herself for her mom's death, why would she want to kill her father?

It made no sense, but it didn't stop her from trying.

Frame (scenario one): Benjamin realizes Caroline means to harm one of them and pushes Grace out of the line of fire.

Frame (scenario two): Benjamin panics at the gun pointed at him and pulls Grace in front of him as a shield from the bullet.

Frame (scenario three): Benjamin knows they are about to die and reaches out to take her hand, trying to tell her in that moment that he will love her forever, but startled by the gunshot echoing in the space, she loses her balance and falls down the stairs.

Try as she might, Grace was never able to reconstruct that final scene, the one she needed most of all. If Benjamin was reaching for her hand as an expression of his love for her, then why would he eventually pick up the gun and point it at his own head?

Dr. Franz was right. There would never be answers.

So, Grace stopped searching. She pushed EJECT, taking the imaginary disk from a slot in her mind and letting it drop to the floor. Her heel dug in, crushing and grinding it into oblivion. She was ready to move forward.

Grace was startled out of her reverie by a bundle of fur throwing itself onto her lap, and she laughed as the puppy planted sloppy wet kisses on every surface he could find. "Jazz, get down." She tried to use her firm voice as she reached for the leash dragging behind the excited little German Shepherd.

"She got away. She got away because she wanted to be by you. I tried to hold her. I did."

Grace stood up from the sand-covered blanket and scooped the adorable blonde boy off his feet to swing him in a circle, completely ignoring the leash tangling around her and the excited puppy trying to join in their happy dance. Lexie was a few steps away, arms loaded down with a pail, shovel, plastic container filled with seashells, and two pairs of sandals, one belonging to her and the other to the rambunctious little boy.

"I have no idea how you keep up with this one. He only asked me about two hundred questions. I think I answered every single one of them, too." Lexie dropped everything in the sand at her feet and unceremoniously plopped down next to the pile, rubbing the tiny bump of her belly. "I'm too old for this. How did I let Sean talk me into this? Put a ring on a guy's finger and he thinks he owns you." She smiled even as she rolled her eyes. She turned her attention back to the boy. "Let's just sit for a minute. Auntie Lexie needs to take a nap." The puppy attacked this new victim with sloppy kisses and she pushed him away, laughing, trying to talk to Grace despite the commotion. "Did you get any writing done?"

"Nope. I'm taking a break from writing today. I decided today is just a 'thinking day.'"

"I'm sure a thinking day will make that book just write itself. You might want to consider a day job." Grace kicked sand onto Lexie's feet, making a face at her friend.

"You can't take a nap," the little voice piped over the sound of the yapping puppy. "Mommy, can she take a nap on the sand? She'll get all dirty."

Grace laughed as she set the squirming bundle of energy down, rumpling the sun-bleached hair before dropping down on the sand next to her friend. Lexie always referred to her adorable little God-son as the universe's way of letting Grace know she was finally with the right man. Grace could do nothing except agree with her. Somehow the universe remained in control, no matter how much they tried to fight it. Planning was almost a joke. They were all just along for the crazy ride.

Jazz ran in circles around the small group.

"We should let her take a little nap. She can use my blanket so she won't get full of sand. You and I should build a castle now." It sometimes took her by surprise when she looked into the big blue eyes in that tiny face and realized just how much he looked like his dad. "But she can't nap long because we really should get going soon."

"Can we get some ice cream?"

"Thomas John, you can't possibly be hungry. You ate a sandwich a little while ago and you've had three snacks. Where do you put all that food?"

He looked up at his mom, scrunching his nose in a totally irresistible way. "You're silly mommy. Ice cream isn't food. It's cold."

The two women looked at one another and laughed. The moment didn't require words. That's the way it is between best friends. Grace sent heavenward a thank you for all the blessings she could call hers. The best friend in the world. This little boy who had become her joy. The husband who had helped her through the toughest part of her life and never gave up because he loved her with all that was in him, and she returned those feelings equally. The new house they would turn into their perfect family home.

She had faced the fears, insecurities and broken pieces of her past and was ready to face whatever the world offered next. There would be good times and bad times, but Grace finally found what she thought was lost forever. She'd picked up all the pieces, fit them together, and was whole again.

"OK, TJ," she said. "Let's get Auntie Lexie off that blanket so we can make your tummy cold."

Mother and son each took one of Lexie's hands and pulled. Just as they thought they were lifting her off the blanket, she tugged them down into the sand, rolling them into one huge pile of arms and legs. Jazz joined in the fun, licking, nipping and barking. The two laughed until they were ready to cry. TJ wriggled his way out of the tangle to stand up and give them his sternest face.

"I don't think you get any ice cream now." He broke into his silly grin. "If you bemember to be good, you can have a lick of mine." Grace couldn't love him more.

"I'll bemember," she solemnly promised him.

The three gathered their belongings, arms filled with the day's adventures on the beach. The two women, the small boy and the bounding puppy made their way across the sand as the sun started its slow descent toward the ocean. Grace smiled, a peace settling over her as she felt her son's warm hand slip into hers, and thinking about her husband waiting for her, hopefully with dinner started and a bottle of white wine chilling, but most of all, with arms wide open to welcome her home.

Acknowledgments

The opportunity to say thank you to those who provided support and encouragement—or a much-needed swift kick in the butt—is one I have anticipated for a long time.

I am incredibly appreciative of the kind souls brave enough to read my earliest drafts. Without your feedback, *Pieces of Grace* would not have been possible: Thank you to Mary Evans, Mona Gresenz, and Joanne Wilson. Sitting on the pontoon on a summer evening listening to the three of you talk about my book was one of the most euphoric feelings I've ever had. Thank you to Betty Rogers. You are a mom extraordinaire and a helpful proofreader! A huge thank you also to Jim Hayes. I'm glad you needed something to read on your flight from Wisconsin to Arizona. Your insights were spot on.

I'm grateful also for feedback from June High, Lorraine Minton, Kathy Immel, Lauree Minton, and Don & Jean Hayes. Every comment made a difference!

A special thank you is reserved for Dean High. You challenge me, make me laugh, encourage me, and love me. I couldn't ask for more.

Finally, thank you to the greatest inspiration in my life: Mallory, Morgan and Mitchell. It's impossible to imagine a mom more blessed. You three will always be my greatest accomplishments—and you've given me enough material to write books for the rest of my life.

About The Author

Karen Gibson is a retired professor who now dedicates her time to writing. She spent a couple decades teaching English and Speech Communication to middle and high school students before joining the faculty of the University of Wisconsin Oshkosh as a member of the Educational Leadership and Policy Department.

Karen divides her time between Wisconsin and Arizona (for obvious reasons!) When she isn't writing, she is cheering on the Wisconsin Badgers, Milwaukee Brewers, and the Green Bay Packers. She spends as much time as humanly possible with her favorite people—her three grown children and her granddaughters.

www.karengibsonauthor.com
Instagram: @kmgibson_author
Facebook.com/KarenGibsonAuthor

COMING SOON BY KAREN GIBSON

In a Heartbeat

Made in the USA
Monee, IL
16 March 2021